AMANDA'S T1

The Lost Collection

Leah Brooke
writing as
Lana Dare

MENAGE EVERLASTING

Siren Publishing, Inc.
www.SirenPublishing.com

A SIREN PUBLISHING BOOK
IMPRINT: Ménage Everlasting

AMANDA'S TEXAS RANGERS
Copyright © 2010 by Lana Dare

ISBN-10: 1-60601-932-5
ISBN-13: 978-1-60601-932-0

First Printing: October 2010

Cover design by *Les Byerley*
All art and logo copyright © 2010 by Siren Publishing, Inc.

ALL RIGHTS RESERVED: This literary work may not be reproduced or transmitted in any form or by any means, including electronic or photographic reproduction, in whole or in part, without express written permission.

All characters and events in this book are fictitious. Any resemblance to actual persons living or dead is strictly coincidental.

Printed in the U.S.A.

PUBLISHER
Siren Publishing, Inc.
www.SirenPublishing.com

AMANDA'S TEXAS RANGERS
The Lost Collection

LANA DARE
Copyright © 2010

Chapter One

Lying on her belly, Amanda Keller remained motionless as she looked down the barrel of her rifle to the group of men moving around below the ridge. Ignoring the fierce sun beating down on her, the rock poking at her hip through her trousers, and the trail of sweat slowly creeping down her neck below her bandana, she waited for Rafael Perez to step out into the open.

The brim of her hat kept the sun from shining in her eyes, but she had to keep blinking against the glint of light reflecting off of her rifle. She could only hope Rafael or one of his men wouldn't spot it before she did what she came here to do. Surprisingly, none of them looked up in her direction.

Desperation burned like acid in her stomach and she had to force herself to keep her breathing steady as she waited for her shot. After she killed him, the others would be easy to control.

She had to kill the man first.

With every deep breath she took, the knots in her stomach just kept growing. She'd never killed anyone before, and the thought of having to do it now made her want to throw up.

But she could see no other way. She'd never be free if she didn't and she didn't have much time. She'd already been away too long.

Rafael, with his stringy black hair and confident swagger, moved among his men, barking out orders. He somehow managed to keep the horses or one of his men between him and the end of her rifle, but she knew that eventually she'd get the perfect opportunity. If not today…tomorrow.

It had taken her weeks to find him, and she'd been following his trail for the last three days, getting a little closer each day. This morning she'd caught sight of him for the first time.

Thanks to the description she'd gotten, he would have been easy to spot, even without knowing he was the leader of his slimy band of thugs. As she watched men all rush to do his bidding, she became more certain than ever that he was the one in charge…and her target.

It appeared Rafael and his men had stopped for a rest and a break from the heat, which gave her the opportunity to study him more closely. He looked younger than she thought he'd be but had the body of a man who drank too much and did too little.

Like her father.

He sat now, leaning up against a rock next to one of his men, who blocked any shot Amanda might have had and drank from a bottle of whiskey. She counted seven other men with him.

A year ago he had eight.

She blinked, trying to clear her vision as sweat trickled into her eyes, watching two of the men walk to the stream nearby and begin to refill canteens. She knew they'd be taking their horses for a drink as soon as they finished and sent a silent apology to Midnight, promising to get her a drink of the cool, clear water as soon as she could.

She'd emptied her own canteen about two hours ago, but knew it would be a while until she could refill it.

Doing her best to ignore the tickle at the back of her neck, Amanda kept her eye on Rafael, tightening her grip when he came back to his feet again. Damn. Her hands had become slick with sweat, but she couldn't stop to wipe them now.

If he would just move away from the tree...yes...now turn just a little...

"Oof!" A hard body landed none too gently on top of her, knocking the air out of her lungs as strong hands wrenched the rifle from her grip and another equally strong hand covered her mouth against her instinctive cry.

"Quiet!" The cold venom in the low tone whispered furiously against her ear had to be the most frightening sound she'd ever heard.

Pressed into the ground by the heavy weight on top of her, she whimpered as the rock at her hip dug in even more painfully, bringing tears to her eyes. She struggled for air, barely able to breathe through the large hand covering her mouth and nose.

Another voice sounded next to her other ear, barely a whisper that she had to struggle to hear. "Be still and be quiet. We're going to back away from the edge slowly. If you resist, Zane, here, will break your neck. Do you understand?"

Amanda nodded once, her vision blurring from lack of air. Oh, God. There were two of them, and they were going to kill her. Her eyes flew open when she felt the hard bulge press at her bottom.

Or worse.

She'd heard stories about men who kept women alive for days, using them over and over until they've had enough of them. Then they'd kill them. She'd rather be killed outright than to have to endure that.

Even in this heat, a shiver went down her spine as fear clawed at her, along with something else, something decadent and dangerous. The man holding her didn't smell sour the way her father did. He smelled like soap, leather and sweat, and the hand covering her mouth was free of grime. Even the slight beard brushing her cheek was soft, and she barely resisted the urge to rub against it. The strength of the body covering hers was apparent, his movements controlled and sure.

Hard-packed muscles pressed over every inch of her back and legs, holding her so firmly that she couldn't move at all.

He bent close, tightening his hand threateningly over her mouth. "I'll take my hand away a little so you can breathe. If you make one sound, you're dead."

Amanda nodded again, gulping in air as soon as his hand moved away, trying her best to be as quiet as possible so he didn't cover her mouth again. She found herself lifted slightly and pulled back from the edge, the man handling her as easily as he would a rag doll. Not until he'd pulled her several feet back and out of Rafael's sight did he loosen his hold, still gripping her arm as he led her down the back side of the rocky ledge to the bottom where she'd left Midnight. The second he let her go, she spun and started backing away, stopping in her tracks when she got her first good look at them.

Holy hell. "Who are you?"

The one who'd just released her put his hands on his hips, his gaze hot as it moved over her. He looked just as muscular as he felt pressed against her. "We're Texas Rangers, ma'am. What were you doing back there?"

She'd never seen such masculine-looking men in her life and found herself tongue-tied. Swallowing heavily, she couldn't help staring, amazed at the erotic thoughts racing through her mind when she saw that their looks matched their voices.

Strong. Authoritative. Blatantly sexual.

The one holding her rifle also looked her up and down, his dark eyes assessing as they moved over her, warming everything in their path. His brown hat kept his face in shadow, not allowing her to see his features clearly, but she saw a flash of white when he spoke as he took a step toward her. "My friend asked you a question. What were you doing back there?"

Amanda flicked her gaze to the other man, the one who'd held her, her breath catching at the sharp emerald gaze she encountered. She took several steps backward, watching them carefully as they kept up with her, matching her step for step, not allowing more than about twenty feet to separate them. Reaching a hand behind her, she stroked Midnight's neck, feeling just a little better to have her horse so close. Fighting the urge to cross her arms over her chest where her nipples pebbled, she lifted her chin, determined not to allow them to see how badly they intimidated her.

Both as a potential lawbreaker and a woman.

The two Rangers didn't stop moving closer until they stood about ten feet in front of her. The one who'd nearly crushed her crossed his arms over his chest and stared at her silently, his green eyes glittering beneath his hat. Both men looked dangerous, in fact downright scary, not the kind of men anyone in their right mind would want to go up against. They stood at least six feet tall. The man on the left with the green eyes stood maybe an inch taller than the other one.

His face, like the other man's, was shadowed under the black hat he wore, but this close she could make out his features. He looked hard everywhere, the harsh planes and angles of his face apparent, even with his short beard, making his expression look unforgiving, his eyes like green ice as they searched her face. His dark blond hair had been tied back at his nape, but from where she stood, she couldn't see how long it hung.

The black hat suited him. Combined with those chiseled features, it made him look like an outlaw.

"We're waiting for some answers."

Amanda snapped her attention back to the man with the dark eyes.

He looked almost as mean as the other man, the kind of man no one would underestimate. His eyes glittered coldly, frightening her a little more but drawing her all the same. His dark hair hung loose over his collar, giving him a slightly wild appearance, making her hands itch with the urge to run her fingers through it.

Holding on to Midnight, she tried to judge her chances of jumping on her and getting away before she did something that would make her look foolish.

"I wouldn't."

Amanda gulped and looked back at the man with the green eyes, tightening her thighs against the look in his eyes. It was the look of a man to a woman, and one who knew his woman well.

How could that be? How had he known that she'd been about to try to escape? No, underestimating either of them would be dangerous.

And she had to deceive them.

Gathering her willpower, she looked away before she became a stuttering idiot. She couldn't very well explain to a Texas Ranger that she'd been about to kill a man. The lie that tumbled from her lips was born of desperation.

"I'm on my way to San Antonio to meet my family. I wanted to stop at the stream for some water, but I saw those men there and I didn't want them to see me. I was just watching them, waiting for them to leave so I could fill my canteen and water my horse."

The green-eyed one folded his arms across his chest. "Stream runs quite a ways."

Closing her hands into fists, she shifted her feet under his scrutiny, inexplicably jealous of every woman he'd ever held against that wide chest.

The man with the deep brown eyes tipped his hat back slightly and took a step closer, holding up her rifle. "And that doesn't explain why you were pointing this at them."

Amanda smiled and shrugged, her stomach dropping when she got a good look at his face. More good looking than the other, his eyes twinkled with what her mother would call devil's charm. "I wanted to keep them in my sights, I mean, just in case they saw me or something. I don't know what you're getting all worked up about. I didn't shoot anybody."

The green eyes narrowed as the other man took a threatening step closer. "What's your name?"

Amanda's mind went blank. She didn't want to reveal her real name and risk having a bounty on her head when Rafael ended up dead, but, for the life of her, couldn't come up with another.

"I...uh...Rose." She hurriedly turned away, giving her attention to Midnight. Cursing herself for using her mother's name, she tried to think of a last name that they wouldn't be able to trace back to her. Before she could think of one, she was grabbed from behind and whirled around.

"You're lying."

Scared he'd try to smother her again, Amanda panicked and struggled to get free. "No, I'm not. Let go of me." She twisted away, trying to make a run for it.

"No."

What felt like an iron band came around her waist, he lifted her with one arm, his other hand covering her mouth again when she started kicking and screaming. "Quiet."

Thankful that his hand over her mouth kept her moan from breaking free, she stilled when his forearm brushed the underside of her breasts.

The other Ranger gathered the reins of her horse and came up alongside them. "We don't want to spook those men. If you make any noise, we're gonna have to quiet you. If Zane takes his hand away, will you promise to be quiet?"

Amanda nodded frantically, desperate for air. Between the heat and lack of air and water, she'd started to get dizzy. When the blond man loosened his grip, she breathed deeply, filling her lungs with hot, humid air as she slumped against him. When she finally got her breath back, she turned to glare over her shoulder at him, alarmed at the flare of need that went through her at being held so closely against him. Knowing her best defense would be a good offense, she snapped at him.

"Do you have to keep smothering me every time you want me to be quiet?"

"Yes."

She kicked at him again, hitting his shin with the heel of her boot, and was rewarded by a grunt before he tightened his arm around her waist painfully. Fearing for her ribs, she panted. "I'm sorry. I'll stop. You're hurting me." Still, she didn't feel the fear she probably should have, perhaps because she knew now that they were Texas Rangers. But damn it, she shouldn't feel this strong attraction.

He loosened his hold, but his deep voice remained threatening, although not as threatening as that bulge pressing at her bottom. "Be still."

The other man led Midnight to where two other horses had been tied to a tree. He secured her horse and moved to one of the other horses, reached into a saddlebag, and brought out a coil of rope, deftly tying her hands and feet together as the other Ranger held her.

"Ranger, what are you going to do to me?" Fear hit her now. Hard. Surely they wouldn't leave her tied up out here in the middle of nowhere! Would they take her horse?

The man holding her carried her to a bit of shade beneath a small outcropping of rocks and set her none too gently on her bottom, making her teeth snap together. "Stay put."

Leaning back against the cool rock, she watched fearfully as he went to his horse and stowed her rifle before reaching for his own and walking away. She'd have to find a way to get her rifle back. She couldn't be left out here defenseless, and she was damned good with her rifle.

The other man crouched in front of her and, despite her struggles, used her own bandana to gag her. His dark eyes glittered dangerously. "We can't trust you to be quiet. And I'm not answering any of your questions until you make up your mind to tell us the truth. Now sit tight, be a good little girl, and stay out of trouble until we get back." He smiled, stealing her breath, when she narrowed her eyes and growled at him. "Spirited little thing, aren't you?" He rubbed his chin where a few days' worth of stubble had grown. "You and I have some unfinished business to take care of as soon as I get the chance."

Amanda tried unsuccessfully to spit the gag out as he straightened and moved away to follow the other Ranger, growling at him when he turned to wink at her over his shoulder. Fighting to get free, she watched them disappear around the side of the rocks heading toward the ledge they'd just dragged her from.

What would they do to her when they came back, and why did she want so badly to see what he would do to check out her spirit?

Damn, what the hell was wrong with her? If he meant what she thought he did, he was in for a big surprise. She hated being physical with a man and, unless he was looking for a fight, he'd be sadly disappointed.

What were they doing here, anyway?

Why were they watching Rafael Perez?

Did they plan to arrest him?

If so, it would ruin everything.

She doubted very much that they'd come back, release her, and go on their way and couldn't afford to take any chances.

Luckily, they'd underestimated *her*.

Thankful that they'd tied her hands and feet together in front of her, she still took several precious minutes before she could get them loose enough from around her ankles to slide them up. Doing that tightened the ropes on her wrists, cutting off her circulation and making it harder to use her hands.

It seemed to take forever to work her pant leg up over her boot, the tight rope impeding her progress. She glanced repeatedly toward the rocks, sweat pouring off of her now as she stuck her hand down into her boot and tried to pull her knife out with two fingers, all the while checking to make sure they weren't on their way back.

The knife slipped from her sweaty fingers twice before she managed to work it out of her boot. It took longer to cut the ropes than it should have, but with her hands going numb, the lack of strength and coordination made the job harder. When she finally got free, she tossed the rope aside and retrieved her rifle, running a hand down Midnight's flank to calm him, the whole time staring toward where they'd disappeared.

A minute later, she was on her way, riding hard back the way she'd come. Now that she knew the direction Rafael and his men were headed, she would follow the stream and catch them again tomorrow.

And somehow stay out of sight of the two Texas Rangers who threatened to ruin everything.

* * * *

Texas Ranger Randall Sloane looked over at his best friend and fellow Ranger. "She's resourceful, ain't she? Feisty little thing, too. She got out of them ropes a lot faster than I thought she would. Is she as soft as she looked?"

Zane Owens watched their captive ride away and turned back to keep an eye on Rafael Perez and his gang. "Yeah."

Rand took a sip of warm water from his canteen, hoping their runaway captive filled her own canteen soon. "Wonder what she wants with Perez. Damn, she's fucking beautiful. Strong and smart, too. Just the kind of woman we need."

Zane's eyes shifted in her direction again as though he couldn't help himself, a muscle working in his jaw. "A woman like that would be nothing but trouble. A man would spend all his time just trying to get into her pants."

Nodding, Rand turned back to see that all but two of Perez's men had fallen asleep. "Since this is our last assignment, I'd say she came along just in time. I wouldn't mind spending my time getting her outta those pants."

He shrugged, his eyes shifting to the cloud of dirt kicked up by their runaway's horse. "The ranch can wait. We don't even know if that's really what we want to do."

Rand was silent as memories assailed him. "It's been three years since Beatrice died. I want a steady woman and a family. You do, too. But I want something more this time."

Zane sighed. "Agreed. A woman like Rose, or whatever the hell her name is, ain't gonna be a sweet and docile wife like Beatrice was. Maybe we should just ask Marjorie Benton and be done with it. She's pretty. I thought you liked blondes."

Rand looked out into the distance at the dust kicked up by the dark-haired beauty's escape. "Marjorie Benton bores you just as much as she bores me. And I find that I have a soft spot for raven-haired beauties. That one sure had pretty eyes. You ever seen that color purple before?"

Exchanging hand signals with the other Texas Rangers hiding in the rocks, Zane clenched his jaw. "Forget it, Rand. One like that would drive us to drink. You ready or you wanna stay here and daydream about a violet-eyed liar while the rest of us go get Rafael and his men?"

Rand grinned. "I got a feeling I'm going to have more than daydreams about her. Maybe we shouldn't have let her get away."

"If we hadn't and somehow lost to Rafael's men, she'd end up being their prisoner. It's better this way."

"Yeah, but if we ever catch up to her again, I won't be so quick to let her go."

Chapter Two

No. No. No. Where the hell had they all come from?

Amanda dropped her head on her arm, burying her face in the sweet grass. Damn it. Just as she'd feared, the Texas Rangers had already arrested Rafael and his men. She should have approached Rafael as soon as she escaped. No, killing him with the Rangers watching wouldn't have helped her at all, and if she'd just gone to Rafael, the Rangers would have suspected her of being in their gang and she would have been arrested with them. *Damn. Damn. Damn.* What the hell should she do now?

Raising her head again, she bit her lip, looking back over the rock she used for cover. To her surprise, she spotted a total of four Texas Rangers. She'd only been gone a couple of hours, so the other two had either arrived shortly after she'd left or had been there all the time and she hadn't seen them or their horses.

Horsefeathers. She backed away and sat down on the grass to think. She didn't know how long she sat there, but she kept glancing back over the large rock she hid behind to make sure they hadn't left. She had to think of something soon or just follow them until she did. She yelped as a large hand grabbed her shirt from behind and lifted her to her feet, all in one movement.

At the same time, another hand ripped her rifle from her hands. "Hi, darlin'. I missed you. I'd hoped you'd be back. Yep, this must be my lucky day."

Flailing her arms to balance herself, she spun, looking up into the dark eyes of one of the Texas Rangers who'd caught her earlier. "You! Damn it, let me go. I haven't done anything to you."

"What did you come back for? Why are you interested in Perez and his gang?" He grinned and wagged his eyebrows. "Unless you're following me?"

Amanda gulped, hating that his hooded gaze made her forget what the hell she'd been saying. She'd been around cowboys her entire life, but this Texas Ranger and his friend made her feel things she didn't understand, and it irritated her. "I don't know what you're talking about. I just figured they moved on by now. I have to stay near the water for my horse."

He regarded her skeptically, crossing his arms over his muscular chest. "Do you have any idea what you're doing? Do you even know how to get to San Antone?"

She didn't, but since she had no intention of going there, it really didn't matter. "Of course." Damn, she'd been telling a lot of lies today.

He grabbed her arm, easily overcoming her struggles, and led her to where the others had begun mounting their horses to start out again. "I think you'd better come with us. I don't trust you at all. I don't want to go to sleep and have a rifle pointed at me, and nothing but lies have been spurting outta your mouth since I met you. Makes me want to shut you up."

"How are you planning to—"

He didn't even let her finish before his mouth swooped down on hers. His lips, warm and firm, moved over hers as his hand cupped her jaw, forcing her mouth open.

Amanda struggled for all she was worth but couldn't loosen his grip at all. Her eyes flitted closed, her struggles growing weaker with each stroke of his tongue over hers. Grabbing his shoulders to keep from falling, she pressed herself against him, her breath catching at the feel of his hard body against her pointed nipples. Swept into a storm, she let it take her. So immersed in it, she lost all sense of everything around her.

By the time he released her, she breathed heavily, and she had to lock her knees to keep from falling.

An unfamiliar weakness assuaged her, forcing her to hold on to him a moment longer than she should have. "Let go of me! My horse."

He turned, pulling her with him. "Your horse is already being taken care of."

Still a little dazed, Amanda looked to where he pointed, surprised to see another man leading her horse to graze with the other horses and found herself reluctantly disappointed that it wasn't the blond man from earlier. Scanning the area, she watched in amusement as the Texas Rangers threw Rafael and his men over the backs of the outlaws' horses.

And then she saw him, her eyes drawn to him as if by some kind of magic, making the others disappear. The blond man with his hair tied back, Zane, happened to be the man throwing Rafael facedown over his own horse, ignoring the man's cursing and fight to get free.

Not wanting Rafael to see her, she began struggling again. "Let go of me. I haven't done anything wrong. I'm not going to shoot you."

"Damned right, you won't." He held up the rifle and grinned. "Once we get these men back to Austin, we'll take you to wherever you have to go. What's your name? And don't lie to me again."

"Well if it ain't Amanda Keller! Did you come lookin' for me 'cause now you want to feel a real man between those thighs? Been alone a long time now, huh?"

Amanda whipped her head around to see Rafael smiling at her with the few teeth he had left. She hid a shudder as he leered at her from his upside-down position over the horse's back. His black eyes raked over her, making her feel dirty, completely wiping away the warm desire she'd experienced in Rand's arms, and replacing it with a cold, slimy sensation. Letting her disgust show, she sneered at him.

"You know where I can find one? How do you know who I am anyway? I've never met you." She sure as hell didn't need the Texas Rangers thinking she rode with him.

A string of angry Spanish followed, only stopping when Zane slapped the other man on the head.

"Answer her question."

Rafael glared at him but complied. "I was in town talking to John and he pointed you out to me. Said he married you and that you was a wildcat in bed. Didn't want me to meet you. Guess he was afraid of you seein' a real man."

Disgusted, she turned from him, facing the man who still held her arm. "That's probably the only thing I can thank him for."

He held her easily and led her to the blond man who was in the process of gagging Rafael with his own bandana. "Zane, you were right. She didn't even realize we'd spotted her."

Zane straightened from his task and nodded, having secured the bandit to his own horse. "So I see. Amanda Keller, huh? Not Rose?"

The man holding her turned her to face him, his firm grip on her shoulders preventing her from turning away. "Keller? John Keller, one of Rafael's men?"

Zane came up behind her, making the back of her neck tingle. "You're married to one of Rafael's men?"

Amanda looked up into the face of the dark-eyed, dark-haired Ranger still holding her. "No. Not anymore."

The brown-eyed Ranger let go of her so quickly, she almost fell. It was clear from the look on his face that he didn't believe her. "Hell. Which one of these men is your husband?"

Amanda moved away and turned, almost running into Zane. Stunned at the fury in his green eyes, she inched closer and closer to her horse.

Zane's arm whipped out, grabbing her and pulling her close. "Which one?"

She gulped, alarmed at the menace in his tone and hurriedly looked away, grateful when one of the other Rangers came forward.

The other Ranger smiled, the amusement in his eyes unmistakable.

"Rand, this little lady givin' you trouble?"

The dark-eyed one shook his head. "No, Jim. We're just fine. Do me a favor and find out which of these men is John Keller."

"Sure thing. Hello, ma'am." The Ranger tipped his hat, smiling at the men on either side of her. "I'm Jim Seton."

Amanda smiled faintly, trying unobtrusively to pull away from Zane. "Hello, Ranger. Don't bother looking for him. He's not here."

He paused, lifting the brim of his hat. "Are you sure?"

"Positive. Rafael killed him a long time ago." She studied the other Ranger, finding him far less threatening than Zane or Rand.

Zane shook her once, bringing her attention back to him. "Are you part of their gang? Did you help them rob the stagecoach?"

Insulted, Amanda tugged her arm free, surprised when he released her. "Do I look like part of their gang? I hate every one of them."

"Your husband cried like a baby when we killed him. I laughed when he died. Then I pissed on him."

Amanda spun, searching for the man who'd spoken out. Spotting him tied across the back of another horse, she smiled slowly. She didn't know his name but he fit in with Rafael's other men, looking just as dirty and slimy as the rest of them. "I'm going to do the same thing when they hang you."

More cursing followed, but the other Rangers started out, leading Rafael and his gang's horses, effectively cutting off the threats and insults she knew would have followed.

Rand folded his arms across his chest and shouted to the other Rangers, keeping his eyes on hers. "We'll bring up the rear. Come on, *Mrs. Keller*, you're coming with us."

Since Amanda had been trying to think of a reason to go with them anyway, she shrugged as though she had no choice, her mind racing. Flanked by the two of them, she mounted her horse, only to have Zane yank the reins from her hands.

"I don't want you taking off on us. I'll be holding on to these."

Amanda shrugged again. She had no desire to take off. Riding by herself had been more than a little scary, and she hadn't slept much at all. It was a relief to have an armed escort to Austin. She wanted to see those bastards hang, but that wasn't what she came all this way for. Lowering her eyes to hide the triumph in them, she nodded. "I understand. I'll go to Austin with you. I want to watch them hang."

Zane eyed her suspiciously. "I don't trust your sudden meekness. Are we going to find out that you should hang with them?"

"Of course not." Since they already knew her identity, she could tell them this. "I married John Keller two years ago. A week later he left with these men, and I haven't seen him since. I found out several months ago that they killed him."

Rand moved his horse closer. "Why did they kill him?"

Amanda shrugged. "Who knows? That's one of the things I wanted to ask them."

"By the way, my name is Randall Sloane. Rand. My friend here is Zane Owens. Why didn't you tell us who you were when you first met us?"

Now that it didn't matter, she told him. "I was going to shoot a man, Ranger. I didn't think it would be a good idea to tell you my name."

Rand turned to face her. "Call me Rand. And now you don't want to kill him?"

Amanda smiled. "There's no point. The law will now, and I don't have to worry about hanging for murder."

His eyes narrowed, the suspicion in them forcing her to look away. "Don't you even think about trying to kill anybody. I'd hate to see them put a noose around that pretty little neck. I have plans for it myself."

Ignoring the butterflies in her stomach, Amanda remained silent, thinking it best not to talk any more than necessary, doing her best to look straight ahead as they covered several miles. Listening to the curses and threats of Rafael's men helped take her mind off the strange feelings fluttering around inside her.

Until she looked at either one of them, and it all came back with a vengeance.

The sense of relief at having the Rangers find her again was something she couldn't quite understand. She'd never met men like them before, men who somehow managed to be both tough and gentle at the same time. Even when they handled her, their grips had been firm but never bruising. Even when their eyes darkened in anger, they didn't lash out or try to hurt her.

She couldn't deny the fact that she'd been thinking of both of them ever since she'd escaped from them earlier. She could admit, only to herself, that she was a little disappointed that they hadn't come after her.

Which was just plain stupid.

Even though their encounter earlier had been anything but friendly, there'd been a familiarity with them that made no sense. She'd been scared at first when they'd grabbed her, but after her escape, she realized that she'd been more curious than afraid. She'd also figured out something else. Not all of her nerves had been fear.

Her belly fluttered, as did the place between her legs. Her nipples hardened uncomfortably every time Zane or Rand eyed the front of her shirt.

For the first time in her life, she experienced the vulnerability, the excitement of being a woman attracted to a man. Of course, like everything else in her life, she even managed to mess that up and got attracted to two of them. She'd already lied to them, and in the present situation, they stood on opposite sides of the law.

She hated the fact that her father would be proud of her now.

"You must have loved your husband very much to want to kill Rafael to avenge his murder."

Turning at Zane's softly spoken observation, Amanda shook her head, finding it hard to look away from the gentle concern in his eyes. "I hardly knew him. My pa made me marry him. I didn't meet him until we were standing in front of the preacher."

"Then why did you want to kill Rafael?"

Damn. She'd been so lost in her thoughts that she'd answered without thinking and ended up saying the wrong thing. Why hadn't she claimed to love her husband? She hated lying, especially when she had her first taste of freedom, at least temporarily, and she vowed that once she managed to escape, she'd never lie again. "He deserves it."

Rand chuckled. "That he does. But the law takes care of men like him."

Amanda nodded absently, watching the Rangers and the outlaws ahead of her. Did they have it with them? Or had they hidden it somewhere? Since Zane rode closer, she turned to him, wanting to change the subject. "How long will it take us to get to Austin?" She didn't think it would be a good idea to let him know that she already knew the answer to that because she lived not far from town. The less they knew about her, the better.

"Day after tomorrow."

Yeah, that's what she figured. She had two days to find out where they hid it.

* * * *

Sitting around the fire that night, Amanda studied Rafael's men, trying to figure out which one would be the best one to talk to and how she could do it without one of the Rangers overhearing their conversation.

The other Rangers had introduced themselves, each man just as hard and compelling as Zane and Rand, but for some reason the two Texas Rangers she'd been riding between all day made her feel giddy and tingly inside, distracting her when she didn't need any distractions.

The Rangers got the men settled for the night amid a lot of grumbling and cursing. The Rangers handled that by gagging anyone who didn't shut up when warned, and they left the gags on for a few hours before taking them off. Everyone got the message, and they all finally stopped talking, even the little man who ran his mouth almost constantly.

Finally they'd all started to fall asleep, and Amanda made sure she knew exactly where Rafael lay. When the Rangers removed his gag to eat, he'd leered at her several times, his eyes pure evil as they roamed over her body.

She met his gaze steadily, determined to not let him see how much he scared her, letting only her disgust for him show. She couldn't deny, though, that when Rand placed her bedroll between his and Zane's, it made her feel much safer.

That is, safer from Rafael and his men.

As soon as Rand lay down next to her, that fluttering got worse. And spread.

She lay stiffly, not daring to move as he settled himself for the night, his hand on his gun. Sneaking glances at him, she couldn't tell whether he watched her or not since he'd propped his hat over his eyes, leaving them in shadow.

"Stop fidgeting and go to sleep. Are you cold?"

She didn't know how he'd seen her shiver since she'd burrowed into her bedroll, but before she could answer, he rolled her to her side and pulled her back against him. She doubted very much that the bulge against her back was his gun. Lying so stiffly it hurt, she jolted when his hand went between her thighs to lift her upper one over his, his thigh pushed up against her center.

His big hand covered her stomach, massaging gently. "You'll be warmer this way. Now go to sleep."

Sleep?

Amanda trembled, her hips rocking of their own accord against his thigh, making the place between her legs burn and tingle. Her breathing became ragged when the side of the hand resting on her belly brushed against the underside of her breasts. Her nipples got that tight feeling again, and she had to bite her lip not to beg him to touch them.

Zane drew her gaze as though willing her to look at him. Everyone else had fallen asleep until only he sat there, sipping coffee and staring at her. His eyes held hers for several long seconds before moving over her body, settling on where Rand touched her, as though he could see through the bedroll to the hand that moved so hypnotically over her stomach. When he lifted his gaze to hers again, she could swear she could feel the heat in them even at this distance.

Did he know what Rand did to her? Could he somehow know what his friend's touch made her feel?

Did he know how his touch affected her when he'd wrapped an arm around her and held her against him?

Averting her eyes, she stared at the fire for a while, the heat from Rand's body soaking into hers and making her lethargic. She snuck another glance at Zane to find him watching her again.

Damn, why didn't he fall asleep?

Rand's breathing evened out behind her, and the hand on her stomach stopped moving. The heat pouring from him warmed her from shoulders to toes. Combined with the sleepless nights she'd had since she left home, she had a hard time keeping her eyes open, but she didn't want to move for fear of waking him before he fell into a deep sleep.

Zane had to be tired, too. As soon as he fell asleep, she could make her way to the man she'd chosen to question.

She looked up again to find Zane still staring at her and hurriedly closed her eyes. The fire burned lower now, but the heat coming from Rand's body kept her plenty warm. She struggled to open them again, wincing at the bright firelight and closing them again.

Listening to Rand's breathing, she gradually relaxed against him, promising herself she'd check on Zane again in just a few minutes.

* * * *

Leaning against his saddle, Zane watched Amanda as sleep finally overtook her. She'd been fighting it for some time now, looking furtively in his direction ever since the others had fallen asleep.

Rand opened his eyes and sat up slightly, a slow smile playing over his face as he met Zane's eyes before lying back on his bedroll.

Zane's own bedroll waited for him right beside Amanda, a fact that stirred his groin uncomfortably every time he thought about it. Who was he kidding? He'd been hard ever since Rand found her again.

He looked away from her, his gaze sliding over Rafael and his men before unerringly returning to her, her slightest movement drawing his attention.

"She's a beauty, ain't she? All that black hair. And those eyes. She looks mighty fine in them pants, too. Surprised she married somebody from Rafael's gang."

At the whispered voice, Zane tensed and looked away from Silas, a Texas Ranger who'd only signed up a few months earlier. He slid a glance toward her again to make sure she still slept. "Said her daddy made her."

Silas stared at Amanda as she slept, and although he had no claim to her, it made Zane's blood boil. "She's a real sweetheart. Makes a man want to protect her. Did you see the way Jim sat between her and Rafael when we were eating? But she's got some fire in her. When we get back to Austin—"

"You'll stay away from her."

A shocked silence fell. "You want her for yourself?"

Zane shot him a look. "Maybe."

Silas shifted beside him. "I see. I heard you and Rand'll be leavin' the Rangers soon. You ain't signing up again?"

"Been three years. We're movin' on." Zane's eyes shifted to Amanda again when she turned and cuddled against Rand, obviously sound asleep and probably cold. The air had grown chilly, and he'd kept the fire low. A bright fire could be seen for miles, and they didn't know if Rafael had any more men out there who might try to find him and break him free.

He could almost hear the questions the much younger Ranger wanted to ask and swallowed his frustration. He'd been thinking about Amanda and Rand's obvious attraction to her. His own attraction to her kept him tense and hard as a rock. She was nothing like Beatrice, the wife they'd shared a lifetime ago and who'd died in an Indian attack.

Beatrice had been docile and shy, the perfect wife.

Amanda carried a rifle and was the widow of an outlaw, completely unsuitable, but he couldn't keep his eyes off of her. His cock sure as hell didn't give a damn.

"I hear a lot of stories about you and Ranger Sloane. You're both heroes to most of the other Rangers. The men have a lot of respect for both of you."

Zane shrugged, saying nothing.

"I heard that you shared a wife and that she got kilt by the Indians, and that you joined the Rangers after she died."

"That's right." Zane had a momentary flash of panic when he couldn't conjure Beatrice's face in his mind. He felt like a heel as her image became dimmer and dimmer over time until he could no longer remember her voice or what her skin felt like beneath his hands. Time and the women he and Rand had shared since then had all but wiped her from his memory.

They'd been married less than a year, but she'd been their wife and he should have carried more of her with him. It hadn't been a love match by any means, but still…

"You plannin' on sharin' another wife? Maybe Amanda Keller?"

Tired of the other man's questions, and not quite sure what he and Rand would do about Amanda, Zane stood. "If you've got the energy to keep yappin', you can take watch. Wake Jim in an hour." He eyed Rafael and his men as he made his way to where his bedroll lay on the other side of Amanda and saw that Rand had placed them *very* close together. He groaned as his cock pressed more insistently against his pants when he lay down next to her. Once he'd settled, he tried to sleep, but Silas' question kept rolling over and over in his mind.

He and Rand had shared women ever since they'd pooled their money together to buy their first whore when they were only fifteen years old. By the time they were ready to marry and settle down, it was as natural as breathing for them to marry and share the same woman.

But Amanda Keller was nothing like their sweet, biddable Beatrice.

Lying beside Amanda now, falling asleep proved difficult. His cock was wide awake, his desire for Amanda sharp and hot, not the comfortable contentment he felt with Beatrice.

Amanda turned in her sleep with a sigh, cuddling against him as she slid farther down inside her bedroll.

Zane barely bit back a groan at feeling her slight weight pressed against him. He put out an arm to pillow her head without even thinking about it, and, as though she'd done it a thousand times, she accepted his offer, and cuddled even closer.

Over her head, Zane met Rand's eyes, unsurprised that his friend woke when Amanda moved. It had been a long time since they'd slept with a woman between them, but some things never changed.

Memories flashed through his mind.

Closeness. Warmth. Contentment. Passion. The softness of a woman held against him through the night.

He turned his head and breathed deeply, filling his lungs with her scent. Even a woman who'd been on the trail smelled like a woman.

Not until that moment did he realize just how much he'd missed it.

Rand smiled, moved closer to Amanda's other side, and settled back to sleep.

Zane closed his eyes, a little unsettled by how good Amanda felt next to him. He and Rand had already decided to quit the Rangers and get married again, and it was obvious Rand had his sights set on Amanda.

Zane wasn't so sure. Amanda was the kind of woman who could rip a man's heart out, not the kind of woman a man took as a wife.

Chapter Three

Amanda couldn't believe she'd fallen asleep last night. She should have known they would leave someone on watch, but even then she'd thought Zane would fall asleep after an hour or two. The last time she snuck a glance, he'd been wide awake, drinking a cup of coffee and staring at her.

That's the last thing she remembered until she woke this morning to find all of the Texas Rangers already awake and busy around the fire. They'd untied Rafael and his men so they could eat and quickly loaded them back up on their horses. Rand brought her coffee and a biscuit, and then went about putting out the fire.

This time, they tied the men's hands in front and tied two of Rafael's men's horses to the horses in front of them. That left Rand and Zane with three men between them, one of them Rafael and the other a giant of a man.

Seeing her chance, she volunteered to hold the reins of the other man's horse so they could focus on the more dangerous of the men, and to her relief, they reluctantly agreed. In an effort to give her the least threatening of all the men, they'd given her the one whom she'd already considered to be the weakest, not just in strength, but in character. Her elation at the opportunity to question one of Rafael's men was short-lived. Rand and Zane both stayed close, as close as they could under the circumstances, and certainly close enough to keep her from asking, what was his name…Billy, the question she needed to ask.

Zane and Rand both watched her throughout the day, but neither spoke to her, as though they didn't want the outlaws to overhear their conversation. Their eyes, however, spoke volumes. Zane eyed her suspiciously as though expecting her to take off at any moment, but his gaze kept falling to her breasts and lingering. Every time she met his gaze afterward, his jaw hardened and he looked away, leaving her feeling bereft.

On the other side of her, Rand watched her, winking every once in a while, his eyes raking over her body from head to toe, silently reminding her of the way he'd held her the night before.

After half a day of riding, the Rangers came to a grove of trees near a small pond. Zane held up a hand.

"We'll stop here and rest the horses."

The midday sun beat down relentlessly, and Amanda did her best to stay covered so she didn't get burned. Her long sleeves protected her arms, her gloves protected her hands, and the brim of her hat shaded her face, but the heat had gotten so bad it made her dizzy.

Zane moved forward as Jim and Rand dismounted and pulled the outlaws, one at a time, from their horses to settle them beneath a tree. He stood guard over them while the other Ranger, Silas, got to work taking care of the horses.

Rafael got to his feet and glared at them. "I'm thirsty, Rangers. Somebody bring me some water."

Jim pushed Rafael back down to the ground. "If you didn't run your trap so much, you wouldn't be so thirsty. You've been talkin' more than your buddy. You just spent all mornin' tryin' to bribe us with gold that don't even belong to you."

That drew Amanda's attention, but she turned her head away to watch the horses drinking so no one could see her interest.

Rafael cursed and began to fight, kicking and screaming until the others joined in. The big man tried to ram Silas in the stomach with his shoulder, and it took both Silas and Rand to subdue him.

With a curse, Rand strode over to her, the hand he placed on her thigh sending heat straight to her center. "You stay here while we get these guys settled, and I'll be back to take him from you."

Amanda nodded, hardly believing her luck as Rand moved away to join the others, not far enough away that she couldn't be rescued right away, but far enough that she could speak in a whisper without being overheard. Keeping her eyes on the other men, she leaned closer to Billy.

* * * *

Rand left the man whose reins he'd been holding with Zane and hurried back to Amanda, not trusting that Billy would be as harmless as he appeared. After all, the man, hardly more than a boy, rode with Rafael's gang, so he must have had to prove himself, and Rand couldn't take any chance that Amanda could be hurt.

As tough as she appeared, she was still a woman and a little one at that, one that fit right against him as though she'd been made for him. Damn, he loved how she'd snuggled against him the night before. He'd been hard as a rock all night, but lying next to her for hours had been worth any discomfort. He hardly knew her, but he already wanted her badly and couldn't wait to get to know everything about her. As soon as he and Zane got these men to Austin, they would be leaving the Rangers and he couldn't help but think they'd met Amanda at the perfect time. They wanted to take a wife again and even though he'd cared for Beatrice, he could see now that she never would have been strong enough to live on the ranch he and Zane wanted.

They'd been taken in by her delicate beauty and should have realized that she was delicate all the way through.

She'd never wanted them to take her the way he and Zane had always taken a woman together. For Beatrice, it had been one at a time and never with any games or exploring. Only at night and only with the covers over them. They'd both been content with her and would have lived out the rest of their lives with her, trading passion for a woman they could build a life with.

He couldn't imagine being *content* with someone like Amanda. She was full of fire and the meekness she displayed since they caught up to her again didn't fool him a bit, especially when her eyes told a different tale. The desire and curiosity in them kept him hard most of the day.

The way she avoided his eyes pissed him off and made him want to turn her over his knee, and that got him hard all over again.

She was up to something, and he had to keep a close eye on her until he figured out what it could be.

He wished he had the chance to talk to her more today, but he hadn't wanted Rafael's men to hear their conversation. Once they dropped off the outlaws at Ranger Headquarters, they'd ride with her to San Antonio and spend the time getting to know her.

Starting toward Amanda now, he looked over to find Zane watching her as he helped water the horses. The expression on Zane's face last night when Amanda had cuddled up to him convinced him that Zane had ideas about Amanda, too, and tried hard to deny it.

She was tough, but an irresistible vulnerability lay beneath the surface that Rand was dying to explore. Combined with the flare of innocence and lust he saw in her eyes whenever he touched her, it made it hard to keep his hands off of her.

Once the horses had been taken care of and everybody had eaten and drunk their fill, most of them napped under the trees while the horses rested. Zane reclined close by, nibbling on some jerky, and kept Amanda under his watchful eyes.

Rand sat down on her other side. "Tell us about your family."

She looked startled at the question. "What do you know about my family?"

Rand exchanged a look with Zane, who'd stiffened and narrowed his eyes suspiciously. He shrugged, attempting to hide that his own suspicions had been roused. "I don't know anything about your kin. You said you were gonna meet up with them in San Antone. Why are they there and you're here?"

Amanda looked away. "I had to do something for my pa so I stayed behind. Now I'm going to meet them in San Antonio."

Aware of Zane's interest, he leaned back and plucked a blade of grass. "So it's just you and your pa? And he's letting you ride all the way to San Antone by yourself? Did you live alone when your husband left or did you live with your pa?"

Amanda stood, her movements jerky and agitated. "Why are you asking me all these questions?"

Rand took in her red face and the fact that she wouldn't look at either him or Zane. She didn't lie very well, but she'd been lying to them ever since they'd met her. She'd learn in a hurry that neither one of them tolerated lies, especially from their woman. "Just curious. We're gonna take you to San Antone as soon as we drop off these men in Austin. It'll be nice to know who we're meeting. Is there some reason you don't want us to know?"

Amanda turned and dusted the dirt off of her bottom, something he would have given his last dollar to be able to do. "No, but I'm tired. I want to sleep before we head out again." She got up and moved away from them, leaving him alone with Zane.

Leaning back on an elbow, he stuck the blade of grass in his mouth. "She's hiding something. We'll have to keep a close eye on her."

Zane nodded and remained silent, but Rand could see that he had something on his mind.

Knowing Zane, Rand waited him out.

"I'm not sure she's what I want in a wife. She sure isn't quiet and docile."

Rand chuckled. "I think she's even more of a hellcat than she's showing. Zane, Beatrice never would have survived on the ranch we want anyway and you know it. This one's strong enough. Beatrice never would have ridden out here by herself." When Zane's eyes narrowed, Rand held up a hand. "I know you're thinking I'm a bastard, but Amanda's more the kind of woman we need than

Beatrice. I never would have left her, Zane, but she was too delicate for us. If we're going to take a wife together, she needs to be strong."

Zane inclined his head. "That same thought's crossed my mind a time or two. I don't know. But you might be marrying Amanda on your own."

Shocked, Rand sat up and looked over to make sure none of the other men could hear him. "Damn it, Zane. What about the plans we have for the ranch?"

Zane shrugged and said nothing.

Rand looked over to see Amanda making herself comfortable beneath another tree, far from the others. Because he watched her closely, he caught the look she shared with Billy, the one she'd rode with earlier. It came and went quickly, but he'd seen it all the same.

"Did you see—"

"Yeah. We're gonna have to separate them. She was talking to him earlier. She's up to something." He stared at her until she averted her eyes, her red face plain to see even at this distance. "Yep, she's up to something, and I don't trust her one bit."

Rand hid a smile. "If you're trying to convince me you're not interested in her because you don't trust her, you're wasting your time. You can't keep your eyes off her any more than I can."

* * * *

The fact that Zane couldn't take his eyes off of Amanda for more than a few minutes at a time really burned his britches.

He could only imagine what life would be like if they married her. He'd never get a lick of work done and would spend all of his time either tumbling her or thinking about tumbling her. Unless she lied to him. In that case, he'd paddle her fine ass and tumble her some more. He'd thought for sure that Beatrice was the kind of woman he needed, but he'd never wanted her the way he wanted Amanda, and it made him feel guilty as hell.

That little catch in Amanda's breath every time he touched her would drive him insane. He could only imagine what it would be like when—if—he touched her more intimately.

After the way she and Billy looked at each other, he and Rand had carefully kept them separated, but it didn't seem to matter to either one of them. They never looked at each other and acted like complete strangers, making him wonder if he'd just imagined the entire thing. He looked over at her again, trying to convince himself that he just wanted to make sure she didn't get into any trouble now that they'd ridden into Austin.

Hell, now she had him lying to himself.

He watched her because he couldn't keep his damn eyes off of her. He imagined what she would look like beneath the men's clothes she wore. He wondered how her skin would feel, how she smelled, how she tasted.

Hell, he had to stop thinking about her or he would have to walk into Ranger Headquarters with his cock tenting his fucking pants the way it had for most of the day. He could only imagine what it would be like if she belonged to him. Damn it, just as he'd feared, she occupied his thoughts when he should have been doing his damn job.

Angry now, he dragged a cursing Rafael and one of his men off of their horses and turned to yell over his shoulder to her. "Tether your horse and go sit in the shade. We'll be out in a bit to take you to the hotel for dinner." Ignoring the look of surprised hurt on her face, he forced himself to walk away without looking back.

Rand walked up, pulling Billy behind him. When the younger man looked over his shoulder at Amanda, Rand jerked him back around. "Keep your fucking eyes off of her."

Zane's movements were hurried, basically handing the men over and going into the captain's office with Rand to officially resign from the Rangers. He had a sick feeling in the pit of his stomach the entire time, anxious to get back to Amanda. He hated leaving her alone out there, and it pissed him off. They were in Austin, with plenty of people in the street, and it was broad daylight. She'd be fine.

Hell, none of that mattered. The need to get back to her had him impatiently pacing as he waited for Jim to finish telling the captain what had happened. By the time he finished, the knot in Zane's stomach had started to burn.

Captain Logan stood, his eyes flicking back and forth between Zane and Rand. "I want to thank you men for your service. I'm going to hold on to your papers for two months. If you change your mind and—"

Zane had already turned toward the door, his instincts telling him to hurry. "Thank you, Captain. We have to go." He raced outside, his stomach sinking when he found exactly what he'd been afraid of finding.

Rand came to a halt right beside him. "She's gone."

Zane cursed a blue streak, his anger mostly at himself for allowing her escape to hurt him. "We don't even know which direction she went"

Rand nodded and turned. "Let's talk to Billy."

Zane had already started back into the building. "I don't like this."

Ten minutes later, they headed back outside, Zane's jaw clenched in anger. "Amanda's no better than the rest of their gang. When we find her, we'll have to bring her in. You know that, right?"

Rand's own face looked as if it had been carved of stone. "We're not Rangers anymore, remember? We'll return the gold, but I'm not giving 'em Amanda 'til I find out what's what."

Zane had been afraid of that. "We'd better find your woman in a hurry, then, before she can get herself into more trouble."

Ignoring Rand's sharp look, he turned his horse and headed out of town, his hand itching to paddle Amanda's ass for doing this to Rand.

Damn it, and to him.

Chapter Four

Amanda rode as fast as she could, heading back toward the rocks where she'd first met the Rangers. She wished she could have found a way to get away from them before now, but they'd been watching her too closely, especially Zane and Rand. They would have come after her in a heartbeat, too suspicious of her to let her get away without answering a lot of questions.

Every time she'd caught one of them looking at her, her heart beat faster and a strange warmth went through her, unlike anything she'd felt with her husband. A giggle escaped before she could prevent it. God, what had they done to her? She wanted them to touch her, *both* of them, and couldn't stop thinking about what they'd look like naked.

John's lovemaking had reminded her of a pig rutting, and if that's what men wanted to do with her body, she would be better off avoiding them.

She knew somehow that it wouldn't be that way with Zane or Rand. It was in their eyes, a gentleness, a strength, neither her father nor her husband had ever possessed.

She couldn't think about it. She'd already seen for herself how horrible having a man could be, trouble she could live without. Even if Zane and Rand would be different, she couldn't afford them right now.

Something told her that she would always remember them and wonder…

Following the now-familiar terrain, she went as fast as she dared, not wanting to tire her horse but needing to put as much distance as she could between her and the Rangers before nightfall. She didn't know whether they'd come after her but had to assume that they would.

Even the thought of seeing them again made her smile.

Darkness had already started to fall by the time she'd gotten only a couple of miles out of town. She slowed, stopping impatiently to let her horse drink. She had to hurry. So much depended on getting back as fast as she could. She had plenty of water but only had enough food to last another day or two, but she had more important things to think about than that.

Her mother and sister depended on her and she couldn't imagine what their lives would be like if she didn't finish this.

God, she was tired. Days of riding, sleepless nights in the open, and fear had just about worn her out.

Hours went by. She didn't know how many, but she knew she'd have to stop soon.

Keeping Midnight at a slow pace, she had trouble keeping her eyes open as they made their way through the night. She slumped over Midnight's neck, intending to just rest her eyes for a minute or two. When Midnight slowed even more, she blinked her eyes open but everything was black and she couldn't make out a thing, so she closed them again.

Just for a minute. She really had to stop.

* * * *

"Well, looky what we got us here."

The voice barely penetrated, and Amanda didn't even get time to open her eyes before she found herself yanked roughly from her horse into the arms of a stranger. A smelly one. Struggling only gained her a few inches, his hold on her arms unbreakable.

Wide awake now, she looked around to see four others, each as disgusting as the man who held her. Reaching for bravado she wished she had, she sneered. "Haven't any of you ever heard of a bath?"

The man holding on to her arms turned her to face him as the other men moved in closer, running their hands over her hair, her arms, her bottom, making her skin crawl everywhere they touched. "You got a big mouth. You should be nice to us. It'll make it easier on you. If you fight us, it's gonna hurt even more."

Amanda struggled and screamed, her mind filled with horror. Her terror got worse when one of the men reached for the front of her shirt and pulled hard, ripping it and baring her right breast. Frantic now, she kept screaming, trying to tug her arms free to cover herself.

This couldn't be happening!

Why had she set out on her own? She should have told Zane and Rand everything and begged for their help. Damn it, they would have probably helped her, and at least she wouldn't be in the situation she found herself in now.

Still screaming as loud as she could, she kicked at the men attacking her, nearly out of her mind with fear and a strange numbness. *Please, God, let this be a bad dream.* She couldn't hold them off for long and soon found herself flat on her back, the breath knocked from her lungs as greedy hands reached for her.

It had to be a bad dream.

Two of the men held her arms down, laughing and taunting each other as the other three ripped her shirt the rest of the way, baring both breasts.

Although she doubted anyone could hear her, she kept screaming, cursing them and fighting them with all of her strength. Just when she thought they would win, a shot rang out.

Startled, she stopped screaming as the men above her froze.

They all turned as one, surprised enough to loosen their hold on her.

She quickly scooted away as they all stood, reaching for the guns at their belts. With their back to her, they blocked her view of whoever had come up behind them. She'd hoped Zane and Rand would find her, but she'd ended up in a place she didn't recognize. Fearing whoever fired the shot was someone else, some other outlaw, she scrambled to her feet, staggering like a drunk while holding the edges of her shirt together. She backed away, looking around frantically for Midnight.

"Come over here, Amanda."

Stunned, Amanda whipped her head around, almost falling when she did. She'd already recognized that deep voice and gulped, her breath hitching in overwhelming relief as she stared straight into the eyes of Zane Owens.

They'd found her.

His eyes looked harder than before but with a gentleness in them for her she couldn't resist.

She took a step toward him and then another before she'd even made the conscious decision to move.

The man who'd pulled her from her horse stepped forward, drawing Zane's hard gaze. "Git outta here before you get hurt. Ain't none of this any of yer business."

Rand, who sat on his horse right next to Zane, smiled coldly, keeping his gun pointed at the man who'd spoken. "Oh, she's our business, all right. And you touched her. Amanda, get over here right now."

On legs that shook, Amanda obeyed him, not looking at the other men as she passed them, her eyes drawn to Rand's. Because of that, it took her by surprise when one of the other men grabbed her and pulled her against him before she even had a chance to struggle.

A heartbeat later another shot rang out and the man went flying backward, almost taking her with him.

Scrambling for balance, she looked up at Zane, his smoking gun still pointed at the man now lying on the ground behind her, and if possible, his expression hardened even more. Seeing that the man had only been hit in the shoulder, she backed away, her eyes moving back to the men who'd attacked her repeatedly as she searched the darkness for Midnight. She had a death grip on her shirt, her hand bunched tightly to hold the ends of it together.

Rand held out a hand. "No. Don't worry about your horse. Come to me, Amanda. Now."

The demand in his voice cut like a knife through the sense of unreality surrounding her. Still holding her shirt together, she walked straight toward him, and lifted her free arm to take his outstretched hand, amazed at his show of strength when he bent and lifted her with one arm. Not until one side of her was plastered against him as he seated her across his lap, did she realize how cold she'd become.

In fact, she couldn't stop shaking.

His solid strength was like a warm haven to her, one she leaned into readily. His arm came around her to hold her securely as the other still held a gun pointed at the men who'd attacked her.

She burrowed against his chest, turning to watch the other men, scared they would try to come after her. She should have known better. The look she'd had of Zane's and Rand's faces scared her even without having a gun pointed at her.

The other men looked mad as hell, sneaking glances at her but they all kept their hands up and backed away, not daring to come forward. Now that she got a good look at them, she could see none could compare in strength to Zane and Rand, but they'd been strong enough to attack her. With five of them, she hadn't stood a chance.

She hated her own weakness, unable to believe how completely defenseless she'd been. She hadn't even been able to go for the knife in her boot. Zane said something to the men, but her heart pounded so loudly she couldn't make sense of it, only the icy coldness of his tone coming through.

Blocking their voices out, she leaned heavily against Rand as he turned his horse away, thankful for his strength in holding her on his lap. She stared into the night, relieved to see Zane ride up on the other side of Rand holding on to Midnight's reins.

"How is she?" The tenderness on his face, so beautiful on such harsh features, brought a lump to her throat that she couldn't even manage to swallow.

Rand's hold tightened. "She's shaking. Bad. We need to find a place to stop so we can check her out. Zane...there's blood on her thigh. It looks like they cut her when they were trying to cut her pants off of her."

Hearing the worry in his voice, Amanda shook her head. She didn't feel anything. No pain. No fear, just...nothing. "I'm all right." Her voice sounded thin and scratchy to her own ears, but she didn't bother to repeat herself. Her teeth chattered, making it difficult to talk anyway. Strangely, she didn't feel cold.

Her fingers were numb where her hand pressed against her breast. She didn't seem able to loosen her grip. Grateful for the dull, gray fog that seemed to settle all around her, she let Rand support her weight and stared in Zane's direction.

She didn't know why Zane tossed a blanket to Rand and helped him pull it around her. She didn't need it, but she just couldn't work up the energy to object. The low murmur of their voices seemed to come from far away, but still she drew comfort from them as they rode through the night. So she just sat there and listened.

Resting her cheek against Rand's chest, she stared at the sleeve of Zane's jacket, not knowing and not caring how long they rode before they stopped. She couldn't work up any energy even when Zane took her from Rand and set her down on top of her bedroll.

How did her bedroll get there?

She sat stiffly, her eyes drawn to the fire that had somehow appeared. The other men had had a fire. She'd had trouble seeing the men's faces clearly because of the fire glowing from behind them, which made them appear even more sinister. But she'd still seen their eyes. She wondered if she'd ever be able to forget that evil look in their eyes or their crazy laughter.

Realizing suddenly that her hand burned, she tried to work up enough energy to move back from the fire.

"Amanda, come on, baby, let go."

It took tremendous effort to drag her eyes away from the flames and look up into Rand's eyes. She'd heard his words but for some reason couldn't make sense of them. "What?" Her voice came out husky and breathless.

His dark eyes looked golden in the firelight. "You have to let go of your shirt so we can see how badly you're hurt."

"Hurt?" She blinked, her gaze dropping to where his hand covered hers. She wasn't hurt. They'd come just in time. Relieved to know that Rand's hand over hers is what had made it feel so hot, she closed her eyes, glad she didn't have to work up the strength to move. She just wanted to sleep.

"Lay her down. It looks small but deep. I'm going to try to get her pants off of her without hurting her."

Amanda panicked when Rand pushed her onto her back. "No!" She fought him, punching and kicking the same way she'd done with those other men, still feeling every place their hands had been. "Don't touch me." Her skin still crawled and she couldn't stand to be touched right now, not even by them.

"Stop it! Amanda! That's enough." Rand leaned close, his face filling her vision. "Zane and I want to check you. You've been hurt. Just let us take care of you."

Amanda struggled to sit up, feeling dazed and a little foolish. Of course it hadn't been those other men touching her, but right now she really didn't want to be touched at all. "No. I'm not hurt. Please let go of me. I don't want to be touched."

Rand ripped her shirt aside. "Look." He kept her arms held at her sides despite her struggles and waited until she looked down at her bared breasts.

Surprised to see scratches on her left breast, right above her nipple, she looked back up at Rand in disbelief. "How—"

Rand's lips tightened. "I don't know. Maybe their fingernails, which were probably dirty, too. We've got some warm water and soap. We need to clean you up so you don't get infected." He spoke to her as he would a child, softly and spacing the words out.

Zane touched her arm, a strained smile curving his lips. "Just lay back and let us take care of it."

Amanda tried to grab the ends of her shirt to pull it closed, but they eluded her. Seeing his worry made her feel better, but she still wanted to take care of it herself. "I'll do it."

Zane's brows went up. "I wasn't asking, Amanda. We're going to deal with this if we have to hold you down and strip you to do it. Now, do you want to do this the easy way or the hard way?"

Rand bristled beside her. "Zane—"

Awareness hit her, the fog surrounding her lifting at Zane's harsh tone. She became conscious of her surroundings for the first time since they'd arrived. Looking around, she saw that they'd bedded the horses for the night and had a pot of coffee and another small pot heating on the fire. With awareness came embarrassment, pain, and the realization that she shook badly, cold all the way to her bones. "Damn, I'm cold. Why the hell are you taking my clothes off when it's so cold?"

Zane smiled faintly and touched her cheek. "There she is. Now behave so we can take care of you."

"I said I can do it." She pulled her hands free of Rand's grip to cover herself again. "You shouldn't see me like this. Just turn your backs and—damn it, Rand."

He pulled her hand away to cover her injured breast with a cool cloth. "We've already seen you and we've got to get you cleaned up. Now lay back like a good girl or we'll have to do this the hard way." He eased her onto her back and rubbed a hand down her arm before releasing her.

She smiled, a little light-headed from the relief that flowed through her, appreciating their attempts to ease the tension. "I've never been a good girl."

Zane reached for the fastening of her pants and chuckled, the sound like a warm blanket wrapped around her. "Now there's a big surprise. Stick with us and we'll teach you how to be really bad. Rand's got a streak of it a mile wide." His low, amused drawl even made her laugh, something she'd thought impossible under the circumstances.

"And you don't?" Surprised that she actually teased him, she lay there, amazed that her skin tingled warmly wherever they touched, the concern on their faces and the gentleness in their comforting touch wiping out the crawly feeling those other men had left behind.

Rand laughed and kissed her hair. "Zane's mean is all the way to the bone."

She held her breath as Zane began lowering her pants, embarrassed that her dark curls could be seen clearly in the firelight. Even with the fire she'd gotten uncomfortably cold, and the cloth Rand held to her breast only made it worse. "That's cold, Rand. Why are you being so mean?"

Rand chuckled. "It was warm when I walked over here with it. It's your fault you wouldn't let me put it on as soon as I came over. I'll go warm it up, and when I come back don't fight me." He tapped her nose and looked down to where Zane had tugged her pants down to her knees. He met Zane's look, his smile falling. "I'll get the whiskey. We're gonna have to get her good and drunk."

Zane sighed and tugged off her boots, shaking his head when her knife fell out. With a look, he placed it close enough for her to reach before he finished removing her pants. "Don't stab me with it. I'm trying to help you."

Now that she knew about it, the pain in her thigh got steadily worse. On top of that, the look that passed between Zane and Rand worried her. "What's wrong with my leg? Why do you want me to get drunk?" Sitting up, she pulled the end of her shirt over her cold breasts, glaring in Rand's direction.

"Stay still, damn it." Zane's sharp demand made her jump.

She gasped when she saw the cut, still oozing blood. "How did that happen without me feeling it?"

Zane sighed and exchanged the soiled cloth he'd been using for another. "You were busy trying to fight 'em off. Just lay back and stop moving around. I gotta get it to stop bleeding, and it's hard enough to do without you squirming."

Rand came back with the damp cloth, a bottle of whiskey, and two tins. He shot another worried look at her leg before he handed the tins to Zane, pulled her shirt out of her grip, and put the warm cloth over the scratches on her breast. With a warning look, he opened the bottle of whiskey and handed it to her. "Start drinking." He quickly stripped the ripped shirt from her with one hand, holding the bottle to her lips with the other.

Amanda pushed the vile-smelling liquor away. "No. I don't drink. Why are you giving me whiskey? That's clean enough. Give me my shirt back." She winced when Rand wiped the cloth over her breast, feeling very exposed at being out here in the open with the two of them and completely naked. Although their gazes raked over her body, neither one of them made a comment or touched her in an inappropriate way, and, to her amazement, she felt perfectly safe. She still wanted her clothes back and reached for them while pushing the bottle of whiskey away and trying to see what Zane was doing. Since they were stronger and she attempted to outmaneuver four hands with her two, they won.

Rand gripped her chin. "You got any clothes in your saddlebags?"

"Yeah, but they're real dirty. I just changed into these before I met up with you two. Just give me my shirt back." A few drops of whiskey spilled on her breast, making her hiss at the sting.

Rand blew on it and hurriedly pressed the cloth to the scratches. "Your shirt's ruined. Hold this here and start drinking that whiskey and I'll go get one of my shirts for you." He tweaked her pebbled nipple lightly, grinning at her gasp before he stood and walked away, adding more wood to the fire on the way back to his saddlebag.

"Drink the damned whiskey."

Turning from watching Rand's swagger, she frowned at Zane. "But I don't want—"

Zane applied pressure to her thigh. Hard. His eyes had a desperate look in them that made her uneasy. "You'll drink it or I'll pour it down your throat."

Amanda yelped and tried to pull away, but Zane had a firm grip on her. "Why do I have to drink this awful stuff?" The smell reminded her of her father and made her sick to her stomach.

Zane sighed again. "I'm gonna have to stitch it closed to get the bleeding to stop. Drink the damned whiskey. If not, it's gonna hurt like hell. At least the whiskey'll warm you up until we can finish and get you in the bedroll."

Scared now, Amanda tried to pull away. "No. I don't want you sticking needles in me. Just leave it alone. It'll stop bleeding. I swear."

Zane kept the pressure on it and gripped her chin. "Listen, honey. I don't want to hurt you. I'll be as gentle as I can, but I've gotta get the bleeding stopped. It's only going to need a couple stitches. Don't worry. Now start sipping the whiskey and keep on sipping it. If you don't, I'll have no choice but to pour it down your throat or stitch you without it."

That scared her even more. Grabbing his arm, she licked her lips nervously. "Please don't do this." She looked up pleadingly at Rand as he came back, shaking out one of his big shirts. "It'll be fine by morning." Uncomfortable with all the fuss, and a little frightened now that she'd become more alert, her thigh had really begun to throb. She kept trying to push them away.

In the end she lost. Rand wouldn't give her his shirt until she'd taken three sips of whiskey. After that it didn't taste so bad. It made her feel warm inside and made her head swim.

Rand kept lifting the bottle to her lips, forcing sips of the whiskey down her throat as Zane tended to her thigh. At least with Rand's shirt on, her breasts and her pussy were now covered.

That didn't keep the back of Zane's hand from brushing her folds as he tended to her thigh.

For some reason she no longer minded at all.

Every time she tried to look down to see what Zane was doing, Rand distracted her, getting her to drink more and more of the whiskey, and kept washing her scratches with the warm water.

Amanda pushed at the bottle he held up to her lips yet again. "It burns. I feel dizzy. I don't want any more. The bleeding's probably stopped by now."

"Too bad. Drink a little bit more. Please. We don't want to hurt you and if you're drunk, it'll help all of us. Don't look at Zane. Look at me. Billy told us what he said to you."

Amanda stiffened, pushing at him clumsily and would have fallen over if Rand hadn't caught her. "I'm not telling you anything."

Rand smiled. "You don't have to. We know everything. You want the gold they hid. Well, you're not going to get it. That's government gold and we're taking it back to Austin with us and turning it in."

Panicked, Amanda reached out to grab his arm and missed. "No! I need it. You have to let me have it. John promised it to Pa. He won't let 'em go until I get it. Damn it. I have to give him some of the gold or he'll never let 'em go."

* * * *

Rand exchanged a look with Zane, who nodded and motioned for him to keep her talking. With an answering nod, Rand turned back to Amanda and put the bottle to her lips again. "Take another sip and tell me about it." Exchanging another glance with Zane, he couldn't resist adding. "We'll help you, no matter what it is." Ignoring Zane's sharp look, he all but poured it down her throat, not the least bit repentant when she coughed and her eyes watered. He wanted to get her drunk enough that she didn't feel the needle that Zane sterilized. He hated like hell to do this to her, but he knew it would be worse if she felt the needle pierce that soft skin. Zane would pour some of the whiskey over the wound before he started to stitch her up, and if she didn't get good and drunk before then, it would hurt like a bitch.

He'd rather have it done to him than to watch Zane do it to her. Hell. He had to keep her talking, to get her mind off of what they had to do. It was hard to keep up with the conversation, though, distracted by her injury and his rage at the men they'd rescued her from. Looking away from her thigh, he met her eyes. "What did your husband promise your pa?"

"Some of the gold." Amanda's eyes kept closing, which would make it harder to get anything out of her if he didn't hurry.

Giving her another sip, he saw Zane also watching her, his look assessing, and Rand knew his friend was trying to determine if Amanda had drunk enough. "Amanda, who is it that your pa won't let go?" When her eyes closed again, he had to shake her, asking the question over and over until she frowned at him.

"My ma and Pamela. They have to go to Albany. On the train. Can't go without the gold."

Zane cursed and took the bottle of whiskey from her and doused Amanda's cut with it

Amanda cried out and flailed. "Stop. It hurts."

Now that she was alert again, Rand continued questioning her, trying to get as much information as he could while distracting her. "Who's Pamela?"

"My sister."

"Why do they have to go to Albany?"

"To get away from Pa. He beats 'em. Uncle in Albanys' gonna take us in. Don't do that anymore."

Rand ran a hand over her hair. "He won't. Relax. Finish telling me. Your pa won't let 'em leave 'til he gets the gold?"

"John was supposed to bring it, but he got killed. Pa said if I got it, he'd let us all go. Gotta get the gold." She passed out before Rand could ask her anything else.

Laying her back, he had a hard time looking away at the beautiful picture she made, lying there in just his shirt, her long, dark hair tangled all around her. Safe.

His hands still shook. He'd never been so scared. He and Zane had started after her, losing her trail in the darkness. When her scream split the night sky, they'd looked at each other, their shock lasting about a heartbeat before they tore after her. Her continued screams had both of them pushing their mounts to the limit, not knowing what the hell had scared her.

Had she fallen? Had an animal attacked? Each second seemed like forever, and he'd been scared to death they wouldn't get to her in time.

When they finally found her, he could have easily killed each and every one of those men with his bare hands. If they'd raped her, he probably would have.

It had surprised him a little that Zane hadn't killed the man he shot at, but he understood it. He understood the look on Zane's face when the other man grabbed her and she'd automatically looked up at them for help. The wild terror in her eyes and her absolute trust in them showed clearly in the light of the men's campfire.

Zane hadn't wanted to scare her anymore.

"Those men just about shit their pants when you told them that if it hadn't been for your woman being there, you woulda killed all of 'em. She got to you already, didn't she? I told you."

Zane's gaze slid to Amanda's face, softening slightly before turning back to gently wipe a trickle of fresh blood from her thigh. "Just hold on to her."

Rand took a shaky breath, eyeing the needle Zane held. Clenching his jaw, he laid one hand over Amanda's smooth belly and another over her thigh to keep her from jerking.

Wincing when Zane pierced her skin, Rand tightened his hold on her when she flinched, gritting his teeth. The second time Zane did it, Rand was the one who flinched when she whimpered. "Hurry up, will you?"

Zane wiped away a trickle of sweat from his forehead and glared at him. "What the hell do you think I'm doing? Just hold her, damn it."

By the time Zane finished and had bandaged her wound, they were both sweating and ready for a drink of that whiskey themselves. Together, they wrapped her wound, put her in the bedroll and settled her for the night, lying on either side of her.

Rand studied the stars, thinking out loud. "If her father wants the gold that much, she won't stop until she gets it." He paused when she whimpered in her sleep and ran a hand over her arm, murmuring to her until she settled again.

"I can't believe a man would send his daughter out to steal from men like this, especially alone. It sounds like she, her mother, and sister are trying to get away from him, and the only way to do that is to get the gold for him. If she's out here on her own like this, she's got nobody to look after her, Zane. I don't care what I have to do. I'm marrying her when we get back to Austin. I want her to belong to both of us the way Beatrice did, but if you don't want her, I still do. Once she's my wife, her father won't be able to do anything like this to her again. I'll go take care of him and put her mother and sister on a train to Albany myself."

Zane didn't say anything for a long time as Rand contemplated what it would be like to have a woman he didn't share with his best friend. Finally Zane sighed. "What if she doesn't want to marry you? What if she wants to go to Albany with her momma and sister?"

"Then I'm gonna do what I have to do to get her to change her mind." Amanda whimpered in her sleep again, prompting him to lower his voice. "Look, are you in this with me or not? I saw the way you looked at her. I saw your face when those assholes touched her. If it's going to be both of us, we need to tell her from the beginning. Or will she be with just me? I mean it, Zane, one way or another I'm taking her as my wife."

The silence stretched as Zane lay back and studied the stars, cradling Amanda's hand that came to rest on his chest when she turned in her sleep. Playing with her fingers, he nodded, smiling faintly. "She sure isn't anything like Beatrice."

"No, she isn't."

Zane rolled to his side, staring down at Amanda's face and brushing her sleek, black hair back. He traced a finger lightly over her pink lips. "Beatrice had your name. I'd want Amanda to have mine."

Rand smiled, relieved. "It's settled then. She'll be wife to both of us."

Zane rolled to his back and closed his eyes, taking Amanda's hand again. "I think it'll take both of us to handle her."

Chapter Five

Amanda woke the next morning with a pounding in her head, the most awful taste in her mouth, and a burning in her thigh. It took several seconds before the events of the previous night came crashing back. She opened her eyes, only to close them again on a moan. The bright sunlight told her that she'd slept late. Very late. She had to blink several times before she could actually get her eyes to stay open and had to shade them with her hand in order to keep them that way. Wincing at the burn in her thigh, she sat up, a little disconcerted to find Rand crouched only a few feet away, watching her.

"What are we doing here? You should have woken me up hours ago. What's going on?"

Rand straightened from where he'd been filling a cup of coffee and brought it to her. "Drink this while I look at your leg."

Amanda accepted the cup, nearly burning herself with sloshed coffee when he yanked the bedroll down the rest of the way to expose her bare legs. Luckily she managed to pull down the overlarge shirt she wore to cover her pussy but not in time to prevent him from looking at her dark curls and smiling in appreciation.

"Stop smiling at me like that. You shouldn't be looking at me like this."

Rand slid his hand higher to hold her thigh in place, his large, dark hand on her skin making her leg look pale and delicate. A slow grin appeared as he playfully reached a finger beneath the hem of her shirt and lightly brushed her curls, the action sending white-hot lightning through her. "I saw your pussy already last night, darlin', and didn't attack you. Hell, the back of my hand brushed those soft curls more'n once when I was holding on to you so Zane could stitch you up. You sure are soft. Thought about having my way with you when you weren't so mouthy but it probably wouldn't have been much fun taking an unconscious woman." He winked, grinning as his finger kept moving, teasing her folds as he kept her thigh immobile.

Amanda sputtered with laughter before she could stop herself. His mischievousness made him damned near irresistible. Jeepers, that felt good. "You...you...I...oh hell!" Her sputtering ended on a gasp when Rand's thumb brushed her clit, the shock of it stealing her breath.

He leaned over her, blocking out the sun, a half-smile on his face. "You like that, don't you, darlin'? God, the look on your face." He lifted her shirt, pushing it back over her hips to expose her completely. "Last night I imagined this little clit peeking out at me." He parted her folds, the more direct touch to her clit making her jolt and surprising another cry from her. "I had trouble sleeping all night."

Stunned by the most amazing thing she'd ever felt in her life, Amanda couldn't work up the energy or the desire to stop him. Oh, God, it felt wonderful. Unbelievable. His big, slightly rough finger sliding back and forth over such a sensitive place made her feel like she was floating on a cloud. She opened her legs a little wider, not wanting this incredible sensation to stop. A large finger circled her opening, adding to the delicious feeling. When it started to press into her, she panicked and closed her legs on his hand. "No. It'll hurt."

Rand bent over her, taking her coffee cup and setting it aside and easing her back onto her bedroll as he touched his lips to hers. "No. It won't. I promise. Open up a little more and let me show you. After last night, you should know that I would never do anything to hurt you."

Mesmerized by his deep growl, Amanda parted her lips and her thighs, not sure which one he wanted, but willing to give him both. She knew it was wrong to let him touch her this way, but she didn't care. She couldn't remember anything in her life ever feeling this good and she never wanted this feeling to end. Her husband's touch had never felt this *right*.

He swallowed her gasp as his finger slid inside her, surprising her by how easily it entered her and the slickness that had formed there.

Slightly embarrassed, she lifted a hand to his shoulder to push him away, but gripped it instead, a surprised moan escaping when his thumb started caressing her clit again. The finger inside her began to move, startling her with the stark intimacy of what he did to her. Still lightheaded from the after-effects of the whiskey, she spread her thighs even wider, crying out softly and wondered if she was dreaming. Without meaning to, she tightened on the finger Rand slid in and out of her, amazed at the heat and tingling at her center. The soft breeze that blew over her reminded her that she lay exposed in the open and somehow made it feel even more decadent. Tears welled in her eyes at the gentle heat in Rand's gaze as he looked down at her, making her feel all womanly inside, as though she was something precious to him.

She'd never been precious to anyone before.

The sensation intoxicated her, stripping away her defenses like nothing else ever could.

Rand swallowed her breathless moans, his touch never faltering as he took her mouth in a kiss so sweet and coaxing, she couldn't resist. His warm lips softened on hers, brushing them with his and sucking gently as though sipping from her.

He continued to stroke her clit, his sure, smooth strokes making her body tighten and close on the finger he moved inside her, the combinations of sweet and blatantly sexual making her head spin.

Amanda opened her mouth wider, loving the feel of his tongue sliding over hers in an intimate dance she found fascinating. Her body tightened impossibly, reaching for something she didn't understand.

But she wanted it. Badly.

Suddenly it was upon her, an overwhelming surge, like a huge wave crashing over her and tumbling her about. Her body sizzled and burned, every inch of her skin tingling with a pleasure that seemed never-ending. She jerked in his arms, gripping his shoulders tightly in both alarm and the need to be closer, a need to be held she'd never before experienced. She clung to him, drawing on his strength to fight the sudden vulnerability that overtook her.

Surprisingly, he seemed not only to understand, but cared, pulling her closer almost immediately. His embrace steadied her somewhat as the strokes from both his finger and his thumb slowed, and she started to shake, her body rocking in time to his caresses. The pleasure had intensified to the point of near-pain when he withdrew and began to caress her uninjured thigh.

Lifting his head, he stared down at her, his eyes hooded and searching. "You act like you've never come before. Didn't your husband do that to you?"

Licking her dry lips, Amanda shook her head, shifting slightly away, not quite comfortable with her need to be held. "Is that what I did?"

She'd heard that women could enjoy being intimate, but learned quickly that she wasn't one of them.

Knowing she didn't like being taken, she'd assumed she'd never experience any pleasure, but Rand had certainly proved her wrong.

God, she'd never even imagined she could experience anything like that!

It had built like a storm inside her, sweeping away everything else.

It was as frightening as it was irresistible and she couldn't wait to experience it again.

Rand chuckled, a sound so deep with warm indulgence, it sent delicious shivers through her. "That's what you did. Real good, too. Now that I've seen your pussy and touched it, you don't have to act shy when I change your bandage."

Amanda slumped back onto the bedroll, a combination of weakness and awe from what Rand had just done to her and the lingering effects of the whiskey from the night before making her efforts to slap at him pitiful. "Is that why you did that?"

Rand unwrapped the bandage, his hand brushing over the moist heat at her center. He looked up at her involuntary moan, his eyes twinkling. "Sorry, honey. I know you're sensitive there. And no, that's not why I did that to you, but if it makes it easier for me to check your bandage, that's good. Be still. Stop lifting that pussy up to me. I'm already on the edge."

Blinking in surprise, Amanda sat up on her elbows, eyeing him suspiciously. "Why aren't you trying to get on top of me?" She looked down as he uncovered her wound. "Where's Zane? Oh, my God! Did Zane really sew that up? I didn't even feel it." She sat all the way up with a start, wincing at the pull of the stitches.

Rand glanced up at her before scooping some sort of salve out of a tin and applying it to her cut, his fingers gentle as he smoothed it in. "Yeah, you felt it. You were just so drunk you don't remember."

But he did.

She could see by the way his jaw tightened that the memory wasn't a pleasant one. It melted something inside her, weakening her resistance to him even more, something she couldn't afford. Too much depended on her doing what she'd come out here to do and, although she would always be grateful that Zane and Rand had rescued her last night, they would be in the way now. She briefly thought about finding them again when she'd finished what she had to do, but knew that neither one of them would want anything to do with her then.

She'd never regretted anything more. Looking away, she sipped at her coffee. "You didn't answer me. Where's Zane?" She couldn't risk running into him when she went to find the gold.

Rand finished bandaging her leg, wrapping a clean cloth around it and tying it in place. "He went to get the gold."

A chill went through her, her entire body stiffening. She turned slowly, staring at him in horror.

He couldn't possibly know. Had they said something last night? A memory of him leaning over her asking her questions flashed through her mind, but she couldn't remember what they'd talked about. She turned away, sneaking glances at him, trying her best to sound as though she didn't know what he was talking about. "What gold?"

Rand's grin told her she hadn't fooled him at all. "The gold you're looking for. The gold Rafael and his gang took from the government stage. The gold you need to give your daddy so your ma and sister can go to Albany."

Stunned, Amanda tried to hide her shock by taking another sip of coffee. "Who told you about that?"

He straightened, standing and moving to the fire, poured himself a cup of coffee and then sat, leaning back against a nearby rock. "Billy told us what you two talked about and told us where to find the gold. You told us the rest last night."

As the implications sank in, Amanda got a cold feeling in the pit of her stomach. "You are gonna let me have some of the gold, aren't you?"

Rand took a sip of coffee and looked out over the horizon, crossing one ankle over the other in a relaxed pose. "Nope."

Even after the way she'd just allowed him to touch her, he would do this to her? Momentarily forgetting her undressed state, Amanda jumped up, earning a disapproving look from him, his gaze narrowing on her bandaged thigh. "You can't do this! I need that gold."

"Don't rip that thing open, damn it. That gold belongs to the government. We're taking it back to Austin and turning it in. Now sit back down before you undo Zane's work."

She went to him without thinking, wincing at the pull in her thigh as she dropped to her knees beside him, automatically putting her hand on his knee. "You don't have to turn in all of it. Just part of it. You don't understand—"

Rand shrugged as he looked down at her hand. "Then explain it to me. You passed out last night before you told us everything. And don't even think about lying to me. I've had enough of your lies, Amanda, and I won't help you if you lie to me again."

She whipped her hand away, her face burning. She had no choice but to tell him, hoping he would see how badly she needed that gold. "We live about two miles northeast of Austin. My pa went to town one day and came home with John and the preacher. John took a hankering to me and pa told him he oughta marry me. I didn't want to and I told him so. My momma agreed with me, and he beat her good for it. It wasn't the first time. She could hardly walk the next day."

A muscle worked in Rand's jaw. "So you agreed to marry him."

"Yeah. I did. I had to or he threatened to beat her again. We had to stay with Momma and Pa. I didn't find out until after John died, but Pa told John he couldn't leave with me until he paid him with the money he'd made from the robberies. He knew John was a bandit and wanted to have a rich son-in-law. But, John didn't have any money left. He'd spent it all on whiskey and whores."

She stood and moved back to her bedroll, covering herself again before retrieving her coffee. She wrapped her hands around the cup for warmth. "We'd only been married a week when John went into town and came back all excited and said he had to leave and that he'd be back for me in a couple of months. I told you that was two years ago. Then, this past winter I heard Rafael killed him last year because he wanted to quit his gang. I still don't know if that's true or not. And I felt guilty because I'd been praying he wouldn't come back. I didn't mean for him to die, though."

"Of course you didn't. So how did you find out about the gold?"

Amanda stared into her coffee. "When Pa heard about John being killed, he was real mad. He told me that John had told him about the stage robbery and all the gold. Pa said he wouldn't have let me leave with John until he got paid. John didn't come back, but Pa still wants his share of the gold. He's counting on it."

If possible, Rand's face hardened even more. "So your daddy got mad and sent you to get it for him."

Amanda nodded. "Pa got real mad, because he already owes a lot of money. Said that since I wasn't untouched anymore, he'd been cheated. Got mad at me because my husband took me without paying for it." It still made her furious every time he talked about her innocence belonging to him. She was the one who'd endured the pain and embarrassment. He'd sold something that belonged to her, something she could never get back, and now he wanted her to pay for *his* loss.

Swallowing the bitterness that rose, she looked away. "By that time Momma decided her and my sister, Pamela and me were gonna leave and stay with Momma's brother, my Uncle Ted. My Aunt Percy passed last year and Momma and me can help take care of the house. She wouldn't even have to find work."

"But your pa won't let her go?"

"He said if I got him John's share of the gold, he'd let us go. I was gonna put aside some of the gold to take with us to Albany and hide it from Pa. I don't wanna be beholden to Uncle Ted and if things don't work out…" Amanda looked over at him pleadingly. "I have to take the gold to Pa. He's been drinking a lot more, and when he does, he likes to hit them. I've gotta get them away from him before he hurts 'em bad." Lowering her voice, she blinked back tears. "He's already talking about what he can get for Pammy. I can't let that happen."

Rand swore. "Has he ever hit *you*?"

Amanda frowned, remembering how much it had hurt. She'd never been hit by anyone, and it surprised her so much she hadn't been ready to defend herself against him. "He did once. I hit him back with the fire poker. He never hit me again after that. I think part of it was because he didn't want to mark me so he could sell me off again." Shrugging, she smiled faintly. "I think he's a little scared of me now. Now he only hits Momma and Pamela when I'm not around. I told him if I came back and saw any bruises on either one of 'em, that I wouldn't give him the gold. But I gotta hurry up and get back.

I've been gone too long already. Please, Rand. You and Zane have to let me have some of that gold. Just enough to appease Pa."

Rand stood and tossed the dregs of his coffee into the dry earth. "No. It's stolen and has to be returned." He raised his hand when she would have spoken. "But we will help you get out of this."

Amanda looked up at him, shading her eyes against the harsh sun. "How?"

Rand set his cup aside and straightened, folding his arms across his chest. "We'll get your ma and sister on a train to Albany if you agree to marry us. You'll be Zane's wife in name but you'll be a wife to both me and Zane."

"A wife? To both of you?" She put a hand to her head, wondering if the whiskey was making her dream crazy dreams. That had to be it. She never would have allowed what Rand did to her when completely sober. This conversation must be just a dream because she'd been thinking about them when she left Austin. "That explains everything. When I wake up, I'll see that none of this happened. I can go get the gold and go to Albany with Momma and Pamela."

Rand chuckled. "It isn't a dream, Amanda."

She shifted uncomfortably, the burning in her thigh telling her that he had to be right. She was wide awake. "But you can't share a wife. I've never heard of such a thing."

He shrugged and looked away. "We did before."

Amanda vowed never to drink whiskey again. Her head hurt. Her stomach felt terrible and her thigh burned like the devil. On top of that, nothing made sense anymore. "Let me get this straight. You and Zane shared a wife?"

"Yes, a few years ago."

"What happened to her?"

"She died in an Indian raid."

"You can't share a wife."

Rand moved to her and knelt at her feet. "It's done quite a bit out in the wilderness, where we come from. Women are harder to come by out there. The women who are married to more than one man feel more secure, that if something happened to one of her husbands, she'd still have another to provide for her."

"And you would both want to, you know..."

"Of course. You'd be our wife."

Remembering what it had been like with John, she shook her head. "I don't like it. It's like being under a rutting pig." Realizing what she'd just said, she clapped a hand over her mouth, surprised at Rand's laughter.

The sound startled her, as did the way it lit up his face. His eyes crinkled at the corners when he laughed and his grin was infectious. The sound of his laughter warmed something inside her and made her want to play, something she never seemed to have the time or the inclination to do. He shook his head as his laughter slowly died.

"You seemed to like what I did to you a little while ago."

Her face burned, which seemed stupid after what they'd just shared, but it felt strange to talk about it with the sun shining in their faces. "That wasn't...you know."

"Sex?"

Nodding, she looked away. She couldn't believe she'd not only allowed him to touch her there but that she'd enjoyed it so much and wanted to do it again.

Rand started to say something, but stopped, coming to his feet. "Zane's back. He didn't get any sleep last night because he left to go fetch the gold. Once he rests up, we'll be on our way."

Zane rode toward them, tossing the reins to Rand as he got off of his horse. "I found it. How's her leg?" He strode toward her with smooth grace, his steps as sure as though he hadn't been up all night. He flipped the end of the bedroll back before she could stop him.

Embarrassed by the moisture that still coated her thighs from the amazing pleasure Rand had just recently given her, she slapped his hand away and struggled to cover herself again with the bedroll. "Rand already changed it. It's all right."

Zane rested his forearm on his knee and narrowed his eyes. "What's wrong with you? Why are you so jumpy?"

Rand came close to kneel at her other side. Without a word, he yanked the bedroll down again and lifted her shirt, exposing her pussy to Zane's gaze. "I already told you that we're both marrying you. Don't try to hide from Zane. Tell him how I made you come. Let him feel the juices all over your thighs. Since I already checked your cut, why don't you open that shirt so Zane can check the scratches on your t…breast."

Zane's lips twitched. "Looks like you two have been busy while I was gone. You didn't take her, did you? I don't want those stitches ripped."

Rand shook his head, smiling. "Nope. I didn't want to ruin your handiwork, but I wanted to wait for you, anyway. Amanda doesn't seem able to get her head around two men marrying the same woman. I think it'll be better if we're both with her the first time or two."

Amanda looked from one to the other. "You mean you'd watch each other do that to me? Stop that!" She struggled against Rand as he laid her back down on the bedroll, holding both of her wrists in one hand while he started unbuttoning her shirt with the other.

"Be still or you're gonna rip something. Let Zane put some more of that salve on your scratches."

The look of awe on Zane's face as he stared down at her now-bared breasts stopped her struggles. Both men bent over her, their shoulders blocking out the sun, the tender heat in their eyes making her heart race, darkening with a look she now recognized. Zane slowly reached out a finger to lightly trace the scratches on her breast that ran almost to her nipple, his eyes glittering as they held hers.

Her breath hitched and she bit her lip in order to hold back the cries that bubbled toward the surface. The gentleness in their touch brought her body to life as though she'd waited her entire life for them. Her nipples tightened and tingled, and, without meaning to, she thrust her breasts upward, offering them to him shamelessly.

Zane's eyes flashed with approval and remained hooded as he reached for her, running his fingers lightly back and forth over her nipple.

Rand smiled. "She likes that."

Nodding, Zane continued to caress her, his eyes possessive as they moved over her exposed body. "You told her about our plans for her?"

Rand released her hands and retrieved the tin of salve from where he'd tossed it earlier. "I did."

"Did she agree?"

Rand chuckled. "Didn't get that far before you rode in."

Zane's lips curved in satisfaction when he lifted his hand to accept the tin. He opened it and scooped out a generous glob, frowning as he began to smooth it over the scratches. "At least they look better than they did last night. You gonna marry us, or not?"

Waiting until he finished, she hurriedly sat up and buttoned her shirt, just now noticing how tired Zane looked. "Can't you give me the some of the gold? A reward or something?"

Zane shook his head as he put the lid back on the tin of salve before tossing it back to Rand. "No. Rangers don't get rewards for doing their jobs. It's stolen property and has to be returned. We'll help you with your daddy, though, and get your momma and your sister on a train to Albany."

She didn't bother covering her legs again, liking the way Zane and Rand looked at them and the way she felt when they did. She couldn't ever remember feeling so feminine and wanted and found, to her surprise, that she was woman enough to be taken in by it. "What if I want to go to Albany?"

Both men shot a glance at each other before turning to stare down at her, their faces unreadable. The silence stretched so long she started to squirm on her bedroll, uncomfortable under their scrutiny.

Zane straightened, his face going blank, making her miss that look in his eyes that had made her feel so special. "If you want to go to Albany, we'll get you on the train with your ma and your sister."

Amanda didn't want to go to Albany any more than she wanted to stay with her father. She hated lies and from now on wanted to be as honest with them as she could. "I don't really want to go to Albany. I don't know anything about work there, and I'd just end up cooking and cleaning for my uncle. I don't want to go someplace where it's cold. I don't want to live in the city. My momma and my sister can't wait to go, but me…" She shrugged, bending her knees to wrap her arms around them. "I like riding and planting and being outside, but I don't want to stay with Pa, either. I never heard about two men sharing a wife before. You wouldn't hit me or anything, would you?"

Zane's lips twitched. "The worst would be a spankin' if you deserve one."

Amanda glared at him. "I thought you were different. You're just as eager to use your strength as every other man. When my father hit me, I got even and swore no man would ever hit me again."

Rand laughed. "I wondered if we'd get to see you again or if I just imagined you."

Confused, Amanda blinked. "What do you mean? I've been here all along."

Zane stretched out beside her on his own bedroll. "I think he means that the woman we found ready to shoot Rafael, the one who cut herself free and escaped, disappeared as soon as we caught up with her again. She's been real quiet since then, and now we know why. You've been making plans all along to steal the gold."

Amanda couldn't find it in her to feel bad about what she'd done. "Can you blame me? You're men. You're free the way women never can be. I wanted to buy freedom for me, my mother, and my sister. Wouldn't you have done the same thing?"

Zane raised himself up on his elbow, leaning partially over her. "If you married us, you wouldn't be completely free, but you'd be treated well and respected. We want to have a ranch. Cattle and horses. We'll be leaving Austin soon. It'll be hard work for all of us, but we'd protect you and provide for you."

"When are you planning on going?"

Rand reached into his bag and brought out some jerky, offering her a piece. "As soon as we take the gold back to Austin and take care of your ma and your sister."

Amanda toyed with the strip of dried meat. She'd been accused of being outspoken more than once in her life, but her happiness depended on her being honest with both of them now. "I like the idea of deciding for myself what I want. I just wish I knew you both better. I can't believe I let both of you touch me the way you did when I hardly know you. The only man who's ever touched me was John, and I didn't like it with him the way I do with you."

Zane chuckled and settled back. "Well that's plain speaking enough. Sometimes it's like that between a man and a woman. It's all right. We didn't do anything that could plant a baby in your belly. At least we know that part of it will be good."

Chewing on the jerky, she smiled. "I hope I like that part of it, but if I don't, I promise to try my best. I think it's only fair to tell you that I have a temper."

Rand laughed. "So do we, as I'm sure you'll learn."

Amanda felt as though a weight had been lifted off of her shoulders and couldn't wait to start her adventure. Feeling light-hearted for the first time in her life, she took a deep breath and nodded, saying a silent goodbye to her old life. "I'd like to go with you and help you start your ranch."

Without opening his eyes, Zane spoke from beside her. "You're not going with us unless you marry us. We want a woman with us who's gonna be there with us forever, not someone who's gonna want to leave when her hands get dirty."

Rand nodded. "Once we get there, we don't want you screaming to go home."

Amanda sipped her now-cold coffee. "The last thing I'll ever want is to go home. But how do you know you want to marry me? You don't even know me." She looked at Zane, who'd already appeared to have fallen asleep and turned back to Rand.

He slid his hand up her leg suggestively. "We know enough. We both want you and you're strong enough to face life out there. You know we're able to take care of you and will provide for you. We should be able to make a good life together."

She hit Zane's leg to wake him up, waiting until he grunted and lifted the hat he'd propped over his eyes. "I'll marry you."

He grunted again and lowered his hat back to cover his eyes. "Good. Now be quiet so I can sleep."

Frowning at his less-than-gentlemanly response, she looked up to find Rand grinning.

"You can marry Zane when we get back to Austin." He tossed her pants to her. "You might as well get dressed. We'll be leaving as soon as Zane wakes up and that pussy's temptin' me every time you flash it."

Embarrassed, she grabbed the pants and put them on, easing them carefully over her injury. As soon as she fastened them, Rand pulled her against him and took her mouth with his, holding her to him with a hand tangled in her hair.

Her knees went weak as he kissed her hungrily, his tongue sliding past her lips to tangle with hers. Leaning into his hard body, she met his kiss, trying to mimic his actions. Thrilling when his moans mixed with hers, she cuddled closer. Soon it seemed as though neither of them could get enough. Tenderness fled as they clung to each other, their kiss becoming wild and frenzied.

By the time he lifted his head, they were both breathing heavily.

Rand lifted her chin and ran a finger lightly down her neck and into her shirt, teasing the slope of her uninjured breast. Touching his lips to her hair, he spoke softly. "You're going to be our wife now.

We'll make a good life together, Amanda. Damn, you're a beautiful woman. I can't wait to see those eyes when I take you."

Amanda closed her eyes, reaching out to grab on to his shoulders as need swept through her. "Yes. Take me." Even if she couldn't get pleasure from the act, she could give it.

He smiled and kissed her forehead. "Not yet. Soon. It'll be fun to teach you some other things we can do. I think you're gonna like 'em."

"Other things? You mean there's more than just that...rutting stuff?"

Rand laughed softly and sat near a rock, leaning back against it and pulling her down beside him. "Let's sit here and let Zane sleep."

Amanda sat next to him, quietly chewing on her piece of jerky, her mind racing with questions. Sliding a glance sideways, she saw that Rand looked out in the distance. Curiosity finally got the best of her. Mindful of Zane sleeping several feet away, she kept her voice low. "What other things?"

Rand turned to her then, lifting a brow as a small smile played at his lips. "Are you sure you want to talk about this? Most women would be too shy to talk about such things with a man, especially in the light of day."

Shrugging, she turned away to hide the fact that her face burned. "You don't know what life's been like at home. I'm not a simpering woman who faints when facing something uncomfortable." Her anticipation in starting her new life also made her a little giddy. Smiling impishly, she touched his knee. "I'm also very nosy."

Rand chuckled softly before he leaned back and sipped his coffee, studying her. "No, you're not a simpering woman. Zane and I wouldn't even think of marrying another woman like that." With a nod, he reached for her hand. "So, go ahead. Ask me whatever you want, and I'll try to explain."

Determined not to let embarrassment keep her from satisfying her curiosity, Amanda nevertheless tugged her hand from Rand's knee to pick at a smudge of dirt on her pant leg. "When you said there are other things…Do you mean what you did to me a little while ago?"

Rand smiled, a combination of tenderness and playfulness that never failed to tug at her. "That's one of the things a man can do to a woman to make her come, and a woman can do the same thing to a man."

Taking a moment to try to figure it out, she held out her cup when Rand offered to refill it. "I give up. What exactly would I do?"

Rand grimaced as he sat back down and adjusted his pants. "I probably shouldn't have started this conversation. My cock's still hard from playing with you. A woman can stroke a man's cock and make him come."

Amanda felt bad that he appeared to suffer after making her feel so good. "Can I do that to you now?"

The flare of lust that appeared in his eyes made her even more determined to try to please him. "Are you sure that's what you want to do?"

Nodding, Amanda set her coffee aside and came to her knees. "I'd like to try. Will you teach me?"

Rand had already started unbuttoning his pants. "Are you kidding? I'd love to have your hands on me. Come here."

She watched, mesmerized, as he worked his cock out, hardly able to believe the size of it. She'd only been intimate with her husband at night and under the covers so she'd never seen his cock. No wonder it had hurt so much! If she learned how to do it using her hand, maybe she could satisfy them and they wouldn't have to stick it inside her as often.

"Are you sure you want to do this, Amanda?"

Unable to tear her eyes away from the menacing sight of the thick cock rising from his lap, Amanda held out her hand to him. "Yes. Show me what to do."

Rand took her hand and wrapped it around his cock. "Like this."

She couldn't get her hand to close around it, but did the best she could, careful not to squeeze it too tightly. She started sliding her hand up and down his length the way he showed her, fascinated by the heavy thickness of his cock and the look on his face as she stroked him. His moans gave her the courage she needed to explore, intrigued that something so hard could also be so soft to the touch. It excited her to think she could give him the same kind of pleasure he'd given her, especially now that she knew just how wonderful it felt.

He released her hand with a groan, clenching his hands into fists at his side as he closed his eyes and leaned his head back. The moans coming from him urged her on and started that same fluttering feeling inside her belly again.

Using two hands now, she continued to stroke him, smiling when a finger brushing up the underside, right beneath the head, elicited a jerk and a low groan from him. So naturally she did it again and again, feeling more brazen and powerful with every stroke. To have such a strong, masculine man melt beneath her hands had to be the most thrilling sensation she could imagine. Hell, she could really learn to like this.

Her own body tingled with excitement from watching him, the sounds that he made, not only exciting, but also giving her a feeling of power that amazed her. "It *is* exciting to watch, isn't it?"

Rand turned his head, opened one eye, and smiled at her. "You getting all excited again, darlin'?"

"I think so. Does this feel as good to you as it does to me?"

Rand groaned. "I'm getting ready to come. Does that answer your question?" His voice sounded raw and gravelly, his body tense, but he didn't stop her.

"What can I do?"

He put his hand over hers and squeezed before releasing it again. "Just keep doin' what you're doin'. Damn, that feels good. Are you sure you've never done this before?"

She'd never imagined experiencing this playful banter before, especially with a man, and at a time like this. It made her feel closer to him, and she liked it. A lot.

She never thought it would be possible to have fun during intimacy, but Rand showed her differently. Enthusiastic now, she used only one hand, using the other to stroke his chest, wishing she could touch his bare skin.

Without opening his eyes, he put his arm around her and pulled her against that hard chest, unerringly finding her lips with his.

Amanda kept stroking him, tangling her other hand in his hair, at first to keep her balance, and then to hold him close. She'd never felt so strong before and yet so weak and utterly feminine. When he groaned into her mouth and stiffened, his cock pulsing in her hand, she tightened her grip on his hair and pressed herself against his chest in her need to be closer. The warm liquid splashing on her hand startled her until she realized it came from his release.

He groaned, his arm tightening around her as he broke off his kiss to bury his face in her hair.

Now she understood why he'd touched her the way he had afterward. Knowing that she'd pleased him, that he'd made himself vulnerable to her made her feel closer to him than she'd ever felt to another person.

And they'd done that to each other.

Did he feel it, too, or was it something only a woman felt?

He put his hand over hers, slowing her strokes, and groaning into her hair. Gradually he brought the strokes to a stop and unwrapped her hand from his cock, forcing her to release him. With a shudder and a sigh, he wrapped both big arms around her to pull her even closer. "You're a quick learner, darlin'."

She kissed his jaw and buried her face in his neck, happiness bubbling inside her. The comfort she experienced by being held this way could quickly become addictive. "You got any more things to teach me, Ranger?"

To her surprise, he fastened his pants again and untied the kerchief around his neck to wipe his seed from her hand. He did it matter of factly, not seeming at all embarrassed by the intimacy of the act. "Me and Zane got lots to teach you, darlin', and as soon as we finish taking care of things, we're going to give you a fine education in lovin'."

"Are you serious? You got more? I mean besides, you know."

"It's called sex, darlin'. Or fucking. I know you've probably been raised where good girls don't say that, but when you're alone with us, you can. No, stay where you are. I like having you cuddled against me like this."

Settling back against him, she said nothing. She still wasn't sure about the rutting part, but if they did it the way John had, at least she could find pleasure with other things, which was more than she'd had with John.

Excited about the future and starting her new life, she couldn't wait to deal with her father and help her mother and sister escape. Once those things were done, she would be free.

It didn't worry her that neither Zane nor Rand ever spoke of feelings. After all, they hadn't known each other very long, and she really didn't expect to ever love them or have them love her in return. Her mother said she loved her father when they got married and look how that had turned out.

No, it would be better to go into this with a level head, and she wouldn't be disappointed. She had no doubts that the men could protect her and provide for her, unlike her father who drank most of the money he made and left her mother to scrape what little she could in order to buy food.

Used to hard work, Amanda knew she could take care of the house Rand said they would build. She knew how to garden and can vegetables, having done it often with her mother in order to have enough food for the winter. She could help with the horses, and although she knew nothing about cattle, she could learn.

As for the rest of it, well at least she wouldn't be living in Albany or with her father, and this time she would take a husband, *husbands*, that she chose instead of having her fate placed in someone else's hands. She had a sneaking suspicion that her uncle would try to wed her and Pamela off as soon as possible.

Snuggling against Rand, she closed her eyes and drifted off, for the first time looking forward to the future.

That soft, warm feeling inside her continued to grow as she thought about having both of these magnificent men to herself. She frowned against Rand's chest. Why did people think they needed love to be happy when safety and friendship were far more important?

* * * *

Hours later, she rode to town between Zane and Rand, a little nervous about confronting her father but anxious to make sure her mother and Pamela were all right. She just wanted to get this over with.

When she slid a glance at Zane, she was a little surprised to find him watching her again. He hadn't said much to either her or Rand since he'd woken several hours ago after sleeping only a little over two hours. It hadn't taken long to realize that he didn't speak much, only when he felt he had to, which made his words that much more important to her.

Rand, on the other hand, talked a little more. Although he didn't run his mouth the way John and her father had, he liked to tease and had seemed comfortable when talking to her earlier. He'd been so easy to talk to that her embarrassment at discussing such an intimate thing, especially with a man, had been replaced by curiosity.

"Have you two been friends for a long time?"

Rand inclined his head. "Ever since I can remember. We grew up in Kentucky. Both our pas worked for the same man, who raised horses."

"What happened to your parents?"

Rand sighed, his jaw clenching. "One night a tornado came through. Flying debris killed my ma straight off. Zane's mom got hit but lingered for days before she died. I didn't have any brothers or sisters, but Zane's little sister and our pas just disappeared."

"Oh, my God! How terrible."

"Yeah. We stayed around a coupla weeks, helping clean everything up and burying the dead. The boss man gave us each a horse for helping and we left."

"And came to Texas?"

"Not at first. We moved around Arkansas for a while until we met Beatrice in Hot Springs. We married her and settled there for a bit, did some construction work."

"And left when she died?"

"Yep. Heard about the Texas Rangers and decided to try our hand at it for a while."

"How's your thigh?"

Amanda smiled at the concern in Zane's voice and understood that he wanted to change the subject. "It's good. You did a good job sewing me up. Thank you."

Preoccupied with her own thoughts, his grunt didn't faze her.

Night had fallen by the time they approached town. Both men rode a little closer to her as they approached Ranger Headquarters, as though sensing her nervousness. She'd hardly ever come to town and never at night. Except for a few men who stood on the corner and greeted the other Rangers soberly as they went by, the town looked deserted. Anxious now, she rode between Zane and Rand to the side of the building where a man waited to take their horses.

The lamp the small man carried cast a strange glow over his face, giving him a frightening look. He ran toward them, limping so badly Amanda feared he would fall. "Rangers! Thank God you came back. What a mess!"

Rand dismounted and tossed him the reins. "What are you talking about? What happened?"

The wiry man's eyes shifted wildly, one more so than the other. Since she saw no fresh blood on him and neither man seemed to notice his limp, she had to assume it to be an old injury. "Them outlaws escaped! Shot the cap'n and a couple of the other Rangers. There's a posse chasin' 'em now. They's headed west."

Zane cursed. "Hell. Where's the captain?"

The other man pointed toward the building. "Inside with the doc. It don't look good, Rangers. Henry said he's gonna die."

Zane leapt from his horse, tossing the reins to the other man. "Rand, stay here and guard everything while I go see what the hell's going on."

Rand's expression hardened into a look much like the one he'd worn when facing those men who'd attacked her. He shook his head when she started to get down from her horse. "Stay on Midnight until we figure out what's going on. If I tell you to go, you ride hard and fast outta here. You hear me?"

* * * *

Zane ran into Ranger Headquarters, alarmed at the controlled chaos that greeted him. The few Rangers who had stayed behind gathered broken chairs and glass, while one of the boys who regularly cleaned up and took care of things mopped blood from the floor. Zane stopped one of the younger Rangers who held a rag covered with blood at his temple. "Henry, where's the captain?"

Obviously dazed and shaken, Henry shook his head and gestured toward the captain's office. "In there with the doc. He's gut shot."

Zane knew as well as anyone what that meant. His captain wouldn't make it. Fighting back his horror, he clenched his jaw. "What the hell happened?"

Henry paled even more and looked as though he might pass out. "I got too close to the cell and Rafael got the drop on me. He got my gun and held it to my head. He made the other Ranger let him and his friends out. Then he hit me over the head with my own gun, shot the captain when he came runnin' out, and Rafael and his men took off. I'm sorry. Tell the captain I'm sorry. It's all my fault. I'm gonna quit. I don't deserve to be no Ranger."

Zane patted Henry on the shoulder, feeling sorry for the young man but impatient to get to the captain. "You learned a valuable lesson. You'll be a better Ranger now than before. You've got a good heart, and the Texas Rangers need you." He turned away, hurrying into the captain's office, stopping just inside and keeping his face a blank mask to hide his horror as he took in the amount of blood the doctor rushed to stop. He shared a look with the captain's wife who knelt at her husband's side, sobbing, and then with the Rangers who stood behind them before looking back at the captain.

The captain's face was as gray as his hair, his eyes pain-filled. When he saw Zane, he smiled faintly. "Good. Come closer." His voice came out thin and weak, a sharp contrast to the loud booming tone Zane had finally become used to.

Zane moved to the cot that the captain kept in his office, hiding a grimace at the amount of dark blood that continued to flow from him, and squatted down next to his shoulder. "Captain, just hang in there."

His captain grimaced. "I'm gut shot. I'm done. You know that as well as I do." He grimaced, reaching out a weak hand to his wife when she sobbed louder. "Rand with you?"

Zane nodded, his gut churning with fury that such a good man's life was taken away by such a worthless outlaw. "Outside guarding the gold we recovered."

The captain laughed weakly, coughing up blood that his wife hurriedly wiped away. "Shoulda known you'd find it. Bring the others closer. I want them to hear this."

Zane gestured for the other three Rangers standing close by to come closer, wondering what the hell was so important. Tom Hensen was one of them, and he shouldn't have even been there. Tom had been a Texas Ranger almost as long as he and Rand had and should have been one of the first to go after the outlaws. "They're here. What do you need?"

"I tore up your resignations. You and Rand been here longer than anybody else. I'm promoting you both to captain. You're in charge now." The captain took a shuddering breath. His last.

Zane cursed and let his head drop.

"Well if that don't beat all. *I* should have been promoted to captain. You and Rand already quit." Tom kicked the captain's desk, bringing Zane's head up.

Zane shot him a hard stare when the captain's wife flinched. "We'll discuss this later." He didn't bother to hide the threat in his voice, knowing that he and Rand would both have a tough time with Tom, just as the captain had. Tom didn't like to take orders or work with others. He'd joined the Texas Rangers for the attention and glory and had been disappointed when it turned out to be a lot of long hours, shitty working conditions, and little sleep.

"We heard what the captain said."

Zane looked up into the face of the Ranger who'd spoken, Ned Tillman, his gaze touching on the other he didn't know, who nodded. A sound from the doorway caught his attention, and he turned to find Henry and Silas both nodding and shooting looks of sympathy toward the captain's wife.

He stood, sighing. It looked like their dream of a ranch would have to wait. Keeping his voice low, he gestured toward the captain's wife, who threw herself onto her husband's chest and sobbed. "When his wife's ready, take care of him. After that, help get this place straightened up for when the other Rangers get back with those men."

He went to the captain's desk, his and Rand's desk now, wrote a message, and handed it to Henry. "Take this to the telegraph office and send it. When you finish, see the doc. I'll be right back." He strode out to the main room and gestured to two of the uninjured Rangers. "Come with me." He and Rand had been on patrols so long he didn't know half of the men anymore. It looked like they'd be spending some time getting acquainted and figuring out just how many Rangers they had.

He went outside to Rand and Amanda, still finding it hard to believe all that had happened.

Rand looked up, reaching for his gun, eyeing the other two Rangers who came out behind Zane. "What is it?"

Zane joined Rand, standing between Amanda and the other Rangers. "The captain's dead. Before he died, he promoted us. We're in charge now and it's a mess. Rafael and his men broke out and are on the run. Take Amanda to the hotel to our room. Several Rangers went to get Rafael and his gang, and they'll be bringing them in any minute. These two are going to bring the gold inside. I already sent a telegram telling the government agent we have it."

He turned to one of the Rangers who eyed Amanda in a way that had all of Zane's possessive instincts clawing their way to the surface. "She's ours. Look at her like that again and, Ranger or not, you'll be eating my fist. Get the gold inside."

The other man paled and then turned red and hurriedly looked away. "Right away, Captain. I'm sorry."

Zane scrubbed a hand over his face. "Amanda, stay at the hotel until we come for you. Every damned man who sees you wants you and right now I don't have the time or patience to deal with it." He regretted his harsh words as soon as they left his mouth. "Shit. I'm sorry. It's not your fault you look the way you do."

Amanda reached out for him, laying her hand on his arm, the sympathetic look in her eyes wiping some of the ugliness of the last few minutes away. "I only want you and Rand. Can't I wait here with you?"

Zane shook his head before she even finished speaking. "No, Amanda. The captain's still inside and Rafael's men aren't gonna cooperate when we lock them up again. It's gonna get ugly and I don't want you here in case they somehow manage to get their hands on you. Go get some sleep. We'll see you later." He patted her thigh and met Rand's eyes. "Our ranch is gonna have to wait. It looks like we're still Texas Rangers."

To his surprise and delight, Amanda removed his hat and ran her fingers through his hair right in front of the other Rangers. "Just remember that you're *my* Texas Rangers now. Please be careful. I'll be waiting for you."

He smiled before he even knew he was going to. "If that doesn't motivate a man to hurry, nothing will."

Chapter Six

As soon as Amanda got to the hotel, she washed off, careful to avoid the bandage on her thigh. Wearing only Rand's shirt, she lay on the large bed to wait, smiling to herself when she realized she already missed having Zane and Rand lying beside her. She'd gotten used to having those hard, warm bodies to cuddle against, and couldn't deny how well she slept knowing that nothing could get past them to get through to her. It provided a feeling of safety she could easily get used to.

Even the warm, spicy scent of male soothed her, and at the same time made her want them so badly she could almost taste it. She couldn't wait to explore all the ways they could touch each other. Physical attraction had always been something she never understood, but she'd had a hard, fast lesson in it and could no longer deny its power.

Sometimes she felt weak with them, occasionally losing track of what she'd been talking about by the way one of them moved, or a certain cadence in their voice. Sometimes they made her feel stronger than she'd ever imagined, as though nothing could hurt her when they were near. The way they looked at her, the way Rand had moaned, his big body shuddering under her hands, made her feel like the strongest woman alive.

Hers.

Their strong characters commanded respect from others around them and most importantly, her. She hated weak, whiny men like her father, and men who were no more than little boys the way John had been. Zane and Rand were *men*, strong enough to do what needed to be done, yet able to be gentle when necessary. That combination of strength and tenderness undid her. She found herself thinking about them every moment they were apart, something completely out of character for her.

Sure, she was grateful for them for their promise to get her mother and sister out from under her father's control, but gratitude had nothing to do with the way she felt when they touched her.

God, she ached for them. She missed them already.

She slept fitfully, waking several times through the night, disoriented and reaching for them only to find the sheets beside her cool to the touch.

Hell. They wanted to marry her because of her strength and she'd only been apart from them for a few hours and already she'd become needy and lonely.

She punched the thin pillow and wrapped her arms around it to hold it close. They'd never know she pretended it was one of them. Gripping it tighter, she fell asleep.

An incessant pounding woke her early the next morning. Groaning, she slid down under the covers waiting for the banging to go away. She'd hardly slept at all and felt irritable and groggy.

"Amanda, open this damned door right now." The knob jiggled and the pounding resumed, shaking the door.

Awake enough now to recognize Zane's deep voice, Amanda jumped up, nearly tripping over the thin blanket in her hurry to get to the door and move the chair she'd forgotten she put there the night before. She swung the door open to find him leaning against the doorframe, alarmed that he looked so haggard and involuntarily took another step toward him. "You look like hell, Ranger." His eyes were bloodshot. His beard was no longer neat and trimmed, and the lines around his eyes had become more pronounced.

Zane smiled as he reached for her hand and brought it to his lips. "You look like a woman who's just been well-tumbled. Come on. The preacher's waiting." He pushed the door wide, stepping into the room, forcing her back and closed the door behind him. Spotting the washbowl full of water she'd used last night, he began peeling off his shirt. "Hurry up and get dressed so we can go."

Her eyes widened at all the sleek muscle he exposed. The only men she'd ever seen without their shirts had been John and her father. Her father had a belly that stuck out, and John had been as skinny as a rail.

Zane looked nothing like either one of them.

The muscles in his arms and wide shoulders shifted as he moved, causing a peculiar heaviness in her belly. His chest looked just as hard, narrowing to a tight stomach and slim hips. Using the small cloth she'd used last night, he began washing himself, turning to look at her, a small smile playing at his lips. "Are you gonna stare at me all day or are you gonna get dressed?"

Her mouth watered as rivulets of water ran down his chest. "I'd rather sit here all day and watch you."

He turned, his green eyes twinkling. "Soon. We got a lot to do today so don't tempt me." He turned back to wash, turning to look at her over his shoulder, and raising a brow when he saw that she hadn't moved.

Amanda caught his look and sighed. "I don't have anything to wear except what I wore yesterday. I need to go home to get my clothes."

Zane's eyes hardened. "You're not going there without me, and we're not going there until you're my wife. I don't want your father having any claim on you."

The door flung open, startling her. Rand came into the room, his eyes widening as they raked over her. "Damn, honey, you look good enough to eat. Did you tell her yet?"

Smiling, Zane shook his head. "I just got here, Rand. I'm trying to get a little of the dirt off me before I get married, but if Amanda keeps looking at me that way, we'll be late for the preacher."

Not about to look away, Amanda grinned. She wanted the closeness with him that she had with Rand, and the look in his eyes as he teased her boosted her confidence. "I can't help it you look so good." The smooth grace in his movements made her wonder just how it would feel to have him between her legs. She could imagine holding on to those wide shoulders as he covered her body with his and pressed his cock into her.

Her pussy clenched in reaction as warm moisture coated her thighs. She licked her dry lips and tried to keep from squirming. "What were you going to tell me?"

Rand scrambled to get out of his own shirt. "You getting all hot and bothered again, darlin'?" He came forward and lifted her by the waist to set her on her knees on the bed. "We're gonna have to stay in Austin for a while. We've got to get Raphael's men and take care of the gold. We also have to meet with a bunch of Rangers we don't know and figure out all the assignments."

A little frightened at the prospect of either one of them getting hurt, Amanda stilled. For the first time the danger they'd be facing every day hit her. But the wife of a Texas Ranger couldn't be a simpering baby. It appeared the tenderness she felt toward them made her more vulnerable than she'd expected. Not only did she miss sleeping between them at night, but would worry every time they left for work.

Trying to hide her fear, she laid a hand on Rand's muscular chest, fascinated by the lines and hard ridges that she'd only felt but had never seen. "You'll be going out on patrols again?"

Rand shook his head. "Not very often. We're needed here to coordinate patrols. But it can be dangerous, I'm not gonna lie to you. You saw what happened to our captain. Have you changed your mind?"

She shuddered under Rand's hands as they went around her and slid inside her shirt to cup her bottom, concerned for their reputations creeping in. Texas Rangers were highly regarded around here, and now she wasn't so sure she'd fit in. "Will the people here accept us?"

Zane tossed the cloth into the bowl and began drying himself, moving to stand beside Rand in front of her. "I have no idea, but we'll do whatever we have to in order to protect you. Is it going to embarrass you? Make up your mind right now, Amanda. You can't change your mind later, no matter what the people here think."

Unable to stop herself, she reached up to caress Zane's jaw. The vulnerability she saw in his eyes humbled her. "It's not going to embarrass me, but you're Texas Rangers…and captains. How will everyone feel about that?"

Zane's hand slid between her thighs, startling a cry of pleasure from her. "I know how I'm gonna feel…and you, especially when I get my mouth on your pussy. Now you gonna marry us or not?"

Amanda moaned, fascinated at the way his eyes darkened. "Are you gonna use your hands like that to get your way all the time, Ranger?"

Zane tapped her clit, smiling when she clutched his shoulders. "Every chance I get."

Amanda laughed, reaching up to kiss his jaw. "You need a shave, Ranger, before we go see the preacher."

Rand grinned and moved to the bowl of water. "She's not even our wife yet and already she's nagging."

With his hands on her waist, Zane leaned in to touch his lips to hers. "I think I'll shave at night from now on. Do you want me to shave it all off?"

Amanda stroked his jaw again, imagining his soft beard and mustache brushing over her breasts. "Not a chance, Ranger."

Rand turned at the waist from the cracked mirror. "I think I'll wait, too. It'll make us look even scarier when we go to face your father."

Zane unbuttoned her shirt, a smile playing on his lips as he slid his hands over her bare skin. "We'll have to stay here at the hotel for about a week. The captain's widow is leaving to go live with her daughter in San Antone." His brow went up. "Seems like a lot of people have kin in San Antone."

Amanda held on to his shoulders, leaning into him. "You know why I had to say that. I won't lie to you anymore. I hate lies. We've been lying to everybody for years, covering for my pa."

Zane's hands went around her to massage the cheeks of her bottom. "You lie to me again and I'll turn you over my lap. Damn, you have the softest ass. Maybe, I'll take a bite of it instead."

Fascinated by the need in his eyes as they slid over her nakedness and the bulge pressing insistently against her belly, Amanda snuggled closer, gasping as her nipples brushed his bare chest. Lifting her eyes to meet Zane's, she did it again, sliding her hands over his shoulders and down to his arms. "The way you touch me…you're not in a hurry. I don't know what I'm supposed to do."

Smiling in a way that made her breath catch and that did strange things to her belly, Zane tightened his hands on her bottom before sliding them around her body to cup her breasts, avoiding the scratches. "We'll teach you what we like while we learn what you like. But right now, we have to go see the preacher and get your ma and sister on a train. Your daddy heard you're back, and he's been looking for you. I want you to be a married woman before he finds you."

Rand finished washing up and got out a fresh shirt. "Yeah, and we've got to get your clothes and get you something to eat. I told Jim and Ned where we'd be today. One of 'em will come get us when the other Rangers bring back Rafael and his men."

Amanda closed her eyes, trying to keep track of the conversation while her body tingled, the now-familiar warmth pooling between her thighs. "The Rangers didn't catch him yet?"

Rand came back to stand beside Zane, bending to touch his lips to her jaw, raising his head to look down at her, and smiling at her shiver. "No, but they will. Get dressed. We have a lot to do so we can get back here and finish this tonight."

* * * *

Zane could hardly believe that the breathtaking beauty in the dirty clothes sitting next to him and eating breakfast belonged to him. To him and to Rand.

This time, though, their wife carries *his* name.

They'd stood in front of the preacher only an hour ago, but the need to protect her, to care for her started long before then.

And it just kept getting stronger. It didn't matter that she was a strong woman. The surge of possessiveness grew each time he looked at her or heard her soft voice and with it, his need to protect her.

The other Rangers had gathered around them as they took their vows, applauding and welcoming her. A surge of pride rose within him at the ease in which she spoke to the other men, despite her obvious embarrassment at being the center of attention.

Tom Hensen was conspicuously absent.

She'd been talking to one of the other men but turned to Zane immediately when he bent to speak to her, as though she'd been attuned to him the entire time.

His possessiveness grew even stronger.

It made his tone gentler than usual. "Let's go to the hotel and get something to eat. You've had nothing but jerky for the last several days."

Amanda's smile lit up the room. "I ate the fruit Rand gave me last night, but I am hungry. Zane, Rand, would it be all right if we shared our meal with these men? After all, they're your family."

Rand looked up, meeting the looks of surprise on the other Rangers' faces. Her generosity and the fact that she immediately deferred to him and Rand despite being just married made him want her even more. "If that's what you want."

Zane inclined his head and drew out some money, but several of the men held up their hands to stop him.

Jim stepped forward. "Please, Captains, allow us to pay for the food. It would be our honor." He smiled at Amanda. "Thank you, ma'am."

Amanda beamed at him, seemingly oblivious to the effect it had on the other men. "You've all been very accepting of me. I don't know how to thank you."

To Zane's dismay, her eyes welled with tears.

"I'll be a good wife to your captains, I promise."

With those words, the sweet smile on her face and a single tear trickling down her cheek, she'd won every single one of the tough Texas Rangers over.

Including Zane.

The joy on Amanda's face along with the kindness she showed young Henry—who clearly still felt guilty about the captain's death—kept Zane from hurrying her.

Although friendly with the men, she kept a discreet distance, smiling at Zane and Rand often and making it abundantly clear that she belonged to both of them. With her beauty, he knew he and Rand would have to watch other men closely, but she appeared completely oblivious to the effect she had on everyone else. Her shy looks and pink cheeks when she looked at his chest, as though remembering this morning, excited the hell out of him and made him want to take her back the hotel right now and bury himself between her thighs.

With a sigh, he willed his cock to behave. They still had a lot to do first. He leaned close to whisper to her. "Amanda, we have to go. The train will be leaving soon and we have to get your ma and your sister on it."

She nodded hesitantly and blew out a breath. "Thank you. I didn't want to rush you, but I really need to get to them."

"We made a promise to you, Amanda."

Her smile warmed his belly. "It's going to take a while for me to get used to a man keeping his promise." Keeping her voice low, she smiled impishly. "It's going to take a while for me to get used to having two husbands, too. Oh, God, I can't wait to see my mother's face when she finds out they're free."

Rand stood and held out his hand to her. "Let's get this over with."

* * * *

Zane's anger grew with Amanda's fear. Although she tried hard not to show it, he could practically see her anxiety at facing her father, and it infuriated him. It would be hard not to fear an evil parent and not knowing what she would find had to plague her.

Her wait until he dealt with the captain's death must have cost her greatly, and yet she hadn't complained. He vowed to make it up to her somehow, starting with keeping her out of the way as much as possible while he handled her father.

He glanced at her as they approached a small rundown house, wondering how the damned thing was still standing. Flowers had been planted all along the front, obviously an attempt to make the place look nice, but their bright colors made the house itself look even drearier.

As they rode closer, he heard shouts and urged his horse faster, sparing a glance at Amanda to see that her face had become deathly white. "Stay back. Rand and I—"

Amanda raced ahead, not even letting him finish.

With a curse, he and Rand took off after her, his fear for her mother and sister growing, especially when the shouts got louder and crashing could be heard coming from inside.

"You git my supper on the table right now!"

A little girl, about ten years old, came running out the front door, her dark pigtails flying behind her. Her face, wet with tears, crumbled when she saw Amanda. "Mandy, thank God you're back. He's gonna kill her for sure this time. He's mad 'cause he couldn't find you."

Amanda leapt from her horse just seconds before he and Rand did, and ran to gather her sister in her arms. "Everything'll be all right now, Pammy. You stay out here. These two men are Texas Rangers. You've got nothing to be afraid of."

The little girl looked up fearfully, her eyes so much like Amanda's, it melted his heart. "You brought Texas Rangers with you? Why'd you do that? Now, Pa's gonna kill us for sure."

Holding on to the little girl, Amanda grimaced as more shouting and crashing came from inside. "They're not just Texas Rangers, honey. They're my husbands. You stay put out here while we go deal with Pa."

Pamela's eyes went wide. "Both of 'em?"

Zane hurried toward the front door. "Yep, your sister has her own Texas Rangers so don't you worry. Amanda, stay out here with your sister."

Of course she ignored him, racing up the steps behind him and Rand. They ran into the house in time to see the man who had to be Amanda's father raise his hand and slap the woman whose arm he held.

Leaping forward, Zane grabbed the older man's arm as he raised it again, surprising him into releasing the woman. "Don't touch her again."

Rand and Amanda both rushed to the woman. Amanda gathered the frail woman as her legs collapsed. "Oh, Momma! How bad are you hurt? Come in here and sit down so I can look at you."

Rand separated them, picked the woman up, and carried her to the only kitchen chair that hadn't been broken. "Are you all right, ma'am?"

"Git your hands off my wife. Git outta my house. You ain't got no call to be here buttin' into my business. Amanda, where the hell you been?" Spittle shot from his mouth. "Did you get it?"

Amanda caught her sister as she raced inside. "Yeah, I got it. The Texas Rangers have it now. *These* Texas Rangers. You wouldn't get it anyway. You hit Momma."

"You stupid—"

Zane whipped the man's arm behind his back, earning a pained cry from him. "I don't take kindly to anyone talking to my wife that way. Amanda, what's your father's name?"

"Wife! You got married without askin' me? You no good—"

Ignoring him, Amanda glanced at Zane as she wiped away the blood trickling from the corner of her mother's mouth. "Fred. Fred Winslow."

Swallowing his anger, he smiled reassuringly at Amanda's little sister. The poor thing looked scared to death. "Well, Mr. Winslow, it looks like you might have had a little too much to drink. You should sit down." Zane consoled himself by pushing Amanda's father roughly onto a stool sitting in the corner instead of slamming his fist into his face as he wanted to.

Hugging her mother, Amanda smiled at her sister. "Hurry up you two and get packed. The train's leaving soon and Zane and Rand already bought your tickets."

"What? They ain't goin' nowhere! Neither are you."

Amanda's mother watched her father warily, her hands clasped together so tightly her knuckles turned white. "Amanda, go. Go with your husband. Can you take Pamela with you?" She looked up at Zane beseechingly, her frail hands grabbing Rand's arm.

"What about my damned gold?"

Zane cut off her father's outburst, knocking him back when he tried to get up again. He gestured toward Rand. "Your daughter has two husbands now, Mrs. Winslow, and we'll both take good care of her. If you want to leave Pamela here with us, that's fine, but there's nothing to stop you from getting on that train. We're gonna put your husband in jail overnight so you've got plenty of time to get away. Maybe he'll cool off by morning."

She grabbed Amanda's arm. "Do you know what you're doing, taking on two men? What if they hit you?"

Rand chuckled, handing Amanda a fresh towel. "She already told us she gets even. When we met her she had a rifle pointed at a man so we believe her. Don't worry about her, ma'am. We're captains in the Rangers, and we'll take real good care of your daughter."

It took several more minutes for them to finally convince Amanda's mother that she really could leave. In the end, she'd wanted Pamela with her and Pamela seemed to want to get as far away from her father as possible.

Through cursing and threats as they took her father to town and handed him over to the other Rangers to be jailed, and tearful goodbyes and promises to write to her mother and sister, Amanda remained strong. Not until the train carrying her mother and her sister pulled out of the station, did she fall apart, breaking Zane's heart in two.

Chapter Seven

Amanda felt like a fool. She blubbered like a baby, soaking the front of Zane's shirt as Rand caressed her back.

Neither man spoke, just held her and let her cry it all out.

Being held, to have such strength to lean on when she needed it, filled her with an inner warmth.

She'd never before had someone she could rely on, someone strong enough—brave enough to fight for her, yet tender enough to hold her while she cried.

Something cold inside her crumbled that had her crying even harder. Still they held her between them, strong hands on her back, her arms, her hair.

Firm caresses to comfort.

And she fell a little more in love.

Once she finished, she raised her head, embarrassed at her outburst and vulnerable enough to cling a little longer than necessary. "I'm sorry. I'm not usually like that."

Rand bent and kissed her hair before taking her hand to lead her back to the horses. "You've had a real busy couple of days and I'm sure there's a lot more than that bottled up. You've been brave for a long time. Let's get back to the hotel and get you settled down."

"I want to see my father before I go back to the hotel."

In the end, they'd insisted on dropping her belongings she'd managed to retrieve from her father's house at the hotel, informing the hotel clerk that they wanted a bath delivered to their room when their *wife* came back.

His lips thinned in disapproval, but he nodded respectfully. "Yes, of course, Rangers."

She waited downstairs with Rand while Zane took her things up to her room, ignoring the looks she received from the two men who sat in the hotel lobby playing cards. She turned her back to them and looked up to find Rand scowling at them. Not wanting any trouble because of her, she attempted to tease him. "You're going to scare them with your Ranger look."

He turned his attention to her, his lips twitching. "Ranger look?"

"Yeah, you and Zane get that mean look that must scare the blazes out of outlaws."

Glancing back up, his eyes hardened again. "Then they can stop staring at you. Stay here for a minute."

"Rand, no." When he ignored her, Amanda sighed and dropped into a chair, recognizing that look on his face and resigned to the fact that he would deal with the men his own way no matter what she said.

The last thing she wanted was for him to ruin his reputation over her.

She wore pants and had a father who was a drunk, a cheat, and caused trouble and folks in Austin had given her and her family dirty looks for years.

She'd been married to an outlaw. Now that she'd captured the attention of not one, but *two* of the town's heroes, she'd be considered a loose woman.

She turned her head to see the hotel clerk frowning at her pants in disapproval. Waiting until he met her stare, she raised a brow, hiding her amusement when he turned red and hurriedly looked away.

Following his gaze, she grimaced at the expression on Rand's face as he spoke to the other men. Although she couldn't hear what he said, his clenched jaw and the ice in his eyes told her all she needed to know.

Zane came back down the stairs just then, his eyes narrowing when he saw Rand talking to the other men and the nervous looks on the other men's faces. "Problem?"

Both men hurried to assure him. "No, Ranger. No problem at all."

She should have known Zane and Rand would feel compelled to defend her, but she wished they would just ignore the disapproval of these people. She didn't know what she would do if the town's opinion of her changed the way they felt about her.

How *did* they feel about her?

Watching their harsh expressions soften as they approached, she struggled to hide her vulnerability.

If they turned away from her now…

As though in a daze, she allowed them to lead her out of the hotel, the touch of their hands burning through her shirt as they led her to their horses.

How could this have happened?

How could she have fallen in love when she knew what love could do to a woman?

And she loved *two* men.

Lost in thought, she mounted her horse, jolting when Rand reached over to touch her arm.

"Those men upset you, didn't they? I knew I shouldn't have let them off so easy." He turned as though to go back to the hotel.

"No!" Amanda reached out to him. "Please don't. Please. They didn't bother me. I was just thinking."

Rand turned back, his eyes narrowing on hers. "About what?"

Forcing a smile, Amanda started off again, forcing him to keep up. "Momma." She couldn't meet his eyes when she answered, finding it more difficult to lie to him now.

Aware of the scathing looks from several of the women they passed, Amanda held her head up high and glared back. Where the hell were these condescending women every time her father beat her mother and sister? Determined not to let them bother her, she smiled as she rode between the men, thinking of the looks on her mother and sister's faces when they finally realized they would be free of her father.

Feeling less guilty now that she really was thinking about her mother, Amanda turned to smile at Rand.

"Momma said she's gonna write as soon as they get to Albany. Did you see the way she smiled? I haven't seen her smile that way in a long time."

Rand grinned. "Yeah, and Pamela's gonna break hearts one day just like her sister."

Her breath caught as she spun toward him. She kept her tone light, not wanting him to see how desperately she wanted to have his and Zane's love. "Are you saying I'm getting to you, Ranger?"

Rand threw back his head and laughed, oblivious to the people staring at them. "Honey, you got to me the first time I saw you aiming that rifle. There's something about a beautiful woman with a loaded weapon that's just plain exciting."

Almost giddy with happiness, Amanda batted her lashes, enjoying their banter immensely. "Are you saying you're going soft on me, Ranger?"

Rand leaned closer, his eyes twinkling and full of fire beneath the brim of his hat. "No, ma'am. I'm saying I'm always hard because of you. I want to finish what we started the other day."

Catching his meaning, Amanda's face burned, earning another laugh from him. She'd already been married and although she'd never made love with either Rand or Zane, she had been intimate with them. "I can't believe you can make me blush. It's not like I've never done that before."

Zane leaned close, keeping his voice low as they approached Ranger Headquarters. "Honey, you're gonna blush all over when we do things to you you ain't never even heard about before."

Amanda climbed down from her horse before either one of them could help her. "Really? Like what?" Curious despite her embarrassment, she cocked her head as she watched him dismount, thoroughly enjoying the sight of all that hard-packed muscle in motion.

Zane's lips twitched as he turned the reins of her horse over to the man waiting and held out a hand to her. "We'll show you later. For now you talk to your daddy, and then you can go back to the hotel and wait for us."

Ignoring his hand, Amanda stepped into the embrace waiting for her, laying her hands on his chest, and smiling as his arms immediately came around her. The brims of their hats touched as he bent his head, shading their faces and providing a welcome intimacy.

"Are you gonna show me some of those things tonight?"

The green in his eyes almost appeared to glow before he sighed and lifted his head. With a hand at her back, he ushered her into the building. "Some. You're still healing, remember?"

Amanda grimaced. "I can't wait to get those stitches out."

From behind her, Rand bent, his lips touching her ear as his arm went around her waist. "I can't wait to kiss it and make it all better."

Amanda gasped and crossed her arms over her chest, flustered to discover that her nipples poked at the front of her shirt. The playful glare she sent to Rand over her shoulder was met by a grin as he leaned close again, his arm tightening around her waist to pull her back against him.

"I want my tongue on that clit, stroking it like I did with my fingers. You're gonna come hard, darlin', screaming my name."

When Rand released her, she looked up into Zane's face, her pussy clenching as a slow smile lit his features.

"Don't look so alarmed. It gets worse." He ran a hand over her shoulder, squeezing it lightly at her sudden stop as they approached her father.

The warm glow created from Zane and Rand's light play disappeared in a heartbeat.

Her father stood and grabbed the bars to his cell. "My daughter's a whore? A liar, a thief, *and* a whore? How could you sell me out to them? I'm your father, damn it! You gotta do what I tell ya."

Zane pulled her closer to his side, his stance threatening. "No, she doesn't. She belongs to us now and you've got no call trying to get her to steal for you. She's not the thief. You are. And what kind of father sends his daughter out on her own to track down outlaws and steal from them? We're just damned lucky we got there before they got a chance to kill her. Now be careful when you talk to my wife or you might just lose the teeth you have left."

Her father's bloodshot eyes narrowed. "Whore! You sold me out to two men who want nothing more than to rut between your legs. What are you gonna do when they get sick of your sassy mouth and move on?"

Both Zane and Rand started forward, blood in their eyes.

Amanda spun and automatically held up her hand to stop them, amazed and humbled that they both actually paused. "Please…he's my father." She could see how much it cost them to tamp down the fury and smiled sadly in appreciation.

Zane glared at her father over her shoulder. "If I don't like what comes out of his mouth, this conversation's over."

Touched when the other Rangers came to attention, their eyes full of encouragement and sympathy when they looked at her, she blinked back tears. "Thank you." Turning to face her father, she grinned. "I beat you, Pa. You can't hit Momma or Pamela anymore. They're not gonna go without food because you drank the little bit of money you made. You can't arrange for me to marry someone else to get something you want. You're on your own now, and you're just gonna have to take care of yourself."

The crazy look in her father's eyes, a look she'd seen too many times in her life, struck her with fear and she almost took a step back, but Rand prevented it. The hands rubbing her shoulders tightened discreetly, steadying her.

Looking up over her shoulder at him, she smiled her thanks, amazed that he would do such a thing, surprised that he'd even anticipated it.

He winked back, obviously trying to make light of it, but it had meant a great deal to her.

Every hour she spent with Zane and Rand reinforced her conviction that she'd made the right decision in marrying them. Every thoughtful gesture, every bit of kindness they displayed made her want them even more and tumbled her a little deeper in love with them. She knew she should tell them, but wanted to get a little more comfortable with it before she said anything.

It was too soon, and she needed to make sure.

"You might think you won, missy, but you're gonna be sorry you did this!"

Amanda forced a smile at her father's empty threat, Rand's touch giving her the confidence that usually diminished when faced with her father's temper. Calm now, she couldn't help but compare her father to her husbands. Her father was a mere shadow against Zane and Rand's strength, making her wonder why she'd ever been afraid of him. He didn't have even the tiniest portion, though, of her husbands' strength of character. With Zane and Rand at her side, she felt invincible. "There's nothing you can do to me anymore. Goodbye, Pa."

She turned and walked away, smiling at the other Rangers as Zane and Rand led her out the back door. Once they got outside, she put a hand on each of their arms. "Thank you for what you both did back there. It means more to me than you'll ever know."

Rand bent and kissed her, apparently not caring if anyone saw them. "You're our wife." He said it as though that explained everything.

Unable to keep from smiling, Amanda looked around at the assortment of Rangers who had gathered, probably waiting for assignments, especially since Rafael and his gang were still loose.

"You seem to know more about being a husband than I do being a wife. I've caused you nothing but trouble while you took time with me you don't have. I'll wait for you at the hotel."

Zane brushed a hand over her hair, exchanging a long look with Rand before smiling down at her. "I think you're going to make a helluva wife." He took her elbow and started around to the front of the building.

Amanda stopped and forced herself to pull out of his hold. God, she loved when they touched her, but she couldn't have them shirking their responsibilities because of her. Smiling, she glanced at Rand, who'd come up beside Zane. "Go back to work. I'll see you later."

Zane smiled back, the polite smile he gave when he wanted to appease her and do what he wanted anyway. "We'll walk you back to the hotel, Amanda."

He started forward again, his brows going up when Amanda slapped her hands on his chest. "You got a burr under your saddle about something?"

Amanda blew out a breath, knowing he knew damned well what she wanted. "I thought you both had a lot of work to do—Rangers to meet and assignments to see to."

Rand folded his arms across his chest, glanced at Zane and smiled, obviously content to sit back and watch the show.

Zane glanced back at him, his lips twitching as he shook his head in apparent exasperation. With his hands on his hips, his fingertips barely resting on his gunbelt, Zane faced her squarely. "We do."

Fighting the urge to leap at him and help herself to a bite of all that raw masculinity, Amanda mimicked his stance. "Then why don't you get to it? The sooner you get it done, the sooner you can get back to the hotel."

Zane's unblinking stare did strange things to her, making it almost impossible to keep from rubbing her thighs together to appease the ache. His eyes narrowed and darkened. "We'll walk you back to the hotel. I don't like the way those men in the lobby look at you."

Allowing a smile, Amanda gestured toward his gun. "What are you gonna do, Ranger? Shoot 'em?"

"If necessary."

If she didn't know him better, she might have believed him. "I thought you said that one of the reasons you wanted to marry me was because I could take care of myself. You said you need a strong woman like me, or did you lie about that?"

Zane's eyes narrowed, sending a chill down her spine, which somehow only made her want him more. "I've never lied to you."

Amanda had learned the fine art of debating long ago. Sometimes it had been the only way to diffuse her father's temper. "Then please explain to me why you don't think I'm capable of walking down a crowded street in broad daylight and cross a hotel lobby where two cantankerous old fools like to sit and play checkers? You think they're gonna attack me with their checkerboard?"

Zane's jaw clenched. "They might say something to insult you."

"And you think I can't handle that? Do you really think I'm so spineless that I'd let a couple of old crusty men get the best of me? You really must think I'm pathetic."

"Damn it, Amanda. I didn't say that!"

Stepping closer, Amanda poked him in the stomach, thrilling at the hard muscle she encountered.

"No. You say you think I can handle myself but then you treat me like a little girl. Just because I appreciated your support when I spoke to my father, you think I'm weak."

Zane grabbed her shoulders, the flare of temper in his eyes telling her that he barely restrained himself from shaking her. "I do not think you're weak. We're you're husbands, damn it. It's our job to support you and protect you."

"And you think I need your protection crossing a hotel lobby?"

"Hell and damnation!" Zane released her abruptly. "Go back to the hotel alone, then." Grabbing her shoulders again, he lifted her to her toes, his nose almost touching hers. "You get into any trouble between here and there and I'm gonna heat that ass up real good."

He released her with a glare and turned to stride away, his long legs eating up the ground as he headed back.

Rand grinned and leaned close, his lips brushing her ear and sending shivers through her. "He'll be like a bear with a sore paw all day. You're gonna have a lot to handle when we see you tonight." He bit her earlobe lightly before turning to wink at her again.

Watching him follow Zane through the back door of Ranger Headquarters she smiled and wondered how she'd managed to marry two such extraordinary men.

She already looked forward to tonight.

Despite the lies she'd told them and her attempt to steal, they seemed to care for her, something that continually amazed her.

It didn't hurt at all that she lusted after her husbands. Still smiling, she started back to the hotel to wait for them. She'd almost made it back when a cold voice called out to her.

"You should be ashamed of yourself."

Amanda spun to the woman who she'd just passed. "What did you say?"

The older woman stuck her nose in the air, giving the appearance of looking down at her even though she stood several inches shorter than Amanda. "You heard me. You should be ashamed of yourself. A woman with two men is unheard of. Your mother would be so embarrassed. A fine Christian woman and she has a daughter like you."

Aware of several other women who'd gathered around, Amanda kept her head held high. She recognized several of them, having seen them speak with her mother on several occasions, but couldn't think of their names. "What I do is hardly your affair. Both Zane and Rand are my husbands, and my mother knows about it. Who do you think helped me get her away from my father? Where were you when he was beating on her and Pamela? I hope you don't consider yourself her friend."

The older woman crossed her arms over her ample bosom. "It's unfortunate when a man hits a woman, but I told her many times that she brought it on herself. My Harold would never dream of hitting me. I keep a clean house and always have his supper ready for him. If your mother would have just done what your father wanted, he wouldn't have beaten her."

"What?" Amanda looked at the others, amazed to see several of them nodding their agreement. "I can't believe you'd think that it was all right for him to hit her."

"Yes, and your daddy should beat you for living in sin the way you are."

Amanda shook her head, hardly believing that someone would have the gall to stop her on the street this way and then claim that her mother deserved to get beaten. "I guess I'm just too much woman for one man. Why don't you go back home and take care of your husband and leave me alone?"

The older woman shared a look with several of the other women before looking back at her, her face scrunched up as though she'd tasted something bitter. "We're not in the wilderness where I hear some men share a wife. We're in Austin and we're real proud of our Rangers. They don't like that you're making their captains look like fools. You're an embarrassment to all of them, but they don't want to show it in front of the captains."

With her nose in the air, she turned and walked away, followed by the other women. A younger woman about Amanda's age brought up the rear. Pausing next to Amanda, she whispered. "Be careful. They're jealous and they're mean-spirited. No one else around here has a problem with you marryin' two Rangers, but these women feel it's their place in life to criticize everyone else. A lot of other folks here are glad to see you and the Rangers happy, and are glad your momma got away. But these women are bullies. Watch your back."

"Come along, girl. Don't be talking to the likes of her."

With an apologetic look, the young girl fled, leaving Amanda staring after her.

Amanda watched her go with a heavy heart as the implications of what the women said sank in.

She'd hoped that with her father dealt with, and becoming a married woman, the talk against her would die.

Apparently, not only the men in the hotel thought badly of her, but these women as well.

What would Zane and Rand do if they found out?

Troubled, she resumed walking back to the hotel, unable to shake the anxiety that the scandal of being married to her could ruin their careers.

What would they think of her then?

* * * *

Looking in the mirror, Amanda grimaced at the old and threadbare nightgown she wore and shrugged, deciding she'd done the best she could do. At least it covered the scratches on her breast and the small, but ugly cut on the front of her upper thigh that Zane had stitched closed. They both seemed to be healing well and she'd washed them thoroughly in the bath that had been delivered. The water had been brought up by two men who leered at her the entire time they brought up the tub and filled it with buckets of water.

Sitting in the tub, she'd cried for a mother and sister she would probably never see again, felt sorry for herself for having the kind of father she had, and worried over whether she'd made the right decision in marrying Zane and Rand and probably ruining their lives.

By the time she finished her bath, she had a headache and a stuffy nose, but she felt better. She would write to her mother and sister, and perhaps one day she could visit. She'd gotten her family and herself away from her father, and she'd started a new life with two of the most incredible men she'd ever met.

Life was good. She wouldn't worry about the rest.

Thinking about the old woman she inwardly winced. She'd *try* not to worry about the rest.

Her stomach rumbled just as she heard footsteps coming down the hall. As they came closer, her excitement turned to trepidation when she remembered the looks of the men who'd brought the water. The words of that woman kept coming back to her. How many people in the town now hated her? What if some of the Texas Rangers Zane and Rand hadn't even met heard about her and decided they didn't want her tarnishing their new captains' reputations?

No. They'd be too scared of Zane and Rand to come up here, wouldn't they?

She couldn't take any chances.

Looking around, she spotted her rifle leaning in the corner. She raced for it, holding it at the ready, careful to keep the muzzle pointed at the floor. Holding her breath, she listened as a key sounded in the lock, her hands tightening on the barrel.

Rand unlocked the door and came through it, his eyes widening when he saw her. "What's wrong? What the hell's going on, Amanda?"

Zane came through the door right behind him, carrying a basket and bringing with him the tantalizing scent of food. His expression hardened when he saw her. "Are you all right?"

Relieved and feeling a little silly, Amanda nodded and handed the rifle over to Rand when he reached for it. "I'm sorry. You startled me and I..."

After setting the rifle aside, Rand gripped her shoulders. "You've been crying."

Amanda shrugged and moved to the basket Zane placed on the bed. "I spent a little time feeling sorry for myself and missing Momma and Pamela. You must have heard my stomach rumbling from Ranger Headquarters. I'm starving." She opened the basket to find a feast inside.

Zane pulled her hands away from the basket to turn her toward him, lifting her chin to study her face. "Are you sure you're all right? No trouble with the men in the lobby?"

Amanda placed her hands over his forearms, once again amazed at the solid muscle she found there. Thankful that she didn't have to lie, she smiled again. "They weren't even there and except for being hungry, I'm great." She reached up to cup his jaw. "You trimmed your beard."

Rand moved in behind her, nuzzling her neck. "We both had a bath and a shave while we waited for supper. We don't want to scratch you tonight." Running his teeth over the spot between her neck and shoulder, he slid his arms around her to lightly cup her breasts. "I want to use my mouth all over you tonight and I don't want you flinching away in pain."

Amanda tightened her hold on Zane, leaning back against Rand and moaning softly as his thumbs moved over her nipples. "Oh, that feels so good."

Rand chuckled, using his lips to tug at her earlobe. "You'll feel even better later."

"Why not now?" To her extreme embarrassment, her stomach rumbled.

Zane laughed softly against her ear and covered her belly with his hand. "That's why. You're gonna need your energy for later. We'd better feed you, and then we're gonna do our best to wear you out." Bending, he kissed her forehead and started to set out the food. "Damn it, they only sent two plates."

Amanda had an idea why but didn't want to mention it. Ignoring the knot in her stomach, she cuddled closer to Rand, rubbing against the bulge at her back. "One of you will have to share with me."

Rand lowered a hand to her abdomen, its heat burning through her thin nightgown. "Hmm, I kinda like the idea of feeding you. I can steal kisses between bites. Then after supper, we can eat *you*."

Sitting cross-legged on the bed between them, Amanda listened as they talked about their day while she ate from both of their plates, each of them tempting her with bites of food as they touched and kissed her. "Did the Rangers find Rafael and his men?" She opened her mouth to accept the morsel of chicken Zane held to her lips.

"No."

Her head shot up at his short, abrupt answer. Looking from one to the other, she got a strange fluttering in her belly when neither one of them would meet her eyes. "What is it? What's wrong?"

Rand sighed and cleared the now-empty plates, stacking everything back into the basket. "They only found Billy. He's dead." At her look of alarm, he tumbled her to her back. "Don't think about him. If he rode with Rafael's gang, he knew what could happen." His eyes narrowed dangerously. "If I were you, I'd be more worried about what was gonna happen to you."

They didn't give her any time to dwell on what they'd just told her. Instead Rand tore her nightgown from her as Zane set the basket aside and reached for her.

Rand made a place for himself between her knees, taking Amanda's hand in his when she tried to cover the unsightly stitches on her thigh. "Do you think I haven't seen this before?"

"It's ugly. You just ripped the only nightgown I have." She couldn't inject the anger into her husky complaint that she wanted to, especially with her thighs spread this way and Rand's lips making their way slowly up her legs.

Zane leaned on his elbow beside her. "Good. I want you naked in my bed. Does your thigh hurt?"

Shaking her head, she gripped his wrist, arching into the palm he placed over her breast. "No. Sometimes it stings, but that's all."

Rand raised himself over her and kissed her hip. "Then I'd better kiss it and make it better." Lowering his mouth to her thigh, he brushed his lips over her injury, sending ribbons of tingling heat to her center. He caught her hand when she tried to push him away. "No, Amanda. Do you remember when I told you there are other ways for men and women to give each other pleasure?"

Zane tugged her nipple, bathing the other with his tongue. "I'm sorry I missed it. When did this happen? And what the hell are you doing? I wanted my mouth on her."

Rand gripped her thighs, carefully avoiding the stitches. "My turn. You were asleep when Amanda and me had a little talk. Amanda learned real fast how to make me come with her hand."

Zane sucked her nipple into his mouth, releasing it with a pop. "Now I know I'm sorry I missed it. Did you show her anything else?"

Something in his tone had Amanda's eyes popping open. The sun had just started setting so the light in the room had dimmed, but she could still see them both clearly.

Which meant that they could also see her.

Rand laughed. "No. Now stop asking me questions so I can have my dessert."

Zane chuckled. "So Rand taught you to use your hand. I'm going to teach you how to use your mouth, the way Rand's using his mouth on you now."

Amanda gasped as Rand slid his tongue through her slit. It had to be the most intimate thing she'd ever felt, and she jerked against the too-strong sensation. "Yes. Oh, God. Feels too good."

Zane tangled a hand in her hair, his mouth hovering over hers. "We're going to do a lot of things to you that feel good, honey. That's it. Don't fight him. Just relax and let us have you." He closed the small distance between them and fitted his lips over hers.

Amanda gripped Zane's broad shoulders in desperation, her moans growing louder as Rand's mouth worked that tight bundle of nerves between her thighs. The heat that formed at her center astounded her. It just kept building, sending sizzles from her center outward and back again. Her weak kicks, an automatic defense against such an overwhelming attack on her senses, only seemed to spur Rand on. She twisted, trying to escape such sharp pleasure, but nothing seemed to stop Rand from devouring her. The need became so great she couldn't keep quiet, crying out at the hot intensity of it, a cry Zane swallowed. Despite how good it felt, she stiffened in apprehension when Rand began circling her wet opening and pressed his finger inside.

Scared now, she pushed at Zane's chest, kicking out again. She kept clenching on Rand's finger without meaning to, her body seeming to have a mind of its own. When Zane lifted his head to look down at her, she turned her face into his chest, unable to look at either one of them. "Please let me up."

Both men stiffened, Zane lifting her face and regarding her searchingly. "What's wrong, Amanda?"

Finding it difficult to speak with Rand stroking her so intimately, she closed her eyes. "I need to…it's wet there. I know it's gonna hurt. Let me just wash…I'll use my hand to make you both come."

The tension left his body as Zane chuckled and kissed her shoulder, running his hands over her breasts again. "You're real soft under all that toughness, aren't you?" He held her, caressing her tenderly as Rand withdrew his finger from inside her and stood.

Rand threw off his clothes and hurried back to his place between her legs. "You're supposed to be wet, honey. It makes it easier to slide a cock into you. When you're aroused, you give up your juices. That's what me and Zane want."

Not knowing what to say to that, she looked up at Zane, who smiled and nodded.

"You'll see. Just relax."

When Rand poised the head of his cock against her opening, she stiffened, remembering how much it had hurt when John did it. Smiling down at her, he pushed his hips forward and began to enter her, his cock stretching her opening. "I love you wet, darlin'. No, don't move. You're real tight, and I don't wanna hurt you."

Zane tugged at her nipple. "No, don't tense up. See how good it feels? Be careful with your thigh and wrap your legs around Rand."

After a brief pause, she nodded and did as he asked, her insides fluttering with nerves. She wanted to please them, to make them feel as good as they'd made her feel, but she didn't really like being taken.

Rand smiled down at her, his eyes tender. "You're not scared of me, are you, darlin'? I won't hurt you."

Amanda's nerves were strung taut, but she forced a smile. "Of course not. Can you just hurry, please?" She kept her hands fisted in an effort to keep from pushing him away.

Rand slid a glance at Zane before slowly withdrawing from her.

Alarmed that she'd done something to offend him, Amanda reached for him just as he gathered her close and flipped over, pulling her onto his chest to straddle him. She pressed her hands to his chest to steady herself, thrilling at the hard muscle she encountered. "What are you doing?"

With his hands at her waist, he lifted her until the head of his cock pressed against her opening. "You do it."

Amanda blinked. "Me? Just do whatever you were gonna do. I don't know how to do this." Oh, God. What had she gotten herself into?

Rand smiled, groaning as the head of his cock slid through her slit. "Time to learn, darlin'. Where's the brave woman who took my cock in her hands and made me come harder than I ever have?"

Amanda stilled, smiling. "Really?"

"Really. Get to it, darlin'. Take me with that sweet pussy."

Zane moved in behind her, taking her weight with an arm wrapped around her waist. "Get higher on your knees. Keep your hands on Rand's chest and lower yourself on him as slow or fast as you want to."

Intrigued, alarmed, and nervous as hell, Amanda followed their instructions, her breath catching when Zane released his hold and she came down, taking the head of Rand's cock inside her. Stiffening in preparation of the expected pain, she sighed in relief when there was none and shifted. "I don't know what to do."

Rand's pained smile gave her a little more confidence. "Just take what you want. Christ, this is killing me."

"It hurts?" She lifted up slightly.

Rand groaned. "The sweetest kind of torture." His hands went to her hips, not guiding her at all, just holding her as he parted her folds with his thumbs and began to stroke her clit again.

From behind her, Zane nuzzled her neck as he looked over her shoulder, cupping her breasts and tugging gently at her nipples. "It's all up to you, Amanda. You do whatever feels good to you."

Without meaning to, Amanda rocked her hips, tightening on the head of Rand's cock, the soft strokes to the too-sensitive bundle of nerves at her center making it impossible to stay still. She moaned softly as the hands at her breasts stroked her nipples, sending little sparks to where Rand's fingers worked magic on her clit. Fisting her hands on Rand's chest, she leaned over him, watching his face as she took a little more of his thick heat inside her.

Sitting on him like this, completely naked and in the light, made her feel like a wanton woman and brought to light needs and desires of her own. She'd never imagined herself the kind of woman who could make love with two men at once, but having them both here this way felt better than anything she'd ever experienced. Having Rand's muscular chest to hold on to, having the freedom to touch him this way distracted her enough to drop down a little more onto his cock, a groan escaping when she did it again. His cock was unforgiving as it entered her, so hard as it forged its way inside her. Instead of being frightened, she reveled in the solid strength filling her.

She couldn't stop tightening on him no matter how hard she tried, and, to her amazement, each time she did, it elicited groans of pleasure from him and made her pussy hungry for even more. "I know I'm supposed to do this, ah…um, fast, but—"

Zane pinched her nipples lightly, kissing her neck when she cried out. "There are no rules, Amanda, except to make it feel good."

The tugs at her nipples and the strokes at her center had Amanda lowering herself more and more onto Rand's cock with each rock of her hips. She couldn't believe how good it felt to have him inside her like this, that even with his cock stretching her and making her feel almost too full, the pleasure just kept getting better.

Rand's features appeared to have been carved from stone. "Hell, Amanda, you're killing me."

Zane's chuckle in her ear made her shiver, the tenderness in his strong hands filling her with a warm glow. "That means it feels good to him. That's a girl. See? It's not supposed to hurt. Doesn't that feel good? You don't have to hold back your cries. Let Rand know how good it feels to have his cock inside you."

Unused to such talk, Amanda couldn't get the words those ladies had spoken to her on the street out of her mind. Shaking her head, she kept rocking her hips, taking more of Rand's length inside her, a gasp escaping at the intimate fullness when she finally managed to take all of him. "I can't." She could hardly breathe, so full she thought she would burst.

Rand eased the pressure on her clit just when she thought she would come, frustrating her. "We'll have to work on that. Hell, you're tight."

When Amanda rocked her hips now, the head of his cock nudged her so deeply it startled her and a cry broke free before she could prevent it. She quickly raised herself up, not sure what to do, but couldn't stop clenching on him.

Zane wrapped an arm around her waist, once again supporting her weight. "Easy, honey. I'll help you."

Amanda gripped his forearm, grateful for his support. It steadied her at a time when she really needed their guidance. No longer able to remain silent any longer, she cried out as she moved on Rand, amazed that the fear of pain had been replaced by something so good she never wanted it to end. She couldn't believe he was actually inside her, filling her. *She'd* taken *him*!

That same tightening, tingling feeling she loved so much, started again, and greedy for more of it, she tried to move faster.

Zane kissed her shoulder and released his grip to cup her breasts again. "Now you do it, honey. Whatever feels good."

The dark need in Rand's eyes as he allowed her to take the lead filled her with a sense of power and wonder. Having his cock moving inside her was all pleasure now, pleasure she couldn't resist. Moving faster, she couldn't hold back her breathless pants, the tension building with every rock of her hips. The strokes on her clit made the sensitive nub burn, and before she knew it, she soared again, whimpering as her pussy clamped down on Rand's cock. Throwing her head back against Zane's shoulder, she groaned, her body jerking clumsily as the feeling continued. She held on to Rand's forearms, grateful when he finally took over.

He gripped her hips his hold firm now, and moved her body on his, lifting his hips to surge into her. His short forceful thrusts made it even better, the desperation in his grip and his harsh moans telling her how good it felt to him, too.

Zane cursed softly from behind her, his hands moving over her body. "Yeah, fuck her hard. She likes it."

She threw her head back again, her body jerking uncontrollably as she screamed her release, not caring if anyone heard, so mindless with pleasure she could think of nothing else.

Rand thrust into her one last time, groaning as his big body shuddered beneath her hands.

She remembered John doing the same thing and knew that it meant he'd found his own pleasure and that it was over. In the past it had always relieved her, but now she crumbled on top of Rand, pleased that he'd found the same bliss in her body that she'd found with his and disappointed that it had to end.

Rand's arms came around her making her feel special even after he'd finished with her, bringing a lump to her throat. He groaned, kissing her hair. "Now do you see why we need to get you wet first?"

Burying her face against Rand's chest, she groaned, unable to work up the energy to be embarrassed. "I can't believe the way you talk."

Zane kissed both cheeks of her bottom, holding her down when she would have jumped. "Ain't no point in being shy about it. If we didn't talk to you, you'd still be scared."

Remembering her embarrassment and fear, she giggled. *Giggled!* "Thank you for being so patient with me. I'll learn how to be good at this, I swear." Suddenly remembering that Zane hadn't taken her yet, she pushed off of Rand's chest. Turning to Zane, she sat up, smiling when she found him naked. "Damn, Ranger." Now that she wasn't so nervous, she took the time to enjoy the view, looking at both him and Rand. Gulping, she reached out a hand to touch Zane's smooth chest, flexing her hand when the hard muscle shifted beneath her fingers.

Zane covered her hand and held it against him. "You get any better at this, and I'm never letting you outta bed."

"Damn it, she's bleeding."

Zane's smile fell, his eyes going flat. "What? Fuck. Amanda, let me see."

Rand lifted her off of him and laid her on the bed to inspect her injury. "Hell, darlin', I'm sorry. Why didn't you tell me I was hurting you?"

Surprised at the fuss, she looked down to see a smear of blood on her thigh that Zane gently wiped away. Shaking her head, she stared at them in disbelief. "What are you talking about? That little bitty thing?"

Rand's jaw clenched as he inspected it as though she had a fatal bullet wound. "It looks like she tore out one of the stitches."

She smiled at the worry on their faces. "I didn't feel anything. It doesn't hurt at all. You're being an old woman." She tried to take the cloth from Zane, but he pulled it away and went to his bag, coming back with another dry cloth.

"Let me wrap it and you'll have to be careful not to pull it again."

Amanda eyed his cock, its thick length not quite as big as it had been moments earlier. Her pussy clenched with the need to have it inside her, thick and hot the way it had been before. After having such a wonderful experience with Rand, she ached to feel Zane filling her. She still didn't have the closeness with him she had with Rand and wouldn't feel right until she did. "But what about—"

He smiled and kissed her lightly before tying the cloth around her thigh. "You're in no shape for that tonight. Is that too tight?"

"No shape? Are you kidding? Zane, please. I want you to take me, too. I can see that you want me. I need it. I need to feel close to you like I do with Rand." Fascinated when his cock jumped, she reached out to touch it, whipping her hand back when he flinched and gasped.

"What do you mean, you don't feel close to me?"

Rand laughed softly and kissed her shoulder. "No, don't pull your hand back. We both want you to touch us. It feels so good when you touch our cocks."

She looked up to see Zane stood with his eyes closed, his jaw clenched, and appeared to be in agony. "Are you sure I'm not hurting him?"

Zane's eyes popped open, glittering darkly as he looked down at her. "It doesn't hurt, honey. It feels too damned good. What do you mean, you don't feel close to me?" He started to pull out of her grasp, stopping when Amanda impulsively reached out to touch his hip.

She got to her knees, careful not to hurt her thigh. "Please, Zane. I want you to take me. Rand has with his fingers and his mouth and his cock, but you haven't. I catch you glaring at me sometimes. Is it because you don't want me?"

"Don't want you? Are you crazy? I don't want to hurt you, Amanda. Tomorrow if—" His sentence ended on a hiss when she reached out to stroke his cock again. "Damn it, Amanda."

The power running through her was as intoxicating as the whiskey they'd made her drink, but much more enjoyable. "I want you to take me. I know now that you'll be careful. Do you want me to use my hand? Do you want to teach me how to use my mouth?"

Zane groaned and shook his head, putting his hand over hers and showing her the touch he liked. "I don't want your hand or your mouth tonight, darlin'. I want to take my new wife, but it can wait 'til you're healed up."

Amanda smiled up at him and kissed his chest. "No, it can't." Amazed at the power she seemed to have over them, she looked up at him through her lashes and pouted, something she'd never in her life done before and hoped she got right. "I need to feel close to you and Rand. You're my family now, aren't you?"

He grinned down at her, the playfulness in his smile making her stomach flutter and warming her even more. "I knew the first time I laid eyes on you that you'd be trouble. You sure you know what you're getting into?"

She kept stroking him, her eyes closing on a moan when Zane released her hand to cover her breasts. "No, but I know that you and Rand make me feel better than I ever felt before."

Rand slid a hand over her hip as he made his way to the bathwater she'd used earlier. "I can't wait 'til that thigh heals. We're gonna have a good time making you feel even better."

Her eyes popped open when Zane took her hand from his cock and placed it on his chest. She couldn't keep from touching him, thrilling at the play of muscle beneath her hand. "You really want me to like this, don't you?" She paused, her hand stilling on his chest. "Why do you care? I mean, either one of you can take me however you want, and I wouldn't be able to stop you."

Zane slid his hands around her to caress her back. "You've got a lot to learn about us, honey. And we've got a lot to learn about you." His hands slid lower to squeeze her bottom. "So, wife, since you're feelin' brave tonight, you up for a little adventure?" He bent to brush his lips over hers, teasing her into following when he retreated slightly, only to advance again. Pressing his lips against hers firmly, he forced them open to kiss her deeply, his tongue tangling with hers and making her light-headed.

Amanda nearly lost her balance when he lifted his head and turned her slightly to kneel on the bed. She leaned back against him for support, moaning when his hands covered her breasts again. He teased her nipples as his teeth scraped her neck and shoulders. Shivers, cold and hot, raced through her, all seeming to gather at her slit.

One hand made its way down her body to her clit, somehow touching her exactly where she needed it most. He parted her folds and slid his fingers through them, his touch sure but gentle.

Rand came back to the bed and knelt in front of her, running his fingers over her other breast, once again carefully avoiding the scratches. He bent and kissed her nipple. "Your little nipples are always hard. It always makes me want to take 'em in my mouth and suck on 'em. I'd better kiss your scratches and make them better, too, don't you think?"

"God, yes!" She reached out to hold on to his shoulders, no longer trying to hold back her moans and cries of pleasure. Rocking her hips in time to Zane's strokes on her clit also moved her bottom against his cock, which had already become rock hard again.

Zane replaced his fingers with his cock, sliding it through her folds. He nibbled her neck, releasing her breast to tangle his hand in her hair. "I'm going to take you from behind. Nice and slow. I won't hurt your thigh. Do you trust me?"

Amanda arched her neck, whimpering when he gave his attention to a particularly sensitive spot. "Yes. Please. Tell me what to do."

Rand moved aside and helped ease her down to her hands and knees. "I hope you feel that way when we're sure you're ready to take us together."

"Together? Oh!" She pushed back against Zane as he started to press into her, her pussy gripping his cock as he entered her.

Zane's hands tightened on her hips. "Hell. She *is* tight." He worked his cock into her, each thrust taking him a little deeper.

Rand stood beside the bed and reached under her, teasing her nipples. "I knew we made the right choice in marrying you. You're a hot little thing in bed."

Throwing her head back, Amanda closed her eyes, absorbing each delicious sensation. Her nipples and pussy were already sensitive from their touch, making each stroke, each pinch feel even stronger. Her pussy clenched on Zane's cock as he continued to thrust into her, his slow, controlled movements stroking her pussy walls and making the tingling between her legs hotter and hotter.

Bending over her, Zane wrapped an arm around her waist to hold her in place, his lips nibbling at her neck and shoulder and making her shiver. "Your pussy was made for my cock, honey. I knew when I met you that if I ever got inside you, I'd never want to leave."

Shocked that Zane would say something like that, she pressed back into him. "I feel like I was made for both of you. Nobody ever treated me so good. Nothing ever felt so good."

Zane chuckled, the sound raw and intimate. "Let's see if we can make it feel even better." He slid a hand down her abdomen and to her slit to part her folds. His rough finger went to her clit and started stroking, the juices he drew from her smoothing the quick flicks of his finger. Lifting himself off of her back, he plunged his cock deeper, his strokes coming a little faster now.

Amanda groaned and arched, the pressure on her nipple and clit and the thick cock driving inside her making it impossible to think about anything except coming again. The combination wiped away all of her inhibitions, her legs automatically parting wider, her bottom lifting to Zane.

Another hand stroked over her back—it had to be Rand's—and reached down toward her bottom. "Keep that ass up." He released her nipple, placed his other hand between her shoulder blades, and gently pushed until her head touched the bed.

Stunned at the touch of a finger on her bottom hole, she jolted. "What are you doing? Why are you touching me there?"

Zane kept her hips lifted high with the hand under her abdomen and doubled his efforts on her clit. "When we take you together, my cock's going in there while Rand fucks your pussy." His words came out stilted and harsh as though he was in incredible pain.

She stilled, hardly daring to move as Rand pressed a finger against her tight hole at the same time Zane pinched her clit. She shivered as it entered her there, just the tip of his finger, but that was more than enough.

They seemed to be everywhere, touching parts of her that had never been touched before, creating such a need in her that she wondered if it could ever be satisfied. Unable to keep up with all the sensations racing through her, she cried out continuously as heated sizzles raced through her, all coming back to center at her slit. Lifted this way, her knees no longer touched the bed and she kicked out, the decadent sensations too incredible to believe. Unable to catch her breath, she gulped in air, whimpering at the pinch of her bottom hole, stealing her breath as the sizzles grew into a fireball.

All of a sudden, it hit her like a storm. She came hard, her body jolting repeatedly as though she'd been struck by lightning. It went on and on, tumbling her into the squall. Fearing it would never stop, fearing it would, she began to mew softly, like a helpless kitten.

"That's it, honey."

Her weak whimpers seemed to trigger something in Zane because he released her clit and straightened, stroking faster now, his short thrusts going even deeper than before, making the fire inside her ignite all over again.

"Hell." His harsh groan accompanied one last thrust as he placed his open hand on her back to hold her in place as his cock pulsed inside her. He groaned again when she involuntarily tightened on him, her own body still trembling.

Rand stroked her hair and took one of her fisted hands in his, withdrawing his finger from her bottom. "I sure as hell don't know what Zane and me did to deserve you, but I'm keeping you, darlin', come hell or high water."

Zane covered her body with his and buried his face in her hair. "Amen to that."

Sleepy and satisfied, her body still trembling, Amanda smiled, too weak to even open her eyes. "You might not think that forever. Even my pa told you I've got a sassy mouth."

Zane bit her shoulder, chuckling softly when she yelped. "If that mouth gets sassy, I'll fill it with cock. I told you I'd teach you to please me with that mouth, didn't I? Hell and damnation, I forgot all about your leg again."

Amanda's pussy clenched frantically at Zane's sudden withdrawal, her body not ready to let him go yet.

His touch gentle, he turned her to her back. "It's too damned dark. Rand, get a lamp."

Amanda blinked against the light coming from the lamp Rand lit and brought over. Looking down, she could see the worry leave their faces, so apparently her thigh hadn't bled any more.

Zane bent to kiss her belly and then leaned over her to brush his lips over hers. "Get some sleep, honey."

Frowning, Amanda lifted her face for Rand's kiss. "Aren't you coming to bed? I have trouble sleeping when you're not here." She couldn't believe how natural it felt to say that, especially since they'd only married that day. After dealing with her father and her scare earlier, she wanted both of them close.

Rand went around the other side of the bed and got under the quilt with her. "You bet. I like how you snuggle."

"I don't snuggle."

Zane got in on the other side and blew out the lamp. "Yes, you do, and you burrow like a prairie dog. It's sweet as hell, but I'm scared to death I'm gonna smother you."

Amanda snorted. "*Now* you're scared of smothering me?"

Zane laughed. "I didn't kill you, did I? Now, come here and keep me warm." He pulled her close, spooning with her, his body hot against her back and bottom.

"You're already hot."

"Then let me keep *you* warm."

Amanda giggled, wondering if there was a better feeling in the world than being nestled between two men she already loved more than she thought it was possible to love a man. She hadn't meant to fall in love. It had never made any sense to her. Now she wouldn't want to live without it. Settling more comfortably, she couldn't help but wonder what it would be like if Zane and Rand could love her, too.

She moved her knee, gasping when she encountered Rand's cock, which had gotten hard again.

Rand pulled her injured thigh over his own and held her hand. "Stop fidgeting and go to sleep."

"But you're—"

"Yeah, and I don't want to be put out of commission with your knee. I got this way watching Zane fuck you. When we take you together, we'll all be satisfied at the same time."

"But how—"

"Hell." Zane's growl sounded low in her ear as he shifted position, his own cock getting harder against her bottom. "Stop talking about it and go to sleep. We'll show you how it's done when you're ready."

Lying in the darkness, Amanda thought about it but just couldn't figure out how it would be possible. "Are you sure it'll fit?"

Zane groaned against her neck, ignoring Rand's soft laugh. "After we stretch you a little. For God's sake, don't talk about it anymore. Just go to sleep."

After several more minutes, Amanda poked Rand, unsurprised to find him still awake. "Rand, you're teasing me, aren't you?"

Rand groaned and reached out to cup a breast. "No, you're teasing me. Go to sleep."

* * * *

Rand listened as her breathing finally evened out and became deeper. "I thought she'd never go to sleep. I can't stop wanting her. I fall a little bit harder for her every time she opens her mouth." He knew Zane lay awake by his breathing and also the fact that the entire time they'd been married to Beatrice, neither one of them slept until she did.

Zane chuckled softly and shifted when Amanda moved in her sleep and attempted to burrow under him. "Yeah, she's gonna be trouble. How the hell could she have been so close to us all this time and we never knew about her? Did you see the way men look at her?"

A swell of fury rose within Rand. "Yeah, like they want to crawl in her pants. Some of them think she's easy, not only because she has two men but because of who her first husband was."

"They'll soon learn different."

"Jim told me that the Rangers are all looking out for her. They like her grit and said that after she called them all kin, they all look at her like a little sister."

"Good to know, but she's our responsibility."

"Yeah." Rand smiled when Amanda sighed in her sleep and stuck her feet between his legs, somehow always touching both of them as she slept. "Damn, she's pretty. Did you see her face when she comes?"

"I like those sounds she makes."

Rand sighed, running his fingers lightly over Amanda's hand where it lay on his chest. "The way she looks at me…Jesus."

"Yeah, she has a way of making a man feel ten feet tall."

"I'm in love with her." Rand held his breath, then blew it out slowly, hardly able to believe he'd blurted that out loud. He'd never said that about the woman they'd married, even though he cared for her and she carried his name. He didn't know why he'd said it now, but already he knew that Amanda meant more to him than any other women ever could.

"I know."

Surprised, Rand lifted his head. "And you're not?"

Zane didn't answer right away, and when he did, he spoke slowly as though weighing every word. "It's easy to be taken in by her. She's the prettiest thing I ever saw. She seems tough but there's no doubt she's all woman."

"But…"

"I don't know. I don't trust her completely. Will she stick around if she finds out people are talking about her? I'm sure she's had her fill of that. Would she stay with us if we end up staying in the Rangers longer than we think we will? You know damned well we haven't heard the last from her daddy. Will she stand up to him when he does come after her? Will she trust us to take care of her?"

"You're scared she's gonna leave."

"If you were smart, you'd be, too. Don't go letting your emotions rule your head or she's gonna end up ripping your heart out."

Struck by the implication, Rand shot up. "Holy hell, you're in love with her."

Amanda groaned and turned in her sleep, his sharp tone and quick movement obviously disturbing her.

Zane murmured to her softly, stroking her arm until she settled again. "Shh, baby. Go back to sleep. It's nothing."

Rand settled back, smiling in the darkness. He didn't get an answer from Zane, but he really didn't expect one. Didn't need one.

Some of the things Zane mentioned had gone through his mind, too, but he'd quickly dismissed them. He could die tomorrow. He didn't want to spend the time he had with her wondering what could happen. He'd rather just enjoy every day as it came.

He slept fitfully, the questions Zane brought up going through his mind all night. Damn it, Amanda wouldn't leave them. He wouldn't let her.

Chapter Eight

Amanda couldn't stay in the hotel another minute.

After eating breakfast downstairs with Zane and Rand, she went back to their room.

Unused to having nothing to do, she quickly became antsy.

When the young girl came up to ask for the laundry, Amanda was so happy to see a friendly face and so bored, she gathered all of their dirty clothes and went with her. It took several minutes to convince the girl to let her help, but when she finally did, the two of them worked together and soon had the clean clothes hanging on the clothesline.

It had gone much faster than she'd expected and she still had a lot of time to kill before Zane and Rand came back. Knowing she wouldn't be able to stand being alone in the room, she made her way around to the front of the hotel with the intention of taking a walk.

Several people stopped to stare at her as she walked by, but she ignored them and kept walking, automatically heading toward Ranger Headquarters. Maybe she could help do something there. She might just stop in at the house behind it and see if the captain's widow needed help with anything.

Thinking about the picture she made as she walked down the street brought a smile to her lips. She wore pants as always, but now she wore her knife attached to a belt Zane and Rand had given her this morning. Not exactly ladylike, but then again, she'd never been a lady like her mother.

Thank God.

She loved her mother dearly but could never understand why she allowed herself and her daughters to be hit. She'd never been in her mother's shoes, though, and wouldn't want to be.

Loving Zane and Rand made her more vulnerable than she was comfortable with, but she couldn't imagine becoming so weak that she'd let either one of them hit her.

It depressed and unnerved her to think that perhaps at one time her mother thought the same thing.

It saddened her to think she had more of her father in her than her mother, and she felt a sense of betrayal that she was thankful for it. She shuddered to think what would have become of them if she'd been like her mother.

A shot rang out, startling her out of her depressing thoughts. And then another.

No one around seemed overly concerned by it, but since it came from the direction of Ranger Headquarters, Amanda broke out in a run. Rounding the building, she came to a halt, smiling in relief when she saw that some of the Rangers had set up cans and a scarecrow for target practice. The tension drained out of her that neither Zane nor Rand were in any danger. Intrigued, she started forward.

Two Rangers worked with Henry, the boy who'd been hurt when Rafael escaped. The men must have sensed her, because they turned at her approach, their smiles like a balm to her soul, but after what the old woman had said, she couldn't help but wonder if they were as sincere as they seemed. Henry greeted her first.

"Hello, Mrs. Owens. Jim and Silas are helping me with my shooting. Would you like to watch?"

Jim shook his head, smiling. "I'm sure she came down here to see the captains, not watch you shoot, Henry."

Henry's face turned bright red. "I'm sorry, I—"

Hellfire, how could someone so young and sweet be a Texas Ranger? Smiling, Amanda nodded, determined to get these men to accept her and appreciating that Henry seemed to want her company.

"I'd love to see you shoot, Henry. I'm sure the captains are busy and I was going crazy sitting in the hotel by myself."

Henry beamed. "Sure, Mrs. Owens."

Jim gave Henry some last-minute instructions before coming over to her. "That was mighty nice of you, ma'am. The captains thought it would be a good idea to get Henry's mind on something else. He's young, but he loves bein' a Ranger."

Over the next several minutes, Amanda stood with Jim as Henry showed off his marksmanship. He hit about half the time, and after he'd emptied his pistol twice, he came over to Amanda as Silas set up more cans.

His face glowing with pride, Henry smiled at Jim. "Thanks for helpin' me. I ain't great at it like you and the captains, but at least I'm better than before."

Jim patted him on the shoulder. "Keep practicing. That's the only way you'll get better."

Amanda grinned. "You did real good, Henry. Jim's right. It took a lot of practice before I could hit anything."

Henry's eyes widened. "You shoot?"

Amanda shrugged. "Yeah. Pa couldn't hunt when he was drunk." Why had she said that? Reminding them of who her pa was hadn't been such a good idea if she wanted them to like her.

Jim whipped around to eye her skeptically. "You can really shoot?"

Henry tugged her arm, dropping it hurriedly when he realized what he'd done. "Sorry, ma'am." His eyes danced as he offered his pistol. "I just reloaded. Would you show us?"

Amanda balked, embarrassed that she'd said anything. She'd gotten so nervous, not knowing whether or not to believe that the woman had spoken the truth about how the Rangers felt about her, and then cursed herself for doubting them after they'd all been so nice to her. If she asked them, though, they'd have no choice but to deny it. "I've never fired a pistol before, Henry. I've only ever fired my rifle."

Jim took the pistol from Henry and handed it to her. "Try. Silas is out of the way." He stood behind her as she got used to the feel of the pistol in her hand while he gave her some brief instructions. Holding her arms, he helped her line up a shot. "Don't jerk the trigger. Squeeze the same way you do with your rifle."

Following his direction, Amanda squeezed off a shot that went wide of the mark. Turning, she smiled at Jim and Henry, her cheeks burning. "I think I need more practice."

Out of the corner of her eye, she saw movement and turned to see Tom Hensen, a Ranger she knew Zane and Rand didn't care for, coming out of the building with Zane and Rand right behind him. None of them looked happy.

Tom scowled when he saw her. "Well. If it ain't the captains' wife. Ain't two men enough for you? You gotta have all the Rangers pantin' for you?"

Amanda had to bite back an insult, not wanting to cause trouble for her new husbands, but she didn't get the chance to say anything anyway as he confirmed her worse fears.

Zane turned and swung, knocking the other Ranger to the ground so fast that all she saw was a blur. He didn't even look back as he strode toward her.

Jim stepped between them. "Captain, we were just showing your wife how to shoot a pistol. We don't mean no disrespect. She was watching Henry and when she said she—"

Rand nodded, shooting a look at Tom as he dusted himself off and glared at all of them before striding away. "We know. We trust you and we trust our wife. You're doing pretty good, Henry. Thanks for working with him, Jim."

Zane reached Amanda first and touched her hair. "You missed, honey. I think you're going to have to practice out here with Henry."

Humbled by their immediate trust in her, she smiled, wrinkling her nose playfully even as she held back tears. "I only practice with my rifle, Ranger."

Zane gestured to the tree stump. "Henry, put a can up there. Let's see if my wife can really shoot or she's just bluffing." He went inside, coming back with her rifle. "It's already loaded. Show us what you got."

Jim's brows went up. "A Sharps rifle? Where'd you get that?"

Rand looked a little nervous. "Do you really know how to shoot that thing, darlin'?"

"John left it behind." Not wanting to talk about her first husband, Amanda lifted the rifle to her shoulder, comforted by the familiar weight, and turned to look over her shoulder at Zane and Rand, including Jim in her look. "I'm not lying. I can shoot, but only with my rifle."

Zane folded his arms across his chest, his eyes hooded. "You hit that can and I'll buy you a Colt myself."

Grinning, Amanda winked at him, not about to let them see her insecurity about how many other Rangers thought the same way Tom Hensen did. "You're on, Ranger." Taking aim, Amanda couldn't resist adding, "It's awfully close, you know. I practice about five hundred yards." She squeezed the trigger, sending the can flying, jumping when two more shots rang out in rapid succession, making the can jump two more times in the air before hitting the ground.

Lowering her rifle, she turned in time to see Zane and Rand holster their weapons. "Show offs."

Rand grinned and closed the distance between them, snatching the rifle away with one hand and hugging her with the other. "We can't have our wife thinking she can outshoot us, now can we?"

Jim grinned, not looking at all surprised. "That was some fine shootin', ma'am."

Henry, however, looked stunned as he turned to Silas. "Did you see that?"

Silas nodded smiling in amusement. "Of course I seen it. I was standing right here. Looks like you got some practicin' to do, Henry."

Zane grabbed her hand. "Come inside. We have some things to talk about. Jim, can you make sure we're not disturbed?"

"Reckon so, Captain. Silas and me'll work with Henry a little more."

Rand nodded once. "Much obliged. Keep an eye out for her father."

Zane pulled her into the building, through the main room, and into their office. He waited until Rand closed the door behind him before lifting her onto his desk, spreading her knees to make a place for himself. His hands went to her thighs, somehow avoiding her injury. "Henry's already smitten with you. You tryin' to get all my Rangers smitten with you?"

Raising her hands to his shoulders, Amanda leaned close, pressing her breasts against him. She didn't want to think of the other Rangers' hatred of her right now. She only wanted to be with Zane and Rand and let them make her forget about everything else.

Looking up at him from beneath her lashes, she closed her legs around him, warmed by the affection in his eyes that accompanied the heat. "You believed that other Ranger? There's only two Rangers I want smitten with me. You got any idea what I can do to get their attention?" She groaned as Rand moved in behind her, removing her hat and tossing it aside.

Rand pushed her hair aside and bent, his lips warm on her shoulder. "I don't think you'd have too much trouble gettin' any man's attention, but I can think of one or two things that might work real good if you want to get mine."

Tilting her head, she moaned as Rand nuzzled her neck at the same time Zane began unfastening her shirt. Drawing a shaky breath, she let it out slowly. "What's that, Ranger?" Her nipples, exposed to the cool air, had already puckered. It felt a little naughty to be half-naked in their office, but she already trusted them so much that she didn't even worry about getting caught, instinctively knowing neither one of them would ever let that happen. It freed her to just lie back and enjoy it.

Zane spread the sides of her shirt and ran his fingers lightly over her nipples, his eyes hooded in that look she'd already come to know so well. "One look at these breasts will make a man forget what he's thinking."

"Is that right?" No one else had ever looked at her the way Zane and Rand did, and she found she couldn't resist it. She let Rand support her weight, arching her back to tilt her breasts upward. "Did you forget what you were thinking?"

Zane followed and brushed his lips over hers, his hands covering her breasts so his palms brushed over her nipples. "No. I was thinking about how beautiful these breasts are. Now I'm thinking about how pretty you are everywhere else." Straightening, he released her breasts and started to work her pants down her legs.

Rand helped her lay the rest of the way back on the desk and bent to take a nipple between his lips. "Funny, I was just thinking about the same thing."

Amanda reached for Zane when he leaned over her, pulling his hair free from the leather strip he wore to hold it back. She tangled her fingers in the long, silky strands, loving the clean feel of it. He still smelled like the soap he'd used to wash up that morning. So did Rand.

Zane slid her pants to her knees and then lower, cursing when he couldn't get them over her boots. "It looks like you're gonna get fucked with your boots on, honey."

She released her hold on his hair to grip his forearms as his hands began to roam over her body, trembling all over at the feel of his rough strength moving so gently over her curves.

From above her, Rand bent to nibble at her lips, thrilling her when he tugged at her nipples. "You ready to learn how to use that mouth, darlin'?"

* * * *

Zane ran a hand down her body to her soft pussy, smiling when she trembled, his other hand lightly tracing over the bandage she still wore. Seeing no sign of fresh blood, he lifted her legs, bending them back to expose her and separate her folds. Seeing the moisture glistening at her slit caused a surge of lust in him, even more powerful than before. "Hmm. Looks like I'll be the first one to take that ass."

Amanda's eyes went wide. "You weren't just teasing me when you said that?"

If she didn't want it, he wouldn't force it on her, but as passionate as she'd turned out to be, he wanted to at least try. She seemed to like being touched there before, but, then again, Rand had hardly breached her. Hell, to have a wife who they could take together...

Zane leaned forward, his chest pushing against the pants bunched around her ankles, effectively lifting her legs higher. "No, I wasn't teasing you." Deciding to test her, he shot a quick glance at Rand and slid a finger through her folds and into her drenched pussy to gather moisture. He pressed deep, and withdrew, curling his finger inside her. Pressed deep and withdrew again. And again.

Her soft moans and desperate whimpers had his cock growing even larger inside his pants, making it damned uncomfortable.

Rand grimaced and loosened his pants to pull out his own cock, touching Amanda's cheek with it. "I'm gonna slide you back so your head's hangin' over the side and fuck your sassy mouth, darlin'."

Amanda let go of Zane's forearms, gripping Rand's as he grabbed her under her shoulders and slid her toward him. "Yes. Teach me."

Zane bit back a groan as more moisture coated his fingers, and she lifted her breasts in offering. He watched, mesmerized as Amanda opened her mouth, taking the head of Rand's cock inside. "Hellfire. I ain't never seen anything that sexy in my life. Suck it, Amanda." His own cock ached to have her lips on it.

Rand's heartfelt groan echoed his own. His best friend gritted his teeth as he leaned over her and reached for her breasts, the effort to remain still hardening his features. "Fuck." He began to move, pressing his cock a little deeper between those full lips. "That's it, darlin'. Damn you're good at this."

Zane couldn't stand it anymore and had to free his cock, the need to fuck her nearly unbearable. Feeling his control slip another notch, he gritted his teeth, the need to know if she could accept both of them nearly overwhelming. He was dying to see how she would respond to more direct attention to her ass. The sounds that came from her and the fact that she clearly enjoyed sucking Rand's cock had his own cock leaking moisture and made him insane to have her.

Fighting for control, he withdrew his finger, circling it around her clit, pressing down on her abdomen in anticipation of her jolt. Leaning forward to lift her ass a little higher, he chuckled softly at the fresh moisture that coated his fingers as he slid them through her folds again. "You like when I touch that clit. Let's see how much you like having your ass opened."

He'd already braced himself for her instinctive stiffening, keeping the pressure on her legs when she tried to straighten them. Aware that Rand watched and knew what he was about to do, he teased all three of them by dipping inside her to gather more of her juices before sliding a hand under her bottom to lift her even higher and touched her bottom hole with his wet finger.

Although muffled by Rand's cock in her mouth, the sounds she made got louder and more desperate as he pressed against the tight ring of muscle at her opening. His insistent pressure was rewarded as it gave way, allowing him entrance. Not wanting to alarm her, he slid only a few inches inside, not stroking her the way he wanted to, instead holding his finger still to let her become accustomed to the feeling. Her ass closed tight on his finger, gripping him so damned hard, he couldn't help but imagine what it would be like when he worked his cock inside her.

"Your ass is so fucking tight. You like that, don't you, honey? You're soaking wet. Damn, I can't wait to bend you over and fuck this tight ass. No, don't turn away. Keep sucking Rand."

With his other hand, he held on to her hip as she attempted to thrash and nudged the head of his cock against her pussy, his cock so hard it bordered on pain. With one sharp thrust, Zane filled her, groaning at the feel of her soft pussy quivering all around his cock.

Rand pinched her nipples a little harder and began to pump more steadily into her mouth. "She's killing me with that mouth. She's too good at—Hell. Fuck her good, Zane. Damn it, she's gonna make me come too soon. Amanda, you gonna swallow my seed when I come?"

When she didn't react, Zane moved the finger in her ass. "You gonna swallow Rand's come, Amanda?"

She bobbed her head and tightened on both Zane's finger and cock. The sensation had both Zane and Rand groaning harshly and tightening their hold on her. A fine sheen of perspiration made her smooth skin glow as she shuddered and trembled under their hands, making her skin slick and more difficult to hold on to.

Knowing he wouldn't last long, Zane began stroking, fucking her tight channel deep, spurred on by her moans of pleasure and obvious enjoyment. Knowing he'd never get enough of this fascinating woman, he looked up at Rand, seeing a look on his face he'd never seen before.

Rand looked and sounded tortured. His groans and harsh breathing as he shallowly fucked Amanda's mouth and played with her nipples seemed more intense than any time Zane could remember.

The prickling at his spine told Zane he was damned close to coming already.

Determined to take Amanda with him, he slid the hand on her abdomen lower, using his thumb to stroke her clit as he thrust harder and faster.

She tightened impossibly on him as she screamed in her throat at the same time that Rand groaned and came, calling out her name harshly. Her scream was cut short as she worked to swallow Rand's cum, her body writhing and shuddering in completion. She milked Zane's cock and finger, making it impossible to hold back any longer. The sharp sparks in his groin all seemed to explode at once as the pressure burst and broke free. With a loud groan that felt as though it erupted from the depths of his soul, he came hard, spurting his seed into her in a seemingly never-ending stream, draining him completely.

Rand straightened and pulled free of her mouth, groaning and breathing heavily, allowing Zane to pull her back toward him. His eyes held shock and amazement as they met Zane's. "Jesus!" He sucked in air like he couldn't get enough.

Zane bent over her and kissed a nipple, smiling against her breast when she shivered. "I knew if I married you all I'd ever want to do was fuck you." Apprehensive when she didn't answer, Zane lifted his head. "You all right, honey?"

Amanda's impossibly purple eyes opened and she smiled. "Am I supposed to like sex this much?"

Relieved, Zane teasingly wiggled the finger in her ass, groaning when she cried out softly and tightened on him again. "Yep, but only with us."

Her satisfied smile made him feel more like a man than any woman ever had. "Ranger, I can't even imagine anybody else touching me, but I'm not a loose woman." Reaching up to tangle her fingers in his hair again, she lifted her head to kiss him, her soft lips inviting him to nibble. "I can't believe you're my husbands. I hope you don't regret marrying me."

Zane slowly withdrew from both openings, nibbling at her bottom lip as she trembled, pleased that she responded with more boldness than she had the night before. "You're turning into a wanton woman. How would I ever regret marrying you?" A little disturbed by the worried look on her face, he helped her up and into Rand's waiting arms. "Is something wrong?"

Her smile seemed a little forced as she leaned into Rand, who helped her right her clothing. "Of course not. What could be wrong?"

Zane lifted her chin with his fisted hand, narrowing his eyes. "If something's bothering you, I want you to tell us."

Amanda looked down to fasten her pants, not meeting his eyes. "I will. I'd better let you two get back to work now. I've gotta go take our laundry off the line at the hotel." Shifting her feet, she looked up at both of them through her thick lashes. "Thanks again for believing nothing was going on out there. I would never do anything to shame either one of you." She smiled and left before they could say anything.

With a curse, Zane went to the window, watching her wave to Henry, Jim, and Silas before starting down the street. "Do you get the feeling something's bothering her?"

Rand stood at the window beside him, also watching Amanda until she disappeared from view. "Yeah, but hell, neither one of us knows her well enough yet to know for sure. Maybe she just needs a little time alone. She always looks a little shaken after she comes, like it surprises her. Maybe it was too soon to take her where we didn't have time to hold her afterward. We'll talk to her tonight. I've got Tom and three other Rangers coming back in this afternoon to deal with the Indian raids going on outside Waco."

Zane nodded. "I'll feel better if Tom's out of the way for a while. I don't like the way he looks at Amanda."

"I'm surprised you didn't rearrange his face out there earlier. You must be getting soft."

Zane went to sit back behind his desk. He hated paperwork and wanted to get everything done so he could get back to Amanda. "I almost did until I saw the look on Amanda's face. She looked like she expected one of us to beat her. With Fred Winslow as her father, I think she's seen enough violence already, don't you? But if Tom looks at her wrong or speaks that way again to her, that fucking grin of his is gonna be short a few teeth."

Chapter Nine

Walking slowly down the street, Amanda paid closer attention to the people she passed, surprised that many smiled and nodded, some of the men even tipping their hats. It was a far cry from the way she'd been treated the day before, adding to the warm glow she already had after being with Zane and Rand. It made her wonder if living here wouldn't be so bad after all.

She'd almost made it back to the hotel when she spotted the woman who'd stopped her the day before coming toward her, this time alone, but with the same bitter look on her face. Determined not to let anyone ruin her good mood, she didn't even look her way as she started to pass her, surprised when the older woman stepped in front of her, blocking her way.

Amanda stopped and, with her hands on her hips, glared at her. "I don't want to hear any more of your filthy mouth. Get out of my way."

To her utter amazement, the woman smiled, surprising Amanda that her face didn't crack at the effort. Looking around, she kept her voice low. "I'm very sorry for the way I spoke to you before. I hope you can forgive me."

Amanda eyed her warily, not trusting the sudden change of heart. "I forgive you. Now, excuse me, I have some things to do."

The older woman grabbed her arm, her grip surprisingly strong. "I was a friend of your mother's, and I hope to be a friend to you, too. Would you come to my home for tea? I know your men are busy and it must be awfully boring at the hotel. I'd like to talk to you about having a housewarming party when you move into the captain's house. It's expected, you know. As the wife of captains of the Texas Rangers, you'll have a lot of responsibilities. As a favor to your mother and to make up for the way I spoke to you yesterday, I'd like to help you."

Damn. What the hell did she know about a *housewarming* party? What the hell was a housewarming party anyway? And what the hell *was* this woman's name?

Amanda didn't want to admit that she didn't remember it, especially now that she'd started being so nice to her. She'd ask someone later. Afraid of shaming Zane and Rand by failing in her duties as their wife, she nodded and added reluctantly, "That would be very nice of you. I have to admit, though, I don't even know what a housewarming party is."

The older woman's lips thinned in disapproval, which quickly turned to a smile. "Don't you worry about that. My carriage is in the livery." Handing Amanda a parcel, she patted her arm. "Be a good girl and take this to my carriage driver. I'll be right along as soon as I stop to get some sugar. I love sweet tea, don't you?"

Amanda took the package pressed at her. "I should go tell Zane and Rand—"

Lips thinned in disapproval yet again. "My dear, you're going to have to learn that you can't be bothering men as important as your husbands for things like that. You'll be back before they know it. Once we have tea and talk a little, I'll have my driver bring you right back to the hotel in time for dinner with your men." She walked away, giving Amanda no chance to answer.

Amanda still didn't trust her, but how much harm could it be to have tea with the old woman and listen to advice on how to throw a party?

God help her.

But if that's what she had to do to be a good Ranger's wife, then that's what she'd do.

Adjusting the lightweight package in her arms, she made her way to the livery, hoping she'd be back from her tea in time to get the clothes off the line before dark.

She glanced down the street toward Ranger Headquarters before walking inside. No matter what the old woman said, she'd just go down to let Zane and Rand know where she'd be. She wouldn't bother them for more than a few minutes and felt strange about going somewhere without letting them know about it. It suddenly occurred to her that she didn't even know where this woman lived, and she had to find out her name.

She'd just put the package in the carriage and ask the driver.

Making her way inside, she was hit with the smells of horse and leather, but her eyes hadn't adjusted enough yet to see either one. "Hello?"

Pain, sharp and hot, exploded in her head, knocking her legs out from under her. And then nothing.

* * * *

Rand whistled a tune as he and Zane made their way up the hotel stairs, his body already tight with anticipation. The picture of Amanda lying across their desk this afternoon played through his mind all day, making it nearly impossible to concentrate on anything else.

He'd hated being away from her, his thoughts consumed with her to the point that it made it hard to concentrate on anything else. He hated leaving the hotel room in the morning and lingered as long as possible, taking his time to dress so he could spend as much time as he could with her before he left for the day.

She looked so damned beautiful, all tousled hair and sleep-soft eyes, making him want to stay in bed all day and tumble her.

"Would you stop that damned whistling?"

Rand grinned at the frown Zane had worn since Amanda left their office hours earlier. "I'm happy. Besides, I don't want to startle her again. It's better if she hears us coming." He held up her rifle. "At least she doesn't have this, but who knows what else she might use? Our woman's resourceful."

He ran his fingers over the rifle she'd used only hours earlier. He'd taken it with him to clean it for her, and in her haste to leave, he'd forgotten to give it back to her. With her father close by, it would be better not to take any chances.

Zane glared at him over his shoulder. "Yeah, well it's getting on my nerves. Something's wrong with Amanda, and tonight I'm going to get to the bottom of it." Zane rubbed the back of his neck, something he'd done several times today. It wasn't a good sign.

Rand sobered. "What the hell could be wrong with her? Do you think she's missing her momma and her sister?" Stopping, he grabbed Zane's arm. "Wait a minute. Do you think she's upset because of what Tom said?" The other Texas Ranger had shown up later than expected to meet the others for their patrol, and when Tom arrived, he'd been full of smug self-importance and that damned smile of his that grated on Rand's nerves.

Zane shook his head, looking down the hall, obviously impatient to get to their room. "I don't know. But I've had about enough of Tom Hensen. If he's pissed at us because he didn't get promoted, he's got no call taking it out on Amanda, and I'll be damned if I'm gonna let him treat her that way. She's been through enough with her father."

Continuing down the hall, Rand tightened his hand on her rifle. "It pisses me off that she's never had anyone to protect her. Not her momma and certainly not her daddy. Hell, even her husband used her and took off without looking back."

"She doesn't have to worry about that anymore."

Rand grinned. "Damned right she doesn't. I want to protect her but I also want to teach her to have a little fun. You and Amanda both need to learn to play a little. You've always been serious, but I don't want it rubbing off on her. She's had enough serious in her life."

Zane's lips twitched. "With Amanda, I'd be willing to play."

Rand reached for the doorknob. "After what she was like this afternoon, I've been thinking of nothing but playing with her all day." He unlocked the door and swung it open, surprised to find the room empty. A kernel of unease settled in his stomach. "She's not here."

Zane went into the room and looked around as though she would appear out of thin air. "Maybe she went to the necessary."

They waited a few more minutes, Rand getting more and more anxious by the second. The fact that Zane kept rubbing the back of his neck only made it worse. "Every time trouble's coming, you rub your damned neck. You've been doing it all day, and it's driving me nuts."

Zane scowled at him. "How the hell do you think I feel? It's got something to do with Amanda, and I know it. I'm going out to check for her."

Rand nodded and went to sit on the bed, smiling when he saw the nightgown they'd ripped from her the previous night. Reaching out, he gathered it in his fist and raised it to his nose. Breathing in the scent of her that still lingered on the thin cloth, he closed his eyes, again picturing the way she looked this afternoon spread out over their desk. Soft skin, high, firm breasts, and enticing dark curls that hid the softest, sweetest pussy he'd ever tasted.

The sounds she made as they pleasured her still rang in his ears, the sweetest sounds he'd ever heard. Once again congratulating himself on choosing her for their wife, Rand let his fingers trail over the soft material.

Amanda's skin was even softer.

His head shot up when the door to the room slammed back against the wall and Zane stood there, breathing heavily, the horror on his face bringing Rand quickly to his feet. "What is it? Where's Amanda?"

Zane ran a hand through his hair, inadvertently ripping out the leather thong that always held it in place. His hair now swung loose past his shoulders, giving him a wild and untamed look. "She's not at the necessary, the clothes she said she was gonna take from the line when she got back are still there, and the hotel clerk hasn't seen her all day."

Rand felt all the blood drain from his face. "Where the fuck is she?"

An hour later, his stomach still burned with fear and anger. They'd talked to several people in town who'd seen Amanda walking toward Ranger Headquarters earlier that day. Some said they'd seen her walking in that direction later that afternoon. "It doesn't make any sense. She didn't come back later on. Unless these people got their times mixed up."

Zane scrubbed a hand over his face, searching the street frantically just the way he and Rand had both been doing for the past hour. "One I can understand, but three different people said they saw her walking back that way this afternoon. If she didn't come see us, where the hell could she have been going?"

They'd been up and down the street talking to everyone in sight and were still no closer to finding Amanda than they'd been an hour ago. Rand turned as a soft voice whispered from behind them.

"Rangers, are you looking for Amanda?"

Rand spun, looking down into the frightened face of a young woman. "Yes. Have you seen her?"

The girl looked back and forth as if afraid to be seen talking to them. "Yes. I saw her this afternoon, but I don't know where she is now. I was going to talk to her but Mrs. Hensen stopped her, so I hid in the general store and watched out the window waitin' for them to finish. I was afraid Mrs. Hensen was gonna say those nasty things again." Her face turned bright red and she looked away. "I know I shoulda come out and defended her, but that old lady scares me."

Rand clenched his hands at his sides, careful to hide his fury at the young girl. It appeared Amanda had been taking abuse and never mentioned it, and no one had stepped forward to defend her. "Hensen? Is she related to Tom Hensen?"

Nodding, the young woman turned away again. "She's Ranger Hensen's mother. She's always talkin' about her son bein' the best of the Texas Rangers. Beggin' your pardon, but she was real mad when her son got passed over and you became the new captains."

Zane touched the girl's arm, turning her toward them when she kept glancing at a group of women who stood several yards away. "Can you come with us to Ranger Headquarters? We'd like to ask you some questions."

"Oh, no! I have to get home. I'll get in big trouble just for tellin' you this, but I—"

Rand had had enough. "You're gonna be in bigger trouble when we put you in jail." Ignoring her terrified look, he crossed his arms over his chest and glared down at her. "Our wife is missing. Tell us what you know or you're goin' to jail. What's your name?"

Crying now, the girl backed up against the wall. "Sissy Farnsworth. Please don't take me to jail. I'll tell you everything."

It took several minutes of questioning, impatient that her sobs slowed down the telling considerably, before they learned all they could. At least now they had a place to start. They'd learned from Sissy where Tom lived with his mother outside of town and both hoped like hell they would find Amanda there.

Rand's fear for Amanda had grown with every word of Sissy's story, but he couldn't let his fear for her or his anger toward Tom and his mother cloud his mind. He and Zane had to stay sharp if they were going to have any chance of finding Amanda. "I can't believe I didn't see it. Tom hated us almost from the first day, but this…"

Neither spoke again until they were on their horses and headed out of town. Zane's stone-like expression hadn't changed at all since they talked to Sissy. "If I find out Tom's behind this, he's dead."

* * * *

Amanda came alert slowly, unable to hold back a moan. Her head hurt so badly she automatically reached up to touch it, unsurprised that her hand came away sticky with what she assumed was blood. It had gotten too damned dark to see. At least there didn't seem to be much of it.

What the hell happened to her?

She had to blink several times before she could focus and then didn't know whether she'd focused or not because she saw only darkness. Thinking back, the last thing she could remember was walking into the livery in town. As hard as she tried, she couldn't remember anything after that. She immediately reached for the knife at her belt, only to find it gone. Of course whoever did this to her would have taken it.

On the off chance that it had merely fallen off, she put out a hand and cautiously felt all around her, finding nothing but cool, damp earth and straw. No knife. Was she still in the livery?

The darkness was so complete she blinked again to make sure her eyes were really open. She couldn't see a darned thing. After several attempts she came to her knees, fighting to ignore the nausea and the pain in her head.

Zane and Rand would be so worried.

Knowing her husbands would be searching frantically for her by now made her feel a lot better and gave her the strength she needed to push herself to her knees and then to her feet. She swayed, catching herself on a nearby wall, the rough wood scraping her palm. Putting a hand to her stomach, she took several deep breaths before her head cleared enough for her to move without falling.

She had to find a way out of here.

It seemed to take forever, but she finally found the door, a sob escaping when she discovered it had been locked.

If only she could see!

Taking another deep breath, she straightened, biting her lip. She wouldn't cry. She'd survived her father, and she was the wife of

Texas Rangers now. She would stay strong and make Zane and Rand proud.

Where the hell was she?

Where were they?

It didn't matter right now. Right now she just had to worry about getting out of here.

She kept moving, groping in the darkness for something to use to break her way out of here and froze when she heard voices. Moving as quickly as she dared back toward the corner, she scraped her shoulder on what felt like a nail sticking out from the wall. She winced, biting her lip to keep from crying out at the sharp pain. The material of her shirt ripped as she pulled away and crouched down to make herself as small as possible.

Not knowing where she was or who could be creeping up outside the door, she reached around on the ground for some kind of weapon, getting on her hands and knees and crawling until her hand settled on what felt like a piece of wood about three inches across.

It would have to do.

She heard the slide of wood as though a beam had been removed, holding her breath as the door pushed open.

"Light a lantern."

Oh no! She recognized Rafael's voice right away. Why would he be coming in here? Did he even know she was here?

"Hey, Rangers' wife. Come on out here where I can see you."

Amanda stayed low as one of his men lit the lantern but didn't have a chance of escaping. The flame lit every corner of what she could now see was a small barn. She held her breath again as Rafael turned and saw her.

"There you are."

Amanda came to her feet, not wanting to cower to him. She'd seen her mother and sister do enough of that and vowed she never would.

"What are you doing here, Rafael? What do you want from me? I don't have the gold. The Rangers took it."

Rafael smiled, the few yellow and brownish teeth he showed making her sick. "I know this. That is why I'm taking you with me. Your Ranger friend took you for me since I can't be seen in Austin anymore. Now you're comin' with me, and we're going to lead your husbands into an ambush. With them dead, the new captain will turn over the gold to me and everyone will be happy."

Amanda forced herself not to show any reaction. She couldn't let them kill Zane and Rand and would have to figure out a way to warn them. "What about me? If you're going to kill me, I'd rather you just do it now."

Rafael came toward her, grabbing the piece of wood she swung at him with ease. Reaching out to touch her hair, he rubbed the strands between his fingers. "John musta been right about you. He said you was full of fire. You have two husbands now, which must mean you're too much woman for one man to handle." Releasing her hair, he ran a finger down a breast and tapped her nipple. "I'm man enough to handle you, and when I'm done with you, I'll let my men here have a little fun. No, I think I'll let you live until I get tired of you, so you'd better do whatever you can to keep me happy."

Not bothering to hide her revulsion, Amanda lifted her chin. "I'll kill myself, or you, if you touch me."

Rafael shrugged as though it didn't matter to him one way or the other. "Either way, your men will come lookin' for you, and I get to kill them."

Knowing he was right, Amanda smiled, hiding her fear for both herself and her husbands. She'd have to go along with him and somehow figure out a way to warn Zane and Rand. "I'm really gonna enjoy watching you hang."

Chapter Ten

Nearly out of his mind with worry for Amanda, Zane searched every inch of the Hensen place and couldn't find a single sign that Amanda had even been here. Striding back into the house, he glared at the old woman who sat at the kitchen table calmly drinking tea.

"Where is she?"

Even attempting an innocent look, she couldn't hide the amusement in her eyes. "Ranger, I already told you I don't know. The last time I saw your wife was in town. We had a few words. I offered to help her with planning a party when you moved into the captain's quarters."

Rand came in from the front door. "Is that why you told her she should be ashamed of herself for having two men? Is that why you told her that even the Rangers were ashamed of her? I got news for you, lady. She's worth more than a hundred of you."

Zane struggled to keep his temper in check. He hadn't been this angry since he'd found those men trying to rip Amanda's clothes from her, but now fear and frustration added an edge to it that he'd never before experienced, making him want to put his hands around the old woman's throat and choke the truth from her. "This is the last time I'm going to ask you before I haul you into jail. Where's my wife?"

The look on her face would have been funny under other circumstances. "Jail? You can't put me in jail! My son's a Texas Ranger." She took another sip of tea and smiled. "Besides, I'm an old woman. Texas Rangers don't put old women in jail."

Zane smiled back coldly. "These two do. Let's go."

"You aren't serious!"

Rand grinned and pulled her from her chair. "It's our way of getting even for what you've done to our wife. We're gonna make sure everyone in town knows you're locked up for being an accomplice to kidnapping Amanda, and that your son's a kidnapper. Let's see how many of your friends even acknowledge you after that and your son's stripped of his badge."

The old woman's face lost all color, her eyes widening in horror. "No! You can't do this. I did it. I kidnapped her. Tom didn't have anything to do with it. I swear."

Hiding his sense of relief that they'd finally gotten through to her, Zane raised a brow and shook his head in pity. "You're never gonna convince us of that, especially since you don't even know where she is."

She grabbed his arm, desperation making her wrinkled hands surprisingly strong. "I'll prove it. I know where she is. I took her to the old barn behind the blacksmith's."

Zane flung her arm off in disgust and started out. "I'd better find her there."

"Wait! Aren't you going to arrest me for kidnapping? Tom had nothing to do with it."

"I don't have time right now. I need to find Amanda."

"She's not there. She's gone."

Zane whipped around, exchanging a look with Rand, who grabbed the old woman by the shoulders.

"What do you mean, she's gone? Where is she?"

Tom's mother seemed to have aged right before their eyes. She slumped in Rand's hold. "That Rafella man has her. He wants to exchange her for the gold, and I figured if you two was out chasing him, my Tom would get to be the captain."

Zane's jaw clenched. "Lady, you don't even know the man's name, and you're trying to convince me that you made a deal with him? You'd never even have the nerve to face *Rafael*. Your son made the deal for Rafael to take us on a wild goose chase and kill us in return for getting the gold from Tom. Your son's the one who planned all of this and it was all for nothing. He'll never be captain and both of you are ruined. You'd better hope we find Amanda alive or you'll both hang for her murder." *Oh, God. Not again. Please, not Amanda.*

Rand pushed her back into her chair and Zane could see the restraint he showed in not flinging her into it. "Rangers will be by to arrest you. In the meantime, you'd better pray like hell we find our wife alive."

Zane turned, racing for his horse, doing his best to tamp down the terror that threatened to choke him. In order to have any chance of finding Amanda, he had to keep a clear head and he would do anything, *anything* to get her back. Riding toward town, he urged as much speed as he could from his horse, the whole time picturing Amanda as she'd looked sitting cross-legged on the bed this morning, wearing nothing but a blanket.

He and Rand had been doing their best to make her feel safe and comfortable with them, showing her how much they both desired her. They both wanted to wipe the distrust and sadness from her eyes and replace it with the happiness they'd seen in them this morning.

The happiness that hadn't been there when she left this afternoon.

He'd known something bothered her and cursed himself for not taking the time to question her about it right there and then. He should have made her tell him everything. His conscience bothered him all day that he and Rand hadn't taken enough time with her after taking her in their office.

She was so vulnerable underneath despite her tough exterior, and having an orgasm always seemed to make her a little weepy.

Now he knew that her trouble had been with the old woman in town, and it made him furious that she hadn't said a thing.

"Now I understand that look on Tom Hensen's face when he came into Headquarters. That son of a bitch already had Amanda."

Zane kept riding, not even sparing Rand a glance. "Yeah."

"Thank God Amanda's able to take care of herself. We just gotta think about it like that or else we'll go crazy until we find her."

Zane said nothing to that, not even wanting to contemplate what was happening to her right now. He'd heard the fear in Rand's voice as he tried to talk both of them into not worrying about Amanda, but he knew both would until they could get her safely back in their arms again.

They rode into town, scanning the dark and nearly deserted street for any sign of her. He prayed that she'd somehow gotten away and even now waited for them at the hotel. He couldn't afford to check the hotel first, though, when she could be lying in the barn hurt, needing them.

Zane tethered his horse outside the feed store, and he and Rand began making their way around the back. In the dark, they snuck from the side toward the old barn behind the blacksmith's. Each step felt like it took forever, but Amanda's life could very well depend on the element of surprise, so neither one of them took any chances. With guns drawn, they stepped over tree roots and rocks, making their way over the uneven ground.

Rand touched his arm, indicating that he would be going around the other side.

Zane barely breathed, listening for any sound at all as he made his way around the barn, scanning the edges of the nearby woods for any sign of life. The knowledge that Rafael would have to ambush them at some point forced him to proceed slowly, while he wanted nothing more than to race inside to get to Amanda.

He knew very well that the only way this plan could work would be if Rafael and his men managed to kill both him and Rand so that Tom would be promoted to captain and therefore have his hands on the gold before the government agent came to collect it.

Fuck. When he got his hands on Tom again…

Pushing thoughts of revenge aside for now, Zane paused as he reached the door, checking the trees for any movement. When a shot rang out from his left, he turned toward it automatically, hitting the dirt and firing back in the direction it came from just as another shot rang out from beside him.

A groan came from where he and Rand aimed seconds before another shot rang out from their right. Getting to his feet, he crouched low and moved toward the trees, sneaking glances around the tree trunk, trying to spot the shooter. As another shot chipped part of the tree trunk close to his head, Rand fired back and was rewarded with a loud, pain-filled moan.

They both stayed low and worked their way toward each of the men, knowing that either one could get up at any moment and shoot again or that another could be waiting. Just as they approached, the one closest to Rand rose and fired again, yelping in pain when Rand fired back and hit the man in the hand.

It took several precious minutes to haul the men out, holding them in front of them for cover in case any of their friends still hid in the trees. Once they got past the trees, they pulled them into the barn and threw them to the floor, closing the door behind them.

Zane lit a match, searching the interior of the barn. "Cover them while I look for a lantern." Spotting one several yards away, he had to blow out the match and light another before he could get the lantern lit. He raised the wick and got a good look at two of Rafael's men, before turning, holding the lamp up high as he searched for Amanda. "Amanda!"

"You're too late. She ain't here no more."

Nevertheless, Zane moved around the inside of the barn, looking for any sign of her while Rand questioned them, pressing on their bullet wounds to get them to talk. One of the men had been shot in the side, the other in the leg and the hand.

Rand's booted foot came down on the one man's leg injury, pressing down hard. "Where is she? Where's Rafael taking her?"

"I ain't tellin' you shit."

Zane saw a small patch of something blue fluttering on the other wall and started toward it just as Rand kicked the other man in his side. "I asked you where he's takin' our woman."

Just then the door burst open.

Zane and Rand both spun, weapons aimed, both breathing a sigh of relief to see Jim and Henry crouched down, weapons drawn.

Jim straightened and moved to stand beside Rand, pointing his gun at the men on the floor. "We heard gunfire and came to check it out. What's goin' on?"

Rand quickly explained everything while Zane went to the piece of cloth stuck on a nail in the wall.

His insides balled in fury when he recognized it as a piece of Amanda's shirt and that it was stained with blood. Pulling it free, he moved back to the others and held it out for them to see as he pointed his gun back at the other men. "She was here. Where the hell did he take her?"

The man who bled badly from his side spat. "Get me a doctor. I ain't—" He screamed as another shot rang out.

Shocked, Zane almost dropped the lantern, holding it up higher to see smoke coming from the end of Henry's pistol and the man with the bullet wound in his side, holding his foot and writhing in pain.

To add insult to injury, Henry kicked him. "Where's Miss Amanda? Tell me right now or I'll shoot your other foot. I swear I will."

Zane, Rand, and Jim looked at each other, more than a little surprised that Henry would do such a thing.

Jim shrugged. "Henry's very loyal and Amanda showed him kindness. He's been practicing real hard. He's gonna be awful upset if he don't get the chance to show her. But he'll be more than happy to keep practicing on you until we find her."

Henry pointed his gun at the other man's foot.

"No. Don't shoot me. Jackson Holler. He took her to Jackson Holler."

Jim waved a hand. "Get goin'. We'll take care of these two and wait for Tom to get back. I'd like to have a word with him."

Zane needed no further urging. He and Rand ran out of the barn like the hounds of hell were on their tail, beside himself with fear and anxious to get to Amanda. "Jim, you're in charge until we get back. Arrest Tom and bring his mother in, but wait until broad daylight, so everyone can see her."

Chapter Eleven

Gagging at Rafael's stench, Amanda leaned forward, trying to put as much distance between them as possible. He held a hand over her mouth as they rode out of town, pulling her back against his body until they were out of earshot. Only then did he loosen his hold to reposition her to lie across his lap. Supporting her head with one arm, he held onto her, occasionally letting his hand wander even while holding the reins, his touch making her sick to her stomach. "It don't matter now if you scream. There ain't nobody around to hear you."

He'd left two men behind in case Zane and Rand tried to follow, telling them to join them, but only after they'd gotten rid of "those fucking Texas Rangers." It scared Amanda to death. She trusted Zane and Rand's abilities, but knew they would be furious and not thinking clearly.

After learning that Tom was the man who'd hit her over the head and dumped her, unconscious, in the barn, she knew they'd be out for blood. She also knew there'd be little chance that they'd ever find her.

She'd have to find a way out of this on her own.

Rafael kept looking over his shoulder upsetting her balance enough that she had to keep grabbing on to him to steady herself.

For years he'd ridden with eight men. Killing John had left him with seven, and killing Billy left him with only six. Leaving two behind in town meant he now rode with only four, and he seemed far less confident than he had the first time she'd seen him.

She didn't know the names of the men who rode with him, but as they rode, she couldn't help coming up with her own names for them in her head.

Sweaty smelled to high heaven, his hair and shirt sticking to him as though he'd fallen headfirst into a horse trough. She'd named the small, nervous, wiry man Tiny. Shut Up never stopped talking, and the other men called out to him every few minutes to shut up. She called the other one Barn because he was as big as one and just as stupid.

Rafael hadn't tied her hands or feet, and she didn't know whether he'd been so distracted that he'd forgotten or he didn't consider her a threat. Either way, she did her best to remain quiet and non-threatening in the hope that they wouldn't tie her, waiting for her chance to escape.

Amanda kept sneaking glances behind him, dreading seeing Rafael's other men catching up with them.

She didn't see anything but it had gotten so dark she doubted whether she could have seen them anyway. With all the noise Rafael and his men made, she knew she would never hear them.

Amanda made a mental note of the trail they took, pretty confident she could find her way back to Austin.

If she could escape.

Now that they'd taken her, they had no reason to keep her alive. If Rafael's men already killed Zane and Rand, she would just be a hindrance. If Zane and Rand survived, they'd come after her not knowing if she'd already been killed.

No, her usefulness to Rafael had ended, except for his threat to rape her. In that case, she'd be better off dead anyway.

Each time fear threatened to choke her, she pushed it back, knowing she'd have to keep her wits about her in order to survive, a lesson she'd learned from her father many years ago. Since they'd taken her knife, she desperately needed to find something to use as a weapon.

Rafael didn't look over his shoulder as often now, appearing to gain confidence with every mile. A few minutes later, she could see why.

They rode into a small town where he was greeted enthusiastically by several less-than-savory-looking men.

He looked down at her and smiled, his breath making her gag. "We're in my town now. If your men dare to show up here, they'll never make it out alive."

To escape, she'd have to shake him—to make him angry enough to make a mistake. If he planned to rape or kill her, or both, she didn't have much to lose anyway.

Forcing a smile even as fear nearly paralyzed her, she snorted. "When my men get here, there won't be anything left of your town."

Shut Up cackled, throwing his head back so far he nearly fell from his horse. "Nobody can touch Rafael in Jackson Holler."

Jackson Hollow? Amanda had heard of the small town, of course. Although she'd never been there, she'd heard her father talk about the town once. He'd laughed because the sheriff had been killed years ago, and every replacement they'd hired had been run out of town. If what her father told her was true, Rafael could indeed bully everyone and run the town, answering to no one.

Sweaty turned to glare at Shut Up. "Shut up. Do you have to tell her where we're goin'?"

Rafael grinned. "It don't matter none now."

It took every ounce of self-control she possessed not to try to run away when Rafael pulled her from his horse, but she knew his men and the others who'd gathered around would catch her right away. She let her fear show, knowing they'd expect it and because of it would think her defenseless. If they knew she depended on Zane and Rand to rescue her, maybe they'd let up their guard.

"You wait until they come. They're going to rescue me and make you sorry."

One of the men in the crowd stepped forward and spat on the ground. "Hey, whatcha got there, Rafael?" He wiped the brown moisture from his lips, making Amanda's stomach lurch.

Pulling her arm, Rafael whipped out his gun and pointed it at the other man. "She's my prisoner. Stay away from her."

Amanda turned to look over her shoulder at the other man, wondering if she could somehow use his obvious attraction to her to escape.

His lips thinned, and he looked like he wanted to say something, but remained silent.

Barn moved toward the other man, standing between him and Rafael, proving to her that there seemed to be no end to his stupidity. "Get outta here, Floyd, before you git yourself hurt."

Floyd backed off, holding his hands up in surrender, but not before giving her a meaningful look and winking at her.

Amanda nearly fell when Rafael yanked her arm, pulling her across uneven ground and into a small house that had seen better days. Her home looked just as bad, but at least they kept it clean. This house smelled terrible, making her gag, and they had stuff piled up everywhere, making it hard to even walk. The faint morning sun could barely penetrate the dirty windows and she imagined if she could see better, the house would look even worse.

Rafael pointed to Barn and Tiny, who'd followed them inside. "Stay here with her. I've got some things to do." He came toward her and lifted her chin. "I'll be back later, darlin'. Try to miss me." He started out, yelling at the other men, "You two come with me."

Amanda allowed her bottom lip to tremble, hiding her smile. It seemed even Rafael felt the need for protection in his own town. "Please don't hurt me."

Rafael turned from the doorway and laughed. "Not so brave now, are you? As soon as I make sure your Rangers are taken care of, you and me are gonna have some fun."

Amanda watched him go, keeping the look of fear on her face, not a hard thing to do. After he left, she paced the front room, her mind racing. She had to find a way out of here before Rafael came back, vowing that there would be no way that she'd ever give that pig a chance to touch her.

Tiny paced, his hands trembling as he tried to roll a cigarette. He moved from window to filthy window, his head jerking from side to side as he looked out, before hurrying to the next window.

His hands shook so badly he spilled more of the tobacco than he got in the paper, but eventually he managed to get a cigarette rolled.

The match he struck flared to life, the smell of sulfur strong, but welcome as it overpowered some of the awful smells in the room.

Amanda glanced at Barn to catch him staring at her. She hid a smile when the giant of a man turned red and hurriedly looked away.

Thanks to her father, she'd learned how to spot a man's weaknesses years ago. Hoping to use these men's against them, she began to move around the room, slowly making her way to the window Tiny just left. Watching out of the corner of her eye as he moved to the next one, she gasped and jumped away from it, holding a hand to her heart.

Tiny spun. "What?"

Keeping her voice at a terrified whisper, she glanced out the window again. "Did you see him?" She hid a smile when both men rushed over with their guns drawn.

Tiny got there first, tossing his cigarette aside and standing on the other side of the window, his head darting out to look outside, before darting back again. "You saw somebody out there?"

Amanda backed away from the window, swallowing heavily and nodded, doing her best to look scared.

Barn, of course, stood directly in front of the window and scanned the area. "What did you see?"

Amanda did her best to instill panic in her voice. "A man. He had a gun. I think it's that man that Rafael pointed a gun at. He was hiding behind the tree but I saw him move. You won't let him come in here and get me, will you?"

Barn scowled. "Nobody's getting' you."

Tiny's eyes widened. "We better go check. If anything happens to her, Rafael'll kill us. You better stay here so she don't escape. I'll go and have a look and be right back."

Amanda waited until Tiny went out the back door before she began to fidget, shifting her weight from one leg to the other. "Oh, I can't wait anymore."

Barn turned from the window. "Wait for what?"

She kept track of Tiny's position through the window. "Rafael frightened me, and now that man outside." She hid her face as though embarrassed. "I really have to use the necessary."

Barn shook his head. "No, you can't go out there."

Amanda went to him, hiding her revulsion as she placed her hands on his chest. From the corner of her eye, she could see through the window on her left and slightly behind Barn. Tiny was moving toward the side of the house and knew she was running out of time.

Making a cry of distress, she pouted and allowed her eyes to well with tears. "Please! I can't wait anymore. Please don't make me have an accident. I'll be real quick, I promise."

Barn looked decidedly uncomfortable.

Seeing his indecision, Amanda took the matter out of his hands and started toward the back door. "Oh, thank you. You're truly a gentleman. Since your friend's out back, will you please watch out front? I don't want that man to get me." Pausing, she widened her eyes. "You'll protect me, won't you?"

Barn straightened, appearing impossibly larger. "Yes, ma'am. I won't let anybody get you."

Amanda hid a smile and opened the back door as he moved to a front window and smiled over his shoulder at her.

"Thank you, sir. I'll be right back." She went out the back door, keeping watch for Tiny as she eased the door shut behind her.

With a glance in the direction Tiny had gone, Amanda hurried as quickly as she could to the trees behind the house. She ran several feet into the woods, not stopping until she came upon a tree with a trunk large enough to conceal her.

Peering around it, she breathed a sigh of relief when she didn't see either one of them.

Knowing they'd discover her absence any minute, she turned and raced through the trees. After about five minutes, she cursed as she came to a steep incline that slowed her down considerably.

Wishing for her gloves, she grabbed at vines, tree limbs, and whatever else she could, until she finally made her way to the top.

Hearing shouts from below, she turned in the direction Rafael had ridden into town and ran as fast as she could.

Already tired and out of breath, she slowed, thankful when the trees thinned and the ground began to slope downward again.

She paused and looked around, guessing that she'd managed to make her way just outside of town. If only she could find a horse to steal, she could make her way back to her husbands.

Frantic that something had happened to them, she blinked away the tears that stung her eyes. She couldn't think about that right now. Zane and Rand trusted her to take care of herself and she knew if she worried about them right now, she wouldn't be able to think straight.

God, she loved them both so much. If she lost them before she'd even told them how she felt...No. They were out there right now, trying to find her.

Scanning the surrounding area, she stilled when she saw two saddled horses behind what looked like an old barn. Making her way down the slope, she did her best to stay hidden as she looked around for their riders.

It took several precious minutes to get down the slope, but she didn't want to alert anyone to her presence. She didn't see anyone as she made her way to the horses, not really looking at them as until she got close.

When she finally got a good look at them, her knees gave out. Kneeling in the dirt, she struggled to her feet, relief making her giddy.

Zane and Rand's horses.

They'd found her.

Spotting her rifle in Rand's scabbard, Amanda grinned as she made her way forward to retrieve it. Luckily, both horses knew her and she had no trouble keeping them calm as she loaded her pockets with ammunition and looked back up at the slope.

From there she would have the best vantage point of the town and would have the best chance of seeing them.

With a burst of energy, she started back up the slope with her rifle, impatient to find her men.

* * * *

Rand eyed the house Rafael walked toward, the house they suspected held Amanda. "I'm gonna go around back." They'd left their horses right outside of town and had spent the last hour keeping out of sight as they made their way around town trying to find Amanda. They'd just narrowed it down to three building when they saw Rafael come out of the saloon and drunkenly walk straight toward this house.

Zane held out a hand. "Wait."

Impatient, Rand cursed and crouched back down. "What the hell are we—"

"Quiet. Listen."

"What the hell happened? Can't you idiots do anything? You can't even watch a *woman*?"

Rand looked over at Zane in surprise at Rafael's thunderous outrage. "She escaped?"

Zane clenched his jaw, scanning the area. "Apparently."

"Then where the fuck is she?"

Zane stood and moved back around the side of the building. "We don't even know how long ago she escaped."

Rand narrowed his eyes when Rafael came back outside with a huge man trailing right behind him. "Once we have Rafael, maybe she'll come out. That big guy might be a problem."

"Yeah, if she ain't long gone by now." Zane inclined his head toward Rafael. "Look, Rafael's sending him around back to check. Now's our chance."

Catching Rafael turned out to be relatively easy. Searching for Amanda and his drunkenness distracted the outlaw enough for Rand and Zane to sneak up on him from either side. Before Rafael knew what was happening, he had two guns pressed to his temple.

Rand quickly drew Rafael's gun from his holster, disarming him. *Where the hell was Amanda?* "Did you really think you would get away with kidnapping our woman?"

Zane threw him to the ground and, with a knee in his back, tied his hands. "Couldn't keep ahold of her, though, could you?"

Rafael struggled, cursing. "I shoulda never left her with those assholes. Don't worry. My men are looking for her, and they'll help me escape. Get the fuck off me."

"You heard him. Let him go."

Rand spun, gritting his teeth when the barrel of a gun pressed against the side of his head. "Fuck." He hadn't expected the much larger man to come back so soon and had shifted his attention to the saloon where Rafael's men were gathered. Worrying about Amanda had apparently fried his brains and would likely get both him and Zane killed.

Zane looked up, his jaw clenching as his gaze went to a spot over Rand's shoulder. Another man came running out of the saloon, and pointed his gun at Zane. Yet another small man appeared and looked around nervously, his gun hand shaking wildly.

Rafael laughed. "I told ya. Untie me, damn it!"

Rand met Zane's eyes as his friend stood, and the little man hurried to kneel beside his boss. He knew that they had very little chance now of getting out of this alive, but at least Amanda had gotten free. Now, if only they could get to her. His mind raced with possibilities.

Suddenly a shot rang out, making all of them jump as the man kneeling beside Rafael screamed and stood, holding a bloody hand with the other, his gun several feet away in the dirt.

"I been shot! Boss, I been shot." He jumped around, howling in pain as he tried to stem the flow of blood.

Rand didn't waste any time, knocking the gun from the startled giant and aiming his own at the man's chest while Zane did the same with the other man. Not knowing who'd fired or who they were aiming for, they kept their prisoners in front of them as they searched the rocky wooded area surrounding the town. "Shooter could be anywhere."

Rafael struggled clumsily to his feet. "I gotta teach my fuckin' men to shoot better. Damn fuckin' assholes. They coulda hit me."

The man holding his hand cried openly. "They shot my hand off, Boss."

The big man struggled, making it hard for Rand to hold him. "Who's shootin'? Is it Floyd? He wants the woman."

Rand hit him in the head with the butt of his gun, knocking him out. "Jesus." He hauled Rafael in front of him to have a shield against the unknown shooter. "Keep an eye on him so I can tie this big guy up before he comes to."

"You're done Rafael. The town and the woman are mine!"

Rand searched the rooftop where the shout came from, keeping Rafael in front of him, despite the man's struggles.

Rafael fought his hold. "Is that you, Floyd? I'll kill you, you son of a bitch! You're not getting' the town or the woman."

Another shot rang out, nearly hitting Rafael. And then another from off to Rand's right. He spun, gun drawn in time to see a man fall from the rooftop to land several feet in front of him. The man with the bloody hand cried harder. "Who the hell shot Floyd?"

Floyd groaned and reached for the gun he'd dropped, but Rand was already there and kicked it away.

Zane searched the surrounding trees. "Same person fired both shots. Rifle. It appears we have a guardian angel. Wanna bet she's got violet eyes?"

Rand scanned the rocks and trees. "I hope you're right."

The man who'd come out of the saloon struggled against Zane's hold. "She's gonna shoot me!"

Zane shook him. "Be still. Jesus, you stink."

Several men came running out of the saloon behind them, guns drawn as they sized up the situation. Rand cursed as he and Zane spun, keeping the other men in front of them as shields.

Rafael fought to get free. "Shoot 'em, damn it!"

Rand recognized the last of Rafael's gang in the crowd and kept his gun trained on him, conscious that an unknown shooter was somewhere behind him. He was betting his life that the unknown shooter was Amanda, and trusted that she wouldn't accidentally hit him or Zane.

Zane kept his gun trained on the crowd. As Rand expected, the man from Rafael's gang came forward.

"Let 'em go. I mean it. Git away from them or I'll shoot."

Rand kept his gun steady. "You try to shoot us, you'll hit your friends, and then we'll shoot you."

"Let 'em go. You can't do this to Rafael. Don't you know this is his town?"

Rafael kicked at the dirt impatiently. "Shut up and shoot 'em for God's sake!"

The other man lifted his gun only to have it go flying from his hand as another shot rang out. The sound of several horses approaching had the crowd scattering, shots coming from everywhere.

Rand and Zane both pulled their prisoners around the side of a nearby store and took cover, grinning when they saw Silas, Ned, and Henry ride into town, guns blazing.

Rifle shots continued to come from behind them and soon the men saw they had been surrounded and dropped their guns. It didn't take long for the Rangers to have the men face down on the ground with their hands tied.

Rand tied several himself, impatient to find Amanda, while Silas and Zane kept their guns on the men on the ground. "It's good to see you. Did Jim get Tom?"

Silas nodded once, kicking the man who wouldn't stop talking in the side. "Yep. And his ma."

Henry beamed, strutting like a peacock. "Paraded her through town in broad daylight. We brung the wagon and Mrs. Owen's horse. Figured when you caught up with Rafael and his gang you'd need a way to get 'em back to Austin. It was Jim's idea, Captain."

Zane nodded, his expression grim. "You men get Rafael and his gang loaded up, but be careful. We've got a shooter up there we think is Amanda. We've gotta go make sure."

"Uh, Captain?"

Rand finished gathering the last of the men's weapons and looked up at Ned, he and Zane answering at the same time. "What?"

When Ned gestured toward the tree-covered slope behind them, he and Zane both spun, weapons drawn.

Rand looked up, grinning in relief, pride, amusement, and lust to see Amanda making her way down the steep terrain, carrying her rifle. "Our guardian angel."

Amanda came forward wearing a cocky smile that made Rand want to strip her naked and sink into her. "You Rangers let that man get the drop on you?"

Zane holstered his weapon and strode toward her, gathering her into his arms, and lifted her off the ground as his mouth swooped down on hers.

Rand smiled as he moved toward them, his smile growing when Amanda's arms went around Zane's neck and she clung, tangling her hands in his hair.

A deep grumble rose from Zane's chest as he set Amanda on her feet. "Thank God, sugar. You all right?"

At her nod, Rand took his place beside Zane, impatiently grabbing Amanda as soon as Zane released her and pulled her against him, cradling the back of her head with his hand, and swung her around. "Damn, darlin'. You had me scared to death." He laughed, so relieved he felt dizzy, aware of the other Texas Rangers' own laughter, and turned to grin at Zane.

His smile widened when he saw the look of love and pride on Zane's face. "I told ya. She's a helluva woman."

Chapter Twelve

Flanked by Zane and Rand, Amanda rode toward Austin in front of the horse-drawn cage that held the prisoners. "I can't believe that woman was the mother of one of the Texas Rangers. I thought she just hated *me*. She hates all of us."

Zane's expression hardened. "Well, they're both locked in my jail right now and these men here will be locked in the cell right next to them. Rafael and his men are going to hang without ever getting their hands on the gold, Tom will never be captain and will have to go in front of the judge, and his momma's going to have a hard time showing her face in town."

Amanda turned to him, placing a hand on his arm. "You really won't keep his momma in jail, will you? She's an old woman."

Patting her hand, Zane nodded slightly. "That's up to the judge. But even after she's released, she'll suffer by being on her own while the law takes care of her son."

Rand rode closer. "It'll be hard enough for her when her friends all turn their backs on her."

Nodding, Amanda rode quietly, so lost in her thoughts that it startled her when Zane touched her thigh.

"What's going on in that head of yours? I swear, Amanda Owens, if you keep anything else from me again I'm turning you over my knee and paddling your backside."

Amanda turned to glare at him. "You try it, Ranger, and you'll be sorry."

Zane leaned close, his hand squeezing her thigh threateningly. "We'll see how tough you are when I shove my cock up that tight ass of yours."

Her jaw dropped, the look in his eyes telling her just how much he looked forward to doing just that. Drawn by that look, she leaned toward him, her heart pounding nearly out of her chest when his eyes flashed dangerously. "I can't wait, Ranger."

Her breathless whisper seemed to take him by surprise for a second or two before a slow, wicked grin appeared. "You won't have to wait for long, sugar."

Surprised by the endearment, she blinked, tears pricking her eyes when he reached for her hand.

Bringing her hand to his lips, he lightly kissed her fingers. "I was so damned scared, Amanda. I thought we'd never get to you in time. I can't lose you now. You're too damned important to me."

Smiling though her tears, Amanda shook her head. "You won't lose me."

Henry raised his voice to be heard from behind them, breaking the spell. "Ma'am, I didn't hear how you got away. I wanna tell the boys when we get back."

Laughing, Amanda looked over her shoulder. "The one I shot off the roof was staring at me when Rafael took me in the house. I kept looking out the window and told Tiny I saw him out there. When he went out to check, I convinced Barn I had to use the necessary."

Rand lifted a brow as Henry laughed and went to tell the others. "Barn? Tiny?"

"I named them." She explained her reasoning behind the names she gave them, a warm glow filling her at their surprised laughter.

Zane leaned toward her. "I'm proud of you. You kept a cool head, and you're a damned fine shot."

Rand moved in from the other side. "You managed to outsmart them and escape. You sure got grit, honey."

Bubbling with happiness and basking in their praise, Amanda burst out laughing. "Outsmarting them wasn't too hard, and I had to go rescue you once the stupid one got the drop on you."

Rand's eyes narrowed. "I let myself get distracted because I was wondering where the hell you were."

Chuckling, Zane reached out to touch her arm. "Maybe you should join the Rangers."

Amanda laughed at Rand's scowl. "No, thanks. Just being married to you two's enough for me."

Zane shot her a cool look. "I'm still a little upset with you, though, that you didn't tell us about all the trouble you were having here in town."

Rand reached out and patted her thigh. "You're not supposed to keep things like that from us. You're not alone anymore, Amanda, and you don't have to take everything on your own shoulders. Damn it, you said it yourself. We're your husbands."

Shrugging, Amanda kept her head held high as they entered Austin. "You're Texas Rangers and very respected in this town. You married someone who's not. There's always been talk about me because of Pa and some people will never accept me. You'll have to get used to it."

A muscle worked in Zane's jaw. "No, I won't get used to it. You're a fine woman who's been through a lot through no fault of your own. It pisses me off that we didn't know about the trouble with your father years ago. Why didn't you tell anyone?"

"Momma didn't want anyone to know, but women like Mrs. Hensen knew. Can you believe she actually told my momma that Pa hitting her was *Momma's* fault?"

Rand moved closer, tugging at her hair to whisper to her. "When I turn that naked ass over my lap, it'll be because you earned it, darlin'. And when I spank you, you'll love it so much that sweet cream will be running down your thighs."

"You try to spank me, Ranger, and I'll shoot you." The image of her naked and over his lap popped into her mind, and had moisture already leaking from her pussy.

Rand smiled, a smile so full of mischief it made her pussy clench despite her best efforts. "Keep shooting that mouth off, darlin', and we'll see what's what when I get you alone."

Riding with the Texas Rangers, Amanda wasn't the least bit surprised at the reception they got. Austin had always been really proud to have the Texas Rangers Headquarters there and most people thought the Rangers themselves could do no wrong.

Amanda smiled at the people who waved and raised her voice to be heard. "Both of you have a lot of work to do. I want to go to the hotel and get a bath. I smell of Rafael."

Their swift and immediate response startled the hell out of her. Rand cursed soundly and reached for her, but Zane grabbed her first, pulling her off of her horse to his lap.

Rand cursed and moved closer, his face a mask of fury. "You told us you weren't hurt, damn it."

Zane cupped her face and turned it toward him, the anger and concern on his own face scaring her. "Did he touch you?" His other arm tightened around her as he bent over her protectively. "Please tell me. I need to know if he hurt you."

Incredibly touched, Amanda ran her fingers over his jaw, thrilling again at the soft beard beneath her palm. "No. He didn't. I swear he didn't do anything like that. It's just that he held me on his lap when we rode away and now he's all I can smell. I need to get the stink of him off of me."

Zane stared at her long and hard. "Don't ever lie to me, Amanda. He was going to, wasn't he?"

Shrugging, Amanda looked away, meeting Rand's eyes. "Yes." Wanting to see him smile again, she wrinkled her nose at them. "In case you didn't notice, Rafael's men aren't too smart and I escaped.

was long gone, and I came across a couple of horses I recognized. Figured you might need some help. Turns out I had to rescue you."

When neither smiled, she sighed. "He didn't. No one did. I swear. You're the ones who came close to getting killed."

Both narrowed their eyes at her even though their lips twitched. Zane tweaked her nose and bent to kiss her temple. "We were doing just fine when somebody started shooting."

Amanda snorted. "Yeah, I could see that."

When they stopped in front of the hotel, Rand tethered his horse and hers before coming around for her. With his hands on her waist, he lifted her, sliding her down the length of his body as he set her on her feet. "Some damned fine shooting, too. Henry'll spread the word, and you'll be a legend in this town before nightfall."

Amanda's nipples tingled at the friction against them. Need clawed at her, the look in his eyes and the slow slide of his hard body over hers bringing that breathless feeling to life. With her hand on his chest, she pushed away slightly, not forgetting his threat to turn her over his knee. "I don't want to be a legend. I just want a bath."

Rand grinned and grabbed her hand, looking over his shoulder at Zane. "Let's go get a change of clothes and take her to the pond." Pulling Amanda close, he wrapped an arm around her shoulders and led her up the steps. "We'll take a bath with you and wash the smell of Rafael off of you ourselves."

Zane nodded. "Get my clothes, too. I've gotta stop in Headquarters. Stay with Amanda until I get back."

Walking into the hotel with Rand, Amanda stopped short when the clerk came around the small counter to stop in front of her.

He shifted his feet nervously. "Ranger, I heard you was comin' into town. I got a bath bein' heated for your wife."

Rand laughed and turned Amanda toward the stairs. "Heard about her shooting, did you?"

Amanda ran as Rand practically dragged her up the stairs, turning to yell a quick thank you over her shoulder. "Keep it hot until we get back."

Once in the room, Rand pulled her into his arms, smiling when she glared at him and tried to push him away again. "You mad at me, darlin', 'cause I said you'd like your spanking?"

Gathering her clothes, she stuffed them into a bag and went to get Zane's. "Damn it, the rest of our clean clothes are still on the line out back." She tried unsuccessfully to ignore Rand, unable to resist the chance to make him think twice before threatening to spank her again.

Rand frowned when she added Zane's to the bag and ignored the ones he'd just put on the bed. "I asked you a question, darlin'."

Amanda released the bag when Rand reached for it. Aware of Rand following her, she went down the back stairs and outside and started to take their clothes off the line.

Rand held out his arms, holding the ones she took down and folded. "Damn it, Amanda. Do you really think I would hit you?"

Sliding him a glance, Amanda pulled his pants from the line and folded them before slapping them into his outstretched hands. "That's what you said."

"No, that ain't what I said at all. A playful spanking between a man and a woman is something different."

With jerky movements, she finished taking the clothes off the line, hiding her laughter and heading back into the hotel. "You're a brute, Randall Sloane."

As soon as they got inside the room, Rand tossed the clothes on the bed, slamming the door behind him. "I'm a brute, am I? Well, then, I might as well act like one." With one arm around her waist, he lifted her and turned, sitting on the only chair in the room and settling her, kicking and screaming across his lap. "You keep screaming and all the people in the hotel and on the street will know you're getting a spanking. Is that what you want?"

Beating on his leg, Amanda arched as much as his hold would allow. Despite her attempt to choke it back, her laughter broke free. "Damn it, Rand. You were supposed to feel bad, not turn me over your knee."

Rand froze. "You little hellcat. You've been teasing me all along. You knew I'd never hurt you."

Amanda giggled and met his eyes over her shoulder. "And you were going to prove to me that you wouldn't hurt me by spanking me?"

With his eyes on hers, he ran a hand over her bottom. "I planned to show you just how hard you'd come after I spanked you."

In her upside down position, she laughed harder, fighting him when he reached under her to unfasten her pants and jerked them down to her knees.

All playfulness fled, replaced by need so wanton and decadent, it stole her breath.

He kept a strong forearm over her back to hold her down as he ran his other hand over the cheeks of her naked bottom. "Well, I can't very well give you a spanking until your bottom's bare, now can I?"

With her legs tangled in her pants, she couldn't kick effectively and couldn't reach the floor with her hands to get any leverage. Having only her bottom bare somehow made her feel more exposed than if she'd been entirely naked. The vulnerable feeling got even worse when Rand slid a hand between her thighs, forcing her legs apart as far as her bunched up pants would allow.

"You didn't answer me, Amanda. Don't you think a spanking should be given only to a bare ass?"

Amanda stilled, gasping at the unexpectedness of his fingers sliding through her folds, and lifted into his caress before she could stop herself. She realized her mistake almost immediately and tried to close her thighs, but his hand already cupped her slit.

"You really do have the prettiest ass."

Biting her lip to hold back the moans that threatened to erupt, Amanda began to struggle, only to freeze again when the motion slid her clit over his fingers. She gulped and took a deep breath, doing her best to resist the naughty pleasure she seemed to crave with them.

"Let me up right now or you'll be sorry." Damn, her demand came out breathless and needy, not the cold tone she'd strived for. Every inch of her body felt alive every damned time they touched her. At times it disconcerted her, but it never failed to delight her.

Rand chuckled, sending a prickling up her spine. "No, darlin'. I think you're the one who'll be sorry." Using the hand of the arm holding her down, he slapped her bottom, earning a cry from her at the unexpected heat, made even stronger by the fingers he ran through her slit.

She cried out in surprise, not pain, because although it stung a little, it didn't really hurt. "Rand, I swear, oh!" Grabbing on to his pant leg, Amanda couldn't hold back her moans any longer as he kept his hand over her bottom, using his fingers to lift and separate her cheeks and exposing her bottom hole. She found herself lifting into his caress despite her best efforts not to.

He circled a finger around her pussy opening. "You're all wet, darlin'. I guess that means you like being spanked after all."

Because of the way she was bent over and because of the strength of his hold, she couldn't close her buttocks against him. The heat from his slap remained and spread, his hand holding the warmth in. She rocked her hips, trying to urge his finger inside.

"You'll pay for this. Oh!"

Rand plunged his finger inside her pussy and began stroking, chuckling when she continued to rock her hips. "Really? Let's see if I can make you take those words back." With his finger moving inside her, he slapped her ass again with the other hand, three more times in rapid succession. Once again, he covered her bottom with his hand and separated her cheeks with his strong fingers as he stroked her folds.

Amanda groaned, writhing on his lap as the place between her thighs went up in flames. Her clit burned, throbbing with the need to be touched, and although she kept moving, she couldn't rub it against his thigh. That familiar tingly feeling began again, amazing her that a spanking could arouse her so much.

But this was like no spanking she'd ever heard of. Knowing that he looked down at her exposed bottom hole made it burn, which got only worse when he tightened his grip. It stung, startling her, her pussy and ass clenching uncontrollably. No longer able to hold back her cries, she called his name repeatedly.

"What is it, darlin'?" His innocent tone didn't fool her at all.

"It's, Rand…oh, God, it's…" Hell and damnation, how could he do this to her? What the hell *had* he done to her?

"It's a spanking, darlin'. Now tell me you don't like 'em."

"Damn it, Rand! Do something."

The door opened, startling Amanda before it closed again almost immediately.

"She's a demanding little thing, isn't she?" Zane's deep tone sounded strained as he approached her. "Appears she likes having her bottom paddled, after all."

Amanda stopped wiggling, her breath catching in her throat when Zane ran a finger lightly over her exposed bottom hole. Amazed at how sensitive it was there, she whimpered in her throat.

"None of that, now, darlin'. Where's the woman who escaped from Rafael and helped rescue her husbands? You're not going to act like a whiny little girl now?"

Insulted, Amanda spun to glare at him. "Whiny little girl? I'll show you a whiny little girl."

Rand released her cheeks to slap her bottom again, withdrawing his finger from her pussy to slide over her clit. "You whined about being spanked and now every time I slapped this pretty little bottom, you lift up into it."

Zane touched her bottom hole again, pressing against it. "Let's see if she likes this. Have you checked her stitches?"

"Ready to come out. Figured it'd be easier after she has her bath and they soften up."

"The pond's out for tonight. It's too dark already. She can have a bath here." He bent near Amanda's head, fisting her hair to pull it back from her face and turned her toward him. "There's my girl. Don't be scared, honey. If you don't like this, we'll stop. I promise."

Amanda tried to press her thighs together, her breath coming in gulps at the slight stinging where Zane pressed. The stinging didn't affect her as much, though, as the heart-stopping intimacy.

Just when she thought she would come, Rand stopped stroking her clit. "Let me have the salve."

"No. Give her to me."

Amanda found herself transferred to Zane's lap, the muscles in his hard thighs shifting under her. "What are you doing?"

"I have to grease up your bottom, sugar."

Little ripples began at her bottom and raced all over her slit, making her swear she could almost feel his touch there already. "Oh God. Is it gonna hurt?"

Rand retrieved the tin and handed it to Zane before crouching down next to her. "It'll sting a little and burn when Zane stretches you."

The sound of the lid of the tin hitting the floor filled her with trepidation. She held her breath when Zane's big hand covered her bottom and lifted her cheeks, exposing her forbidden opening to his gaze.

"Did you do this with your wife?" She didn't know what made her ask the question, but she had to know. Being jealous of a dead woman didn't make any sense, but she couldn't help it.

Zane froze. "No. She didn't let us touch her together. If you feel the same, we'll respect that."

Amanda turned her head to look over her shoulder at both of them. "Don't either one of you dare leave me!" Now that she knew what it felt like to have four hands on her body at the same time, to have the two men she'd fallen in love with sharing the intimacy of marriage, she'd quickly become addicted to it.

Rand smoothed a hand down her back. "Nobody's leaving you, darlin'. As soon as Zane gets your bottom greased up, we'll do things to you you'll never forget."

Amanda gasped and stiffened as Zane's finger slid into her, the salve easing his way. She automatically reached for Rand's hand, which he readily held out to her. Shivering, she squeezed it, moaning harshly at the incredible sense of vulnerability from having Zane penetrate her this way. Although she instinctively tried to tighten her bottom to keep him out, it didn't seem to make any difference. The raw intimacy of what he did to her made the entire thing seem a little unreal.

Zane withdrew his finger, entering her again almost immediately with more of the salve. "That's it, sugar. Let me get more of this in you so my cock will slide right in."

Rand kept hold of her hand, running his other over her hair. "Stretch her a little more. Look how she lifts up. She loves having something in her ass."

Withdrawing again, Zane rubbed the cheeks of her bottom while he likely gathered more of the salve. "Yeah, she gets two fingers this time. Get her boots and her pants off so I can spread her."

Rand released her hand and moved to her, taking longer than necessary to remove her boots and pants. She would swear she could feel the heat of his gaze on her bottom and shivered. It seemed like forever until he came back to her, murmuring something to Zane she couldn't make out. Holding her hand again, he knelt close and pressed an arm down on her back, his hand cupping her shoulder. "I've got her."

Amanda didn't know if either one of them knew what their conversation did to her. Her trepidation rose, and with it, her hunger. She bucked frantically as Zane spread her thighs even wider and lifted his leg to make her bottom stick higher in the air. With his left hand, he covered her cheeks and lifted them again, his fingers firm as he spread her wide.

She couldn't stop moving, her clit throbbing so badly it made her whimper. Her whimper became a cry when Zane poised two fingers at her tight opening and began to press them into her. Her body gave way under the firm pressure, her bottom hole now slippery from all of the salve.

Shivers continued to race up and down her spine, the sounds passing her lips unlike any she'd ever made. The fingers in her bottom felt huge and she froze as Zane stroked her there, his fingers going a little deeper each time.

"This is how I'm going to work my cock into your ass." His voice was barely recognizable, so harsh and deep it scared her a little. "Your ass is gripping my fingers tight. Let me stretch you a little more." She could tell he tried to keep his tone gentle but failed miserably.

Rand's lips touched her back. "Damn, my cock's about to burst."

"Just a little more. Hold on to her, damn it."

Amanda struggled to catch her breath against the overwhelmingly naughty feel of having her husband sliding his fingers in and out of her bottom hole. "I can't believe you're doing this to me. Oh, God. It feels too private."

With his lips against her shoulder, Rand groaned. "Nothing should be too private between a husband and a wife. Do you know how good it's going to feel to all of us to take you this way? That's it, darlin'. You took that real good. Now that Zane has you greased up, I want to lick that little clit."

Zane withdrew his fingers. "Yeah, she's suffered long enough. She's soaking wet and needs some relief before we get her ready to take her." He lifted her onto his lap with an ease she wondered if she'd ever get used to and positioned her so that she lay back against his chest. Deft fingers undid her shirt and pulled the ends apart, quickly ridding her of it.

She watched as Rand threw off his clothes and knelt between her thighs, spreading them wide and pulling her toward him. Holding on to Zane's forearms, she moaned as his hands covered her breasts at the same time Rand lowered his head to her slit.

Zane's voice sounded rough in her ear. "I know, sugar. I know. It's too much. I'm sorry, I didn't mean to tease you but I wanted to get your ass good and ready for me." He pinched her nipples as Rand sucked her clit into his mouth, sending her immediately over the edge in a series of little ripples that she feared would never stop. "That's my girl. Yes, let us hear you. I love those sounds you make. That's it. Easy, honey. Now, doesn't that feel better?"

Amanda slumped against him as her orgasm subsided, jerking each time Rand's tongue moved over her clit. The pleasure was too much, too unreal. She held out a hand to his shoulder and pushed weakly. "Please stop. It's too much."

Rand looked up at her, his eyes darker than she'd ever seen them. "Just relax, darlin'. Me and Zane will have to get you all worked up again before we can take you the way we want to. As tight as you are and as worked up as both of us are, we won't last long at all. We want you to come with us." His light touch had those feelings stirring inside her again, her weakness from already coming so hard making it difficult to fight them.

The awareness of her bottom distracted her so much that Rand's finger sliding into her pussy took her by surprise. She cried out weakly, digging her short nails into Rand's shoulders. "I can't."

He lifted his head to kiss her belly, using his thumb to lightly stroke her clit. His grin had a hard edge to it, telling her just how aroused he'd become. "Yes, you can. You're already milking my finger."

Zane pulled her back against him and pinched her nipples, tugging them away from her body. His cock pushed insistently against her bottom, and he groaned each time she shifted on his lap. "I want that ass. Now."

Amanda moaned, covering his hands with hers as he pulled her nipples again, pinching them over and over. The sharp pain sent ribbons of white-hot heat to her slit, where the still-rippling effects of her recent orgasm lingered. Writhing in Zane's arms moved her bottom over his stiff pants, the sizzling heat a reminder of the spanking Rand had just given her.

They seemed to ignite fiery pleasure everywhere they touched, and with two sets of hands roaming over her naked body, it seemed to be everywhere. Lost in the wonderful feeling, she felt as though she floated when Rand reached for her and carried her to the bed. Unlike before, he took charge this time and lowered her onto his cock, his hands firm on her hips as he pulled her down onto his thick heat.

Amanda shuddered as he filled her, a moan escaping as her hands fisted on his chest. "Oooh, that feels good." She started moving, the memories of what it had felt like last time urging her on.

"No. Don't move, Amanda. Hell, just stay still, darlin'." Rand's hands tightened on her hips, holding her still.

Her eyes flew open when Zane moved in behind her, his hands coming around her to cup her breasts and tease her already sensitized nipples. She gripped his arms, tilting her neck when he began to nibble there. The cock pressing at her back was a sharp reminder of their intentions.

Zane released her breasts and firmly pressed her down into Rand's waiting embrace. "Hold on to her good, damn it. She bucks hard when I push into her ass." He held her against Rand's chest with a strong hand at her back while he positioned his cock at her forbidden opening.

Amanda shivered, chills racing up and down her spine as Zane began to work his cock into her. "Oh, God. I'm scared now."

Rand tightened his grip on her, his lips caressing her hair just as the head of Zane's cock began to enter her. "Don't be. We'll stop whenever you say. Fuck, she won't stop clenching."

"Yeah, but I have to go slow. Don't want to hurt her." The desperation in his voice and in his hold had Amanda gripping Rand fiercely.

"It burns. I don't know if I can do this."

Rand's hand tangled in her hair, cupping the back of her head while the other held her like a solid band around her waist. "Just feel, darlin'. Do you know how good it is for both of us to take you like this? Think about us filling you. In just a minute or two, you'll be stuffed full of cock. When we start moving, it'll feel so fucking good, you're going to scream."

She could tell Zane did his best to go slowly, his short strokes easing his cock into her bit by bit. It felt so strange to her, this invasion of her most private place, that her mind struggled to adapt as well as her body. Panting, she held as still as she could, nothing existing for her except the huge cock relentlessly stretching her bottom hole to accommodate its thickness.

Zane combined curses and groans with praise and pleas as he continued to work himself into her, his hands now firm on her hips to hold her in place. "Fuck. Oh, hell. Sugar, you're squeezing my cock so damned hard."

Amanda's toes curled as his strokes went deeper. It amazed her that her bottom seemed to open up, giving in to his insistent demand. After the way he'd teased her there, she wanted him inside her, needed both men to be a part of her. The restraint to stay still had her scratching and biting Rand.

"Damn it, you *are* a little hellcat, aren't you?" He tightened his hold on her, grabbing her hands to force them behind her back. Looking up at her, he smiled, a strained smile, full of desperation. "Open up that ass and let Zane in so we can fuck you good, darlin'.

By the time we get done with you, you'll be so worn out you won't be able to move."

Amanda cried out, surprised and delighted at the feel of Zane's cock going deep. "Move. I can't stay still, damn you."

Zane groaned. "A little more, sugar. You're so fucking tight and I don't want to hurt you. Almost. Yeah, that's it. Let me in."

Twisting restlessly, Amanda marveled that each time she moved, shivers went through her to combine with the tingling heat of her pussy, clit and bottom. The sensations layered one on top of another until she couldn't tell them apart. Never had she needed relief this badly.

Zane pushed deep, growling in his throat. "I'm in." He slid his hands from her hips to her upper thighs, keeping her spread wide and lifting her knees from the bed so she had no leverage at all. "Now, sugar, you're going to get fucked good."

Rand helped her lift slightly, his thumbs teasing her nipples as he lifted her. "Here we go, darlin'. Be ready for the ride of your life."

Amanda clenched her fists on his chest, tilting her head back in abandon as they began to move.

Rand's hands slid to her hips to move her on his cock while Zane used his grip on her thighs to move her. Between them, they set up a rhythm, Rand sliding deep and withdrawing, just as Zane slid deep into her bottom.

Moaning between pants, Amanda closed her eyes, absorbing every sensation of the most decadent and erotic experience of her life. At all times, a cock surged into her, their pace robbing her of breath. Filled completely, she couldn't keep her body from repeatedly clenching on both of them, which made her feel even fuller.

The sounds they made, their words of encouragement, of praise washed over her, but it was the raw hunger in their voices that got to her the most.

Her bottom tingled hotly around Zane's cock, the feeling of his thrusts so unfamiliar and disarming, so damned *forbidden* that it took her to another place. Her body became so overloaded on sensation that she could only hold on and let them do as they wished to her. Her clit rubbed against Rand, making the tingles stronger, and it seemed that after only a few strokes, her body tightened unbearably.

Having both of them this way, their cocks filling her even as they surrounded her with their heat and strength pulled her into a world of decadent pleasure, all of her senses filled with nothing but them.

"Oh, God. It's…it's…" She couldn't say any more as the sizzles inside her exploded.

Rand groaned, lifting her with every thrust. "Damned right it is. Fuck, I'm coming." He groaned roughly as he surged into her, his cock pulsing, his final thrust sending her impossibly higher when she thought she'd already reached the top.

Zane growled like a wild animal when she tightened on him. He stroked once more and thrust hard, holding his pulsing cock deep inside her bottom, both men now completely filling her.

It took several seconds before she realized that the frantic whimpers she heard came from her, but she could do nothing to stop them. Her scream came out breathless and tortured, her body milking them in spasms she couldn't control. It went on and on, and she'd started to fear it would never end before she slowly began to pull back from the peak.

Her body slumped, drained of all energy.

They seemed to have anticipated it because Rand caught her easily as Zane wrapped an arm around her waist and together, they lowered her to Rand's chest.

Hands moved over her, caressing her quivering flesh. The only sounds in the room were of labored breathing and moans as they all struggled to recover.

She had no idea how long she lay melted on top of Rand before Zane moved. The brush of his lips on her back and shoulder made her tremble, her bottom and pussy squeezing them again in reaction.

Both men moaned, making Amanda giggle.

Rand cupped her chin and lifted her face to his. "Something funny, darlin'?"

Touching her lips to his, Amanda smiled. "It makes me feel good that I pleased both of you."

Zane eased his cock from her bottom, rubbing her back when she shivered and moaned. "Then you should feel great. Hell, sugar, I think I died and went to heaven. I'll wash off and go downstairs to tell 'em to bring up a bath. I think we could all use one."

Amanda lifted her head. "Hell, I have to get dressed."

Rand sat up, lifting her with him. "No. I do. Nobody'll see you."

In the end, Rand kept her standing behind him, wrapped in the blanket, as the men carried the tub and buckets of water into the room. He stood with his arms over his chest and what she could only assume was his "Ranger" face because after one glance in his direction, the men didn't look their way again.

As soon as they left, Rand unwrapped her and helped her into the tub. Kneeling beside it, he grinned, his eyes moving over her. "Now let's get you all cleaned up." He rubbed a handful of soap flakes into a cloth and started washing her.

Amanda squealed, jerking up and sloshing water all over the floor. "What are you doing? I can wash myself."

Grinning, Rand started to wash her breasts, dropping the cloth and using his hands. "Yeah, but it's more fun this way."

Instead of the relaxing bath she'd assumed she'd have, bath time became a time of play, with Amanda laughing so hard at their antics she feared drowning. "Stop! I give up."

Kneeling on either side of the tub, they washed her everywhere with the cloth and their hands, both men having to strip when their clothes became soaked. Zane kissed her hard and lifted her out of the water. "Now I have to take care of your bottom. The salve's waterproof, and it won't come off until I wash it off."

Amanda didn't get a chance to do any more than squeal as Zane flipped her over his arm, holding her bottom out of the water. With

Rand kneeling in front of her, caressing her breasts, and Zane spreading her legs to wash her slit thoroughly, Amanda amazingly found herself aroused once again. "Oh, God. Look what you two do to me."

Rand kissed her, little kisses and nips that sent her heart soaring. "Looks like we'll have to take care of you again, darlin'. You're such a demanding woman."

Zane dropped the cloth, using his fingers now to wash her inside and out. "You've got to love a woman who never gets enough."

Amanda's breath caught at the word "love," but not knowing whether he really meant it or not, chose to ignore it. "It's your fault. I was fine until you two started in again."

Zane bent and bit her bottom cheek, making her yelp. "It's your fault for being so damned beautiful. This time I get to eat your sweet pussy." He rinsed her off and lifted her over his arm and headed back toward the bed.

Amanda couldn't hold back her giggles. "I'm all wet!"

Zane tossed her onto the bed, quickly flipping her over. Using one of the towels to dry her with one hand, he slid the other between her thighs. "You sure are. Let me take care of that for you."

Rand chuckled as he stepped into the tub. "Make her wiggle around. I want to see a show."

Amanda laughed again, delighted in this intimate play. "I'm not going to put on a show for…oh, hell."

Zane lifted her bottom several inches off of the bed and buried his face between her thighs, plunging his tongue into her pussy. Using his shoulders to keep her lifted, he slid his mouth to her clit and began sucking at the same time he reached up to fondle her nipples.

Her already swollen clit flared to life immediately, the sharp ribbons of pleasure from her nipples travelling straight to her clit and making it throb even harder. Between one breath and the next, she came, pressing her feet into his back to lift herself harder against his mouth as she went over.

His fingers tightened on her nipples, increasing the pleasure as he used his tongue on her clit to drive her wild.

She come hot and fast, and, worn out, began to come down again. This time, though, when Zane released her, she could barely move. The sound of water sloshing had her opening her eyes, straining with the effort, to see Rand getting out of the tub.

Zane leaned over her and kissed her deeply before nuzzling her neck. "As soon as I get all the grime washed off me, I'll hold you. Rand, come over here and keep her warm 'til I get a bath." He dressed quickly and went out the door.

Rand finished drying her, and then himself, before wrapping her in the blanket again. He put on his pants and pulled her to sit on his lap, rubbing his hand over her thigh.

Zane came through the door, smiling when he saw them. He stepped aside, admitting the other men to dump the tub and refill it.

Not once did the men even glance in her direction.

Once the men left and the three of them were alone again, Zane stripped off his clothes and lowered himself in the tub. "Dinner'll be here in about twenty minutes. The hotel clerk is falling all over himself to be nice to Amanda now."

Zane leaned back in the tub, his green eyes hooded. "It seems the whole town's already heard about Amanda Owens' shooting. They've also heard she has Texas Rangers falling all over themselves to make her smile and has the hearts of the two captains in the palm of her hand."

Amanda couldn't breathe.

Staring at him, she wondered if they could hear how loudly her heart beat. "Who…who told you that?"

Zane's lips twitched. "The hotel clerk was real happy to tell me. Twice."

Rand didn't say a word, just held her close and continued to caress her thigh.

Tightening her hands on the blanket, she shifted on Rand's lap, unable to look away from Zane. A huge knot formed in her stomach as the lump in her throat grew until she feared it would choke her. "What did you say when he told you that?"

Zane came to his feet, the water running off his sleek muscular body holding her enthralled. He reached for a towel, waiting until her eyes met his again.

"I told him he heard right. I also told him that I'm crazy in love with my wife."

A sob broke free before Amanda could prevent it. And then another. And another.

Gulping in air as tears ran freely, she turned her face into Rand's chest.

His arms tightened around her. "Amanda, honey, please don't cry. I love you so much. Seeing you cry breaks my heart."

Amanda found herself being transferred to Zane's arms and settled onto his lap.

Tilting her face up, Zane wiped her tears. "You must have known that we love you." He tightened his arms around her when she shook her head.

"How could we not fall in love with you, sugar?" He rubbed her back and held her closer, his big body absorbing her shudders.

Her sobs made it difficult to get the words out. "You. Really. Love me?"

Zane tilted her face to brush his lips over hers.

"I didn't stand a chance." He took her hand in his to press his lips against her palm. "I'd die without you."

To hear such a big, masculine man say something so incredibly sweet made her sob even harder. Pressing her face against his chest, she clung to him "I love you, too. So much…it hurts."

"Shh, sugar. Don't cry." Zane rocked her as he would a child until her tears subsided, wiping her face with the corner of the blanket when she looked up.

It occurred to her that she seemed to cry a lot around them lately. The last time, though, they'd done nothing to stop her tears. This time her tears seemed to make them uncomfortable.

It hit her suddenly.

This time her tears were because of them.

Nothing could have made her more confident that they both loved her.

Held in Zane's arms with Rand crouched down beside her, Amanda was once again surrounded by them.

Both men stared down at her with love shining from their eyes and she knew there was no place in the world she'd rather be.

Rand slid a hand over her hair, his dark eyes twinkling. "I think I fell in love with you the first time I saw you."

Amanda smiled, her breath hitching. "I love you, Rand. When I said I love you so much it hurts, I meant that for both of you."

Looking from one to the other, she gripped their hands in hers. "I never wanted to love anyone, but you two are so wonderful, I couldn't help it."

Zane tightened his arms around her and kissed her again. "You're the one who's wonderful. I couldn't help falling in love with you either, sugar."

He looked up, cursing when a knock sounded at the door. "Rand, that's dinner. Get the door."

Rand slid his arms under Amanda and lifted her high against his chest. "No. You took her away from me before I could kiss her. *You* get the door."

Zane kissed her forehead as he released her, the reluctance in his expression prompting Amanda to hold out a hand to him.

"Hurry."

Flashing a smile, Zane turned for the door. "Stay covered."

Rand sat with her on the bed, keeping her completely covered with the blanket.

With a muffled laugh, she objected when he covered her face until he lifted the end of the blanket to screen them, kissing her as Zane quickly got rid of the clerk, who'd delivered their meal himself.

Amanda never imagined she'd ever find such happiness and to her chagrin, she started crying again.

Rand lifted his head, frowning as he looked up at Zane. "She's crying again. She'll make herself sick."

Zane brought the basket of food to the bed, placed it beside Rand and scooped her into his arms. "Between coming and crying, she's weak as a newborn kitten. Let's get her fed."

Amanda reclined between them, leaning heavily against Zane. So tired she could barely keep her eyes open, she allowed them to feed her, letting their conversation wash over her.

She could hardly believe that only a few short weeks ago she didn't even know them and now they were the most important people in her life.

"You're not saying anything, honey. What do you think?"

Amanda blinked and looked up to see Rand offering her a forkful of food, both of them staring at her, their concern apparent.

"I'm sorry. I wasn't paying attention."

Zane lifted her chin, leaning her back over his arm. "What do you think of us staying with the Rangers a few more years before we start the ranch we talked about? They need us here and it'll give us a chance to save more money for livestock."

Amanda blinked. "You're asking *me*?"

Zane frowned. "You're our wife."

Smiling, Amanda turned her face to press her lips against his bare chest, taking the time to do it again. "Whatever you want is fine with me. As long as I'm with you, I'm happy."

Rand touched her arm. "I know you'll get scared when we're out on patrol."

"Not if I'm with you." She lifted a hand when they both started to speak. "You know I can help you. I'll stay out of your way and do whatever you tell me to do, but you already know I can handle myself."

She smiled at Rand and lifted her face for his kiss, before turning to Zane. "Tomorrow you can buy me that Colt you promised me so I can start practicing."

They stared at each other silently for several minutes before nodding and looking down at her again.

Zane slid a hand over her abdomen. "Until you're carrying a child."

Rand's hand covered her breast. "Something about seeing you handle a loaded weapon gets me every time."

Sighing, Zane gestured toward the food. "We've got a big day tomorrow. The captain's wife left today, so we're moving into the captain's quarters."

Amanda jerked upright. "Hell. Now, I have to throw a housewarming party."

Rand frowned. "What the hell's a housewarming party?"

"I don't know, but Mrs. Hensen said—"

Rand toppled her onto her back. "I wouldn't pay attention to anything Mrs. Hensen said. If she wants a housewarming party, she can throw one for herself when she gets out of jail."

Chapter Thirteen

Pacing restlessly around the house they'd moved into a month ago, Amanda called herself all kinds of a lily-livered fool. She'd wanted to go to Rafael's hanging, had thought of nothing else for the last two weeks, but this morning when she got out of bed, weak from her husbands' lovemaking, she hadn't been able to do it.

Damn it, as the wife of the captains of the Texas Rangers, she should have been there.

Watching Zane and Rand getting ready to leave, all she had in her heart was love, and she couldn't work up any hatred for Rafael.

Unable to stay inside any longer, she grabbed her hat and went out the front door and to the side yard where she'd planted her garden. Pulling weeds with more force than necessary, she cursed under her breath.

This morning Zane and Rand had looked surprised by her decision, but accepted it. They'd appeared a little preoccupied when they left, and she hoped she hadn't let them down.

She tossed weeds aside and sat on her heels, her head bowed in regret.

"Thought you'd be at the hangin'."

Amanda lifted her head, jumping to her feet in automatic defense when she heard her father's voice. "Is that why you came by, because you thought I wouldn't be here?"

Her father looked even worse than ever. His clothes looked as though they hadn't been washed in weeks, he'd lost weight, and his face had become more heavily lined.

What really surprised her, though, was that he looked sober for the first time since she could remember.

Her father smiled faintly. "I never could fool you. You're smart as your momma and as hardheaded as me. Pretty tough combination. I can't say I cotton to you havin' two husbands, but I hope they know what they got themselves into."

Uneasy, she fought the urge to shuffle her feet, not wanting to show any kind of weakness. "What do you want, Pa? If you're trying to cause trouble, I'm not interested."

He nodded sadly. "Don't blame you for thinking that. I ain't been a real good father to you and I'm sorry. Sorry for a lot of things, but mostly for makin' you marry John Keller. He didn't deserve you."

Crossing her arms over her chest, Amanda fought back bitter memories, reminding herself that they had nothing to do with her life now. "No, he didn't. I don't worry about that anymore. I'm happy with the husbands I have now."

Her father winced. "They good to you?"

Amanda couldn't help but smile, thinking about how sweet and loving her two Texas Rangers had been ever since the night they'd told her they loved her. They even played more often now, usually after Rand initiated it. "Real good, Pa."

He nodded sadly. "I know I wasn't much of a pa to you and your sister and even less of a husband to your ma." He looked away studying the outside of her new home, but she had the feeling he didn't really see it. "Did your ma ever tell you we lost a son?"

Stunned, Amanda could only stare at him. He'd said it so matter-of-factly that at first she thought she must have misunderstood.

"You had a son?"

Her father nodded. "A boy. Named him Jack after my pa. Our firstborn."

Amanda's jaw dropped. "Your firstborn? Why didn't I ever know about him? What happened to him? Where is he?" A knot formed in her stomach when her father's eyes met hers again and she saw that his had filled with tears.

"I killed him." At her horrified look, he shook his head. "Not on purpose. Your ma was expectin' you and I took him with me fishin' 'cause your ma was feelin' poorly. He fell in. I'd fallen asleep and didn't know about it until it was too late."

Amanda stepped closer, reaching out to touch his arm. "Oh, Pa. I never knew. It was an accident."

"Your ma was so struck with grief the doc didn't think you'd make it."

"And that's when you started drinking?"

"And that's when I started drinkin'." He sighed, running his hand through his thinning hair. "I drank to forget. It got so I couldn't look at your ma anymore without feelin' guilty. Then I had a daughter, and then another. It was like God wanted to punish me and not give me the son I wanted."

The knot tightened as the insult struck home. "I see."

Her father shook his head. "I doubt that you do. I couldn't be happy. I couldn't let myself be happy. I'd kilt my son. I didn't deserve to be happy. You was always a pretty thing. Everybody said it. 'Amanda's the most beautiful baby I ever seen.'" He looked away again, staring out into a nearby field. "And you were. Even more beautiful than your momma, and I didn't think that was possible. I was so proud, but every time I wanted to smile at you or play with you, I'd remember Jack. And I'd drink some more."

Amanda led him to the small front porch and gestured for him to sit down while she took one of the other chairs. "Pa, I don't know what you want me to say."

He shook his head sadly. "Tain't nothin' for you to say. I just wanted to tell ya." He lifted his head, a sad smile playing at his lips. "When you hit me with that poker, I knew there was some of me in you."

"How come I never heard about it? How come nobody told me?"

Her father turned to her then. "We didn't move to Austin until you was born. Nobody here even knows." He slumped back in the chair as if all the air went out of him. "I'm sorry I made you marry John. I wasn't thinkin' straight and knew I was losin' your ma. Lost every job I had and needed the money. Thought if I had the money to provide for her, she wouldn't leave me. Stupid."

Nodding, Amanda stared at him as though seeing him for the first time "Yeah, it was. Momma never cared about the money. She just wanted enough to feed Pammy and me. She just wanted her husband. Do you know how many times she told me how much she loved you when you got married? I knew I wouldn't ever marry any man I loved because you showed me how fast a man could turn it against me." Amanda didn't even try to keep the frustration and anger out of her voice.

He waved his hand negligently. "I know. I messed up, Amanda. I made a big mess of everything. But if you don't love them Rangers, you could maybe come home with me. We'll see what we can do about getting' your ma and sister back."

For the first time in her life, she felt she understood her father, at least a little, but trusting him would never be easy. "I'm not coming home with you, Pa. I said I didn't want to love Zane and Rand, but it happened anyway."

Her father slumped. "I understand why you can't come home. I'm glad you found some happiness, honey. After what I've put you through, you deserve it."

Amanda watched him get to his feet, alarmed at how frail he looked. "Pa, my place is with my husbands now, but as soon as I get a letter from ma, I'll write back to her. I'll ask her and Pammy to come home, but you have to promise me, no more drinking."

Her father's eyes lit up and he smiled, the first real smile she'd seen from him in years. "I promise. I ain't had a drink since the night I heard you was kidnapped. Thought you might need me. If anything happened to you…Well, I'da known it was all my fault. If I hadn't made you go after the gold—"

Amanda touched his shoulder, saddened to see her father such a broken man. "That's all in the past, Pa. We'll all have a new start. That's what I'll tell Momma when I write to her."

Her father straightened, standing just a little bit taller. "Got myself a job now, working at the mill."

"Oh, Pa, that's—"

"Touch my wife and I'll kill you."

Amanda spun to see Zane approach, his face as hard and cold as marble, with Rand closing in fast. "Zane, I—"

"I'll take care of it, Amanda. Get in the house."

Knowing her husbands well enough to be scared of what they might do, Amanda stepped in front of her father and stood her ground. "Stop! It's not what you think."

Alarmed at the look on their faces, she hurriedly put an arm around her father. "Everything's all right now."

Relieved that both Zane and Rand stopped, she knew she'd have to explain quickly to diffuse the situation.

"Pa explained everything. He stopped drinking. He has a job now and we're going to have a fresh start."

She hugged her father, smiling reassuringly as he kept looking warily at Zane and Rand. "And we're going to try to get Momma and Pammy back."

Zane and Rand's eyes narrowed. They shot a look at each other and then back at her, but still looked far from convinced.

Zane came forward, climbing the steps to the small porch and making it feel even smaller.

"Explained what? Explain it to me."

Amanda nodded, careful to stay between him and her father. "I will. Let's all go inside."

Over an hour later, her father took his last bite of the cold chicken sandwiches she'd put together, and smiled at Zane and Rand. "I couldn't've picked better men for my daughter. Just so you know, I told her I didn't approve of her havin' two husbands."

When Zane and Rand both stiffened, he shook his head. "But now that I see all three of you together, I can see that it works. Never woulda expected it."

Rand lifted his cup of coffee. "Just so *you* know, we're watching out for her, and won't like it at all if she's not happy. When her momma and sister get back, we'll still be watching."

Amanda's father stood. "I know. Nothing like havin' two Texas Rangers watchin' you to keep a man straight." All amusement fled. "I just want my family back. I learned my lesson. Just don't make the same mistake with my daughter."

Zane's brow went up. "I have no intention of ever hitting my wife."

Amanda's father shook his head sadly. "Neither did I." He shook hands with both men, and smiled at Amanda. "I gotta get back to work, and I gotta lot to do to get the house ready for your momma."

Nodding, Amanda watched Zane and Rand walk her father out. Blinking back tears, she smiled as the three of them stood in the front yard talking for several minutes before her father smiled, and with a short wave to her, went on his way.

She dropped into one of the kitchen chairs and looked up as soon as Zane and Rand stepped inside. "You must think I'm lily-livered because I didn't go to the hanging." She hadn't meant to blurt it out like that but it had been bothering her all day.

They looked at each other and then back at her in that way they did whenever she said something that surprised them.

Rand poured himself another cup of coffee and sat down next to her. "You've had quite a morning, haven't you, darlin'? Talking with your father, finding out you had a brother, and beating yourself up for not going to a hanging."

Amanda shrugged, picking at a crumb she'd missed. "I'm the wife of the captains of the Texas Rangers. I should have—"

"No." Zane took his usual seat at her other side. "You don't have to go to hangings. I'd actually prefer it if you don't."

Amanda's heat shot up. "But you didn't say anything. I've been talking about going and neither one of you ever said a word."

Zane got up to refill his own cup and hers. "If you wanted to go, I figured you had the right."

"So you don't think I'm a coward?"

Taking her hand in his, Zane smiled in a way that curled her toes.

"Sugar, the last thing you are is a coward." He pulled her from her chair to settle her on his lap. "You're a strong woman who brings me to my knees so often, I'm starting to get calluses on 'em."

Amanda nearly choked on a laugh. "You're full of it, Ranger, but I love you." Her laughter died as she snuggled against him, still reeling from her father's visit. "Will you just hold me for a minute?"

Tightening his arms around her, he nuzzled her hair. "Of course, baby, I'll hold you as long as you want."

Rand slid from his chair to the one she'd just vacated, moving it closer. "I want in on this." Wrapping an arm around her waist from behind, he bent and kissed her shoulder.

Amanda went limp, letting them support her weight, and let the tension of the morning fade away.

After several minutes, Rand chuckled in her ear and rubbed her stomach. "I know something that'll make you feel even better."

Tilting her head back, Amanda met his lips with hers in a brief kiss. "I'll bet I know what that is."

Rand grinned. "I'll bet you don't. You got a dirty mind, darlin'."

Giggling, Amanda stroked the arm Rand wrapped around her and the hand Zane rested on her hip. "It's your fault. And you and Zane already made me feel better, but tell me your news."

Zane slid his hand over her thigh, caressing her from knee to hip and back again. "Another time, Rand. She's had enough for today."

Amanda released his arm to cup his jaw, sliding her palm over his trimmed beard. "You don't think I'm too soft because I didn't go to the hanging, do you?"

Zane slid a hand to her mound, a small smile playing at his lips. "I love your soft parts just fine, sugar."

She laughed as she was sure he'd meant her to. "You really are smitten with me, aren't you?"

Zane touched his nose to hers. "Couldn't help it."

Rand tugged her hair. "How come he's getting all the loving?"

Turning her head, Amanda grabbed Rand's hair and pulled him down for a kiss. She was the aggressor this time, sliding her tongue past his lips before he could react, to stroke his tongue with hers.

She poured all of her love for him into it, retreating only to nibble at his bottom lip before advancing again. By the time she broke off the kiss, they were both breathing heavily.

Rand blinked, his slow smile spreading. "Damn, woman. I can't feel my toes. Who taught you to kiss like that?"

Pleased with herself, Amanda smiled. "That's how you kiss me."

"Come over here, then. I want more than just a kiss. Zane's being selfish."

Zane helped her sit up and turn on his lap until she faced Rand. "Don't listen to him. He's got a burr under his saddle because I got to have your pussy last night for dessert."

"It was my turn!"

Amanda shook her head, both amused and a little disconcerted by their teasing. She couldn't help but wonder if their banter sometimes held real jealousy. The last thing she wanted was for either one of them to feel neglected. "Tell me what you were talking about."

Rand pulled her closer and draped her thighs over his. "Last night some men got drunk at the saloon and started a ruckus. Silas and Henry locked 'em up to sleep it off. They told us about it this morning and when we went in to let 'em go we got a nice surprise."

Curious now, Amanda smiled. "What?"

"They're the men who attacked you that night when you went to get the gold. You should have seen their faces when they recognized us."

Amanda gasped at the remembered horror of that night. "Are you serious?" With them in her life, she'd never felt safer, and decided she wanted just a little revenge. "I'll have to stop by later on to see you and Zane at work."

Rand grinned and kissed her. "Wear your Colt."

Giggling, Amanda leaned into Zane and reached for Rand, suddenly needing more than just to be held. "I need both of you so much. Take me to bed."

Zane stood with her in his arms and strode toward the bed. "With pleasure."

In no time at all, Amanda lay naked in bed between her equally naked husbands. Pushing their hands away before they made her forget her intentions, she scrambled to her knees, ignoring their looks of concern.

Letting her eyes roam over all that hard muscle and raw masculinity, it amazed her once again that they belonged to her.

She slapped away the hands that reached for her. "No. I need something from both of you. I want you to let me touch you first." The sight of the two thick cocks on either side of her almost made her forget everything and beg them to take her.

Zane and Rand glanced at each other, making her smile that she'd managed to surprise them once again.

Rand's wicked grin sent a sharp jolt of need through her as he lifted his arms and stretched before folding them behind his head. "Well now, darlin', that sounds like fun."

Zane didn't look as happy, his gaze hooded as he clenched his hands into fists at his side. His beautiful eyes glittered, promising retribution. A muscle worked in his jaw as he nodded once.

Pressing her lips together to hide a smile, Amanda leaned forward to run her hands over their gorgeous chests.

"Thank you. I didn't think you'd let me."

Rand's grin grew. "Anytime you feel the urge to touch me, darlin', is fine by me."

Zane shot a look of impatience at Rand. "I have a feeling you'll regret those words."

Staring back at her, Zane's expression softened. "It doesn't appear there's much we wouldn't do for you." His gaze sharpened and slid to her breasts. "But it's costing me, so hurry up."

Marveling at the muscles that quivered and tightened under her hand, Amanda smiled and arched her back, amazed, as always, at the flare of heat in their eyes as they roamed over her, as though seeing her for the first time.

She smiled and pouted again, fascinated by the way it drew their gaze to her mouth, making her lips tingle. "That's not fair. I don't tell you to hurry."

Rand groaned when she teased a male nipple. "Sure you do, darlin'. You're always screaming at us to hurry up and fuck you."

A giggle escaped before she could prevent it and she slid her hands lower to touch their flat stomachs.

"Yeah, but you're big, brave Texas Rangers. I'm sure you can take it better than I can."

Other than the time she'd been with Rand while Zane slept, she'd never been intimate with either one of them without the other present. Although she loved being with them together, the fact that she hadn't been alone with either of them had started to make her a little uneasy, especially with comments like the ones Rand made only minutes earlier.

Rand arched his hips upward, growling at her when she lifted her hand away.

Amanda glared at him. "You promised."

He sat up, reaching for her. "I never said I wouldn't move. Why don't you forget all this and let Zane and me—"

Amanda slapped a hand on his chest. "No. Please."

Something in her tone must have come through because both men looked at her in concern.

Rand ran a finger down her cheek. "What's wrong, honey?"

Smiling to reassure them, she cupped his smooth jaw. "Nothing's wrong. I love both of you. It's just…" Would she sound stupid putting it into words?

Sitting up, Zane brushed her hair back from her face. "Tell me."

Amanda took a deep breath and blew it out slowly. "Does it bother you when I touch Rand?"

He blinked, clearly confused. "Of course not, Amanda. Sugar, I thought you understood—"

Cutting him off, she turned to Rand. "How would you feel if you walked in and found Zane and me in bed together?"

Rand frowned and glanced at Zane. "I'd feel like jumping in and joining you. Darlin', what are you getting at?"

Smiling, she touched each of their beloved faces. "I love when you both take me, but it overwhelms me so much that I don't get a chance to touch you the way that I need to."

Zane's jaw clenched. "I'm sorry, honey. We got a little carried away with the chance to take you together. I should have realized—"

"No, Zane. There's nothing wrong with the way you make love to me." Amanda put her arms around him, pressing herself against his chest. She kissed him, soft little brushes of her lips over his.

Holding his face between her hands, she smiled, "I just want a chance to show both of you how much I love you and how much your love means to me." She winked. "And I want the chance to make you both as wild as you make me."

With a last brush of her lips, she moved to Rand. She grabbed fistfuls of his hair and kissed him deeply, rubbing her nipples against his chest and moaning into his mouth at the sharp pleasure. She pulled away before she gave in to temptation, pleased to see raw hunger in Rand's dark eyes.

Sticking out her bottom lip, she looked up through her lashes. "You won't stop me, will you?"

Rand's eyes narrowed on her lips. "You're really asking for trouble, aren't you? What do you have in mind?"

Rubbing her nipples against Rand's chest, she tugged his bottom lip between her teeth.

"Since Zane's so proud of teaching me how to use my mouth on him, I thought I'd let him watch me use it on you."

Rand grinned. "Hell, yeah!"

Zane groaned and fell backward onto the bed, closing his eyes and dropping his forearm over them. "I'll never survive it." He lifted his arm to peer at her. "Can I touch you while you're sucking Rand?"

Hiding a smile at his disgruntled tone, Amanda ran a finger over Zane's cock, tracing a bulging vein. When he hissed and clenched his hands into fists again, she couldn't hide her smile any longer. "No. You have to watch, and then Rand has to watch while I do the same thing to you."

A sound somewhere between a groan and a growl passed Zane's lips as his cock jumped against her hand.

More moisture coated her thighs, and knowing just how much pleasure that cock could give her had her pussy clenching.

Rand frowned. "And no touching?"

"One condition." Zane's fight for control could be heard clearly in his deep tone, sending her arousal soaring.

She never really got to see them like this. She was usually so far gone that she missed it. Deciding that this was something she'd have to do more often, she grinned and ran her fingertips up his thighs. "What condition?"

His features appeared carved from stone as Zane jerked upright and gripped her hair, winding it around his fist to tug her head back.

"When we tell you to stop, you have to stop. I'm spilling my seed in your tight pussy, not in your mouth." He leaned close until their noses almost touched. "Agreed?"

She slid her gaze to Rand as he leaned close, closing her eyes on a moan when he scraped his teeth down her neck.

"And my seed's going deep in that tight ass."

Anticipation made her heart beat faster, her body already flushed and trembling. Closing her eyes, she fought back the almost overwhelming urge to forget the whole thing and beg them to take her.

She took several deep breaths and opened her eyes, the fierce heat in Zane's eyes strengthening her resolve. "Agreed."

Dying to make them both out of their minds with need, she put a hand on each of their hard chests and pushed, drawing a shuddering breath as soon as they lay back. "Both of you better behave."

Zane reclined on his side as though prepared to watch, the cool intent on his face filling her with trepidation. "Until it's our turn."

Amanda had seen her husbands aroused many times but she'd never seen quite that blatantly sexual look before. She met it with a teasing look, but inside a fire raged, tightening her abdomen and making her clit feel swollen and hot.

Making a place for herself between Rand's thighs, she hid a smile when he groaned. She ran her short nails up the inner part of his muscular legs, something she'd already learned they both loved, and bent her head to lick the drop of moisture from the tip of his cock, humming her approval of his taste.

His reaction was more than she bargained for.

"Fuck!' His body bowed, his hands clenching at his sides as his eyes squeezed shut.

Zane never took his eyes from Amanda as he spoke to Rand. "I told you you'd regret being so damned cocky."

Smiling, Amanda kept shifting her gaze between them as she opened her mouth wide and took as much of Rand's cock inside as she could. It added to her excitement to see Zane watching her, making her shift to rub her thighs together, to Zane's obvious amusement.

Her eyes widened when Zane took his own cock in his hand and began to stroke it. A rush of heat flowed from her pussy and she squirmed restlessly as she tried to focus on what she was doing.

She sucked gently, moving her lips up and down Rand's length. Using one hand to stroke the part of his cock she couldn't fit into her mouth, and the other to lightly caress his sack, she kept shifting her gaze from his face to Zane and back again.

Distracted by the sight of Zane working his own cock, she jumped, startled, when he spoke.

"Use your tongue the way I taught you."

Rand's groans got louder when she followed Zane's demand, his body tight as he started to reach for her, cursed, and grabbed the headboard instead.

Zane nodded in approval. "Good. I'll bet your thighs are soaked, aren't they, sugar? Do you know what we're going to do to you? You'll beg for it this time. You're going to get cock shoved in your pussy and your ass, and we'll fuck you until you're ready to come. Then, we'll stop."

Amanda's eyes widened, her pussy and ass clenching as though already full. She sucked Rand a little bit harder, gratified by his answering moan as his body arched again.

Zane continued to run his hand slowly up and down his length. "When you settle again, we'll start all over. When we finally decide you've suffered enough, we'll fuck you hard while I hold you against me and rub that clit on me."

Amanda closed her eyes as a wave of need washed over her, trying to ignore the fire at her center and focus on sucking Rand's cock. She ran her tongue repeatedly over the underside, thrilling at his taste.

His thighs trembled, the sounds coming from him sending her hunger soaring.

Zane's deep voice held an underlying layer of ice that sent Amanda's arousal even higher. "Open your eyes, Amanda. You wanted us to watch you. I want you to watch us."

Stunned by the strength of her hunger, Amanda cupped Rand's sack, startled when he grabbed her hair.

"Stop! No more, Amanda. No more, damn it."

His raw, gravelly voice and the pained look on his face told her just how close to the edge he'd allowed her to take him.

She released him slowly, teasing him with her tongue as she lifted her head. Unable to resist, she took her time releasing his sack, giving it a last caress before she lifted her hand and sat back on her heels.

"I guess I did good. I'll get even better with practice."

Rand shot up, eying her hungrily. "Just wait until I get my cock up that ass. You'll see how good you did."

He looked over at Zane. "Fuck, I need to cool down some before I take her ass."

Amanda ran her hand over his cock again. "Don't you dare." Pleased when he sucked in a breath, she scooted out from between his thighs and moved to Zane, smiling at him as he rolled to his back.

"I want both of you to feel the way I feel when you take me."

She eyed Zane's cock hungrily before looking up to meet his eyes. "I like seeing you both this way."

Remembering how exciting it was to watch him touch himself, she decided to do the same thing to them. Reaching up, she cupped her breasts, lightly pinching her pebbled nipples, moaning at jolts of pleasure.

Both men watched, their eyes hooded, as she massaged them before sliding her hands down to her pussy. They both sat up when she spread her thighs, their eyes widening when she parted her folds.

Zane's hands reached for her before he remembered, and pulled them back with a snarl. "When I finally get my hands on you…"

Sliding a finger over her slick folds, Amanda moaned as her finger moved over her clit.

Rand moved to her side. "Don't you dare fucking come. Move your fingers so I can see."

Amanda hid a smile and gave him a stern look. "I'm the one in charge here, remember? There were no rules about me touching myself. I can come if I want to."

Zane bent forward, getting right in her face. "You come and I'm giving you a spanking you won't ever forget. Get your fucking hands away from your pussy and suck my cock."

He smiled coldly. "Or are you ready to move on?"

An idea hit her and she decided she'd found a way to get even. "No moving on until I'm done. Lay back, Ranger, and take it like a man."

Zane reclined back on the pillows and gestured toward his cock. "Have at it, sugar. But I'm warning you, I'm already on the edge from your fucking games. Don't push me."

Amanda shook her head. "You agreed to the rules before we started and even made a few of your own. You said I could suck you, while Rand watches."

Zane's eyes blazed. "I can't wait until I get my cock up that pussy. You're going to pay for teasing me."

Moving over him, she grinned. "Then I'll just have to make sure I get my money's worth."

She moved up beside him and hooked a leg over his stomach, positioning herself so her slit was over his chest before bending to take his cock in her mouth.

She didn't tease him the way she'd teased Rand, just sucked him in as far as she could and began to move on him.

Rand shifted on the bed beside them. "Hell and damnation. Christ, Zane, look at her."

Amanda lifted her head. "Rand, you're supposed to be watching me."

"Suck, Amanda." Zane's tone was like iron.

"Fuck." Rand moved to sit beside her. "You got that ass up in the air good, darlin'. I'm watching you, but I'm getting the salve. As soon as Zane says to stop, I'm greasing your ass."

The bed shifted as Rand moved away, but he came back just as quickly.

Zane lay stiff as a board beneath her, his big body drawn tight, making her wish she could see his face.

With her thighs spread wide, she knew he had to have a good view of everything. The knowledge made her pussy burn, and even more of her juices flow.

She began to rock on him, using her knees to move her up and down on his cock instead of her neck.

Curses flowed out of Zane, the tone of each more desperate than the last.

She used her mouth on him, doing everything he'd taught her to do, her own sharp need growing with every stroke of her tongue. Holding on to his thighs, she felt the muscles quiver, but knew her own did the same.

Suddenly Zane bowed. "Stop."

He grabbed her hips before she could move, yanked her back, and buried his face between her thighs.

Amanda cried out at the first swipe of his tongue through her slit. Holding on to his thighs, she struggled to escape, the pleasure so sharp it bordered on pain.

Zane held strong, his hands holding her securely as he stabbed his tongue into her and all around her folds.

Amanda could no longer reach his cock with her mouth, but she could with her hands, and used them to stroke him again.

A hard slap landed on her bottom, startling her so much she let go.

Rand smoothed a hand over the place he'd just slapped.

"Enough, Amanda. We played your game. Now, it's our turn."

His harsh tone, nothing like the playful one she'd come to expect from him, surprised her and gave an edge to their play she hadn't expected.

The heat from his slap made the entire area more sensitive, drawing whimpers from her as she fought to get Zane's mouth on her clit. She pressed her face against Zane's hard stomach, kicking her legs in frustration.

Focusing on getting Zane's mouth on her clit, she groaned when Rand parted the cheeks of her bottom. It focused her complete attention there, the vulnerability of having that part of her exposed both thrilling and frightening.

To her surprise, Zane held her away from him as he slid upward, positioning her so that her head lay over his cock again.

"Suck, Amanda."

Keeping her legs spread wide and on either side of his hips, Zane sat up, slightly, his hands on each of the cheeks of her bottom, holding her open.

"Go ahead, Rand. Grease her up good. I told you to suck, Amanda."

The sight of his cock, long, thick, the drop of moisture leaking from the tip only inches in front of her took her breath away. She opened her mouth wide to take him in, moaning around his thickness as Rand pressed a slippery finger against her bottom hole.

Knowing that both of them watched close-up as Rand's finger started to enter her drew a whimper from her and made her stiffen.

Zane rubbed her bottom as he held her. "Don't tense up. Easy, sugar. Just let us make you feel good."

Rand withdrew, almost immediately touching her bottom opening again. "Let me in, darlin'."

He slid his finger deep, the salve he'd already applied allowing him to slide his finger in with ease. When he moved it inside her, she whimpered again, her body trembling so hard she held on to Zane for support. Chills raced up and down her spine, somehow adding to her pleasure, a different kind of pleasure—one that stole her ability to think.

It was more intense, more decadent than any other pleasure and sent her to another place, turning her into a creature of need.

It was a wildness that she couldn't fight, but one that Zane and Rand seemed to love.

But even though the fire inside her burned so hot she wanted to struggle against it, the helplessness of having something in her ass created such turmoil inside her, she could barely move.

Shuddering as Rand withdrew again, she turned and went to Zane as soon as he reached for her.

He wrapped his arms around her, pulling her against his chest before tilting her face upward. "There's my kitten inside my hellcat."

Lowering his mouth to hers, he kissed her, sliding his tongue past her lips to dance with hers in a slow, sweet dance that melted her heart. His hands moved up and down her back, soothing her while kissing her as though she was the most precious thing in the world to him.

Between one heartbeat and the next, the gentleness turned to heat.

He took her mouth hungrily, pulling her more firmly against him and letting her feel his cock against her stomach.

Rand moved in from behind, kissing her shoulder as his hands came around to her breasts and began to pluck at her nipples.

"I want that ass." Rand's voice had lowered, the hint of steel in it even stronger than before.

Zane broke off the kiss, and lifting her by the waist, lowered her onto his cock, inch by incredible inch.

"And I want that soft pussy wrapped around my cock."

Amanda didn't even try to hold back her moans, the sensations too strong to keep inside. Grabbing onto his shoulders, she threw her head back as he filled her, her pussy stretching to accommodate him.

She placed a hand over her abdomen as he seated himself to the hilt inside her, his cock going so deep she always wondered how she could take him.

But, God, it felt so good.

Once he'd lowered her, he held onto her hips and scraped his teeth over her jaw. "Hot, wet, and tight, just the way I like it."

He lay back, pulling her with him while Rand helped lower her with a hand at her back.

Zane's cock shifted inside her, drawing a gasp from her, and a moan as her clit touched his abdomen.

Anticipation made her grip Zane's shoulders tighter. Lifting her face from where she'd tucked in under his neck, she moaned, crying out as Rand positioned his cock at her bottom hole.

"Thick, hard, and hot, just the way I like it. Oh! I'm gonna come."

Zane kept her chin lifted. "No. You wanted Rand and me to watch each other because you were afraid we'd be jealous. Now I want you to tell me what he's doing to you."

Amanda couldn't believe she'd heard him right. Crying out as the head of Rand's cock breached the ring of muscle, she panted, her body clenching on both of them.

Zane ran a hand over her hair, gripping it in his fist the way he had before. "Tell me, Amanda."

"I can't. Oh, God."

"What's he doing?"

"You—ah—you know what he's doing."

"Does it hurt?"

"It burns."

Rand groaned. "Fucking tight. Easy, honey."

"I want to come."

Zane tightened his hand in her hair. "No."

Her clit felt swollen and throbbed insistently, but she couldn't move on Zane enough to get relief. Her pussy kept clenching on his cock, making her bottom burn where Rand held the head of his cock just inside her.

Curses flowed from Rand as he paused, groaning each time she tightened on him. "Hold her, damn it. She's already milking me like she's coming."

Zane stared into her eyes and spoke through gritted teeth. "You're not coming, are you, sugar? No, but you want to bad, don't you?"

He looked over her shoulder. "She's close."

Amanda panted through her moans as Rand worked the rest of his thick cock into her ass, the salve allowing him to slide over tissue so sensitive it made her shiver.

Full to bursting, she could feel every bump and ridge of their cocks as her flesh quivered all around them. Her clit burned, but they wouldn't let her move enough to give herself any relief.

They held still for several minute, the only sounds in the room their harsh breathing and groans.

As one, they began to move.

The rhythm of their strokes stole her breath, the constant surge and withdrawal caressing her pussy and ass making it impossible to think.

Giving herself over to them, she clung to Zane and threw her head back as the pressure kept building in that way which she'd come to crave. Secure in their arms, she let herself go. Every time with them, it got easier. Her love for them grew stronger every day and along with that, her trust.

Just when she was about to go over, they stopped, their hands tightening on her, the tension in them showing her just how difficult they found it to stop. Hanging on the edge, she fought them, trying to move on them to give her what she needed.

"Don't stop, damn you. Move."

Zane groaned, his cock jumping inside her. "No." He drew a deep breath and blew it out on another groan.

"After all that teasing—"

Amanda punched his shoulder. "Fuck me, damn it."

Rand moved, withdrawing slowly, only to thrust back into her again. "I can't stop." Another groan followed, as he began to move in earnest.

Zane cursed, his eyes brilliant as they met hers. "Come, honey. Too close."

None of them said anything coherent for the next several minutes as they moved together toward completion.

Her cries of pleasure drowned out their words until the only thing she heard was the deep timber of their voices.

Two thick cocks worked her pussy and ass, the unbelievable fullness and stretch of such sensitive places inside her leaving her teetering on the edge.

When they started to move faster, Amanda gripped Zane tighter and held on for the ride, the friction on her clit sending her over.

It was like a storm.

Her skin tingled the way it did during a lightning storm, but this time the sizzles went all the way through her, encompassing her clit, her pussy, and her ass where it stretched around Rand's cock. Her nipples hardened to the point of pain as the pleasure exploded.

She cried out, gulping in air between cries as her body stiffened. Her pussy and ass clamped down on Zane and Rand's cocks, making her feel impossibly fuller.

Rand's hoarse cry thrilled her as he surged deep one last time, wrapping an arm around her from behind and covering her back with his big body. "Fuck. So good. So tight."

Amanda whimpered as his cock pulsed and shot his hot seed deep into her ass.

Zane thrust twice more, his thrusts lifting her against Rand, before he, too, held himself deep, and shuddered.

Her orgasm seemed to go on forever, the slightest movement by each of them setting off more tremors. Lost in sensation, she threw her head back against Rand and just let herself feel.

She didn't know how much time had passed, but she gradually began to come down when Zane gathered her close, wrapping his arms around her, holding her as Rand slowly withdrew.

She couldn't prevent a whimper and a shudder as the head of Rand's cock passed the tight ring again, pressing her face against Zane's shoulder.

Rubbing his hands up and down her back, Zane murmured softly to her, holding her close and absorbing her tremors. He kissed her hair, running a hand over her bottom before caressing her back again. "You all right, sugar?"

"Hmm." Amanda snuggled closer, not even bothering to open her eyes. She could hear Rand washing up and knew he'd be back soon to cuddle with her.

Zane chuckled. "My tough girl."

Lifting her head, Amanda narrowed her eyes at him. "I'm tough when it counts. I didn't hear you complaining."

He grinned, his hooded eyes twinkling. "No, ma'am. No complaints from me, but I don't want to make a habit of that. I like touching you."

Amanda glanced at Rand, needing to make sure they both understood. "I just need to make sure that it doesn't bother either one of you. I spend time alone with each of you, but never for sex. It started to make me a little uneasy."

Rand came back and plopped down beside her and took her hand in his. "We want that, too. Both of us want to spend time alone with you, but..." He trailed off as he shot a look at Zane.

Amanda stiffened and sat up. "What?"

Zane smiled at her, his eyes gentle. "When we were married before, our wife didn't like it. We're both so crazy in love with you that we both just jump in anytime we can get you naked."

The apology in his eyes and his voice melted her heart. "So, you lose your head whenever you see me naked?"

Zane chuckled, the relief on both of their faces at her teasing apparent. "Sugar, I lose my head far too much around you."

Rand sat up and pulled her from Zane's arms to hold her on his lap. "And we get you naked every chance we get."

Amanda grinned. "I noticed."

Sobering, she pulled the quilt over herself, feeling a little vulnerable. "I just need to be alone with each of you sometimes. I feel like I never get to show you just how much I love you. It's not that I don't want you both together. There's nothing in the world I love more than lying between you."

Zane pushed the quilt off of her breasts and bent to kiss a nipple, a small smile playing at his lips. "Nothing?"

Running her fingers through his hair, she giggled, amazed at how much she'd changed since meeting them and how happy she was now.

She'd never known it was possible to be this happy.

"Well, maybe one or two things."

Rand kissed her slowly, brushing his lips over hers as Zane chuckled and slid out of the bed to go to the wash basin.

It occurred to her that they often left her alone with the other, even for just a few minutes, after lovemaking and she vowed to make sure she let them know how much it meant to her.

Snuggling against Rand as he lifted his head, she kissed his jaw. "I love you."

Sliding his hand over her hip, he leaned close, keeping his voice low. "I love you, too, darlin'. I fell in love with you the first time I looked into those violet eyes."

He laughed and pulled her closer. "You were spitting mad that we pulled you off that ledge, and your eyes were flashing fire at us. Had me hard as a rock and thinking of nothing but sinking into you."

Zane turned from the other side of the room, a teasing glint in his eyes. "Kind of makes you wonder what would have happened to Rafael and his gang if we hadn't come along."

Amanda flung the quilt away, jumped off the bed and, stark naked, stood toe-to-toe with him. "What? You don't think I could have handled them?"

She poked her finger into his stomach, struggling to keep a straight face when his lips twitched. "Don't forget. I escaped from them and had to rescue the two of you."

Zane's brow went up. "Oh, really? And what—"

A knock at the door interrupted what he was about to say.

All amusement left his face as he reached for his pants. Once dressed, he went into the front room, closing the curtain behind him.

Rand dressed just as quickly, and patted her bottom as she pulled on her on pants, before following Zane through the curtain.

Amanda threw on clothes, eavesdropping on the conversation in the next room, and peeking through a hole in the curtain.

As soon as the door opened, she heard Henry, his voice full of excitement. "Captains, a couple men from Paul Wilson's spread just rode in. It's them cattle rustler's again. Looks like they was headed North. Got about two days headstart."

Zane was already strapping on his gun belt. "Jim won't be back for a couple of days and—"

"No, Captain. Jim just rode in about an hour ago."

Amanda opened the curtain to find Zane and Rand ready to go. She donned her boots, excitement racing through her veins.

Rand reached for his hat. "We can't send Jim and Silas on this. They'll be exhausted. They'll have to hold down the fort while we're gone." His gaze went to Amanda.

"Darlin', we're gonna—where the hell do you think you're going?"

Amanda grabbed her own gunbelt, and the Colt she was so proud of. She also grabbed her rifle. "I'm going with you. We talked about this already, remember? Hello, Henry."

Zane cursed as he and Rand grabbed their saddlebags and ran after her.

She walked out with Zane and Rand following close behind, with Zane still cursing.

Rand laughed. "We'll have to tell Jim not to let those drunks out before we get back. I want to see their faces when they see Amanda wearing that Colt."

Zane stopped and spun, glaring at him. "Are you crazy? I don't want her with us. I want her to stay here where she's safe."

Ignoring them, Amanda kept walking.

Rand came up beside her. "You've seen for yourself the kind of trouble she gets in when we're not around. I'd rather have her with us. We can keep her safe."

Henry ran up behind them. "Cap'ns, I'd like to go with you. I've been practicin' and I'm a real good shot now. I could help you."

The wiry man she'd first met weeks ago waited for them and already had Zane and Rand's horses ready. His eyes widened when he saw her, and sent a questioning look at Zane and Rand.

Rand nodded. "Saddle Midnight and Henry's horse, Vern. They're going with us."

Ignoring Henry's whoop, Zane glared at Amanda before handing Rand his saddlebag and heading for the office. "I'll go tell Jim he's in charge until we get back."

Rand smiled and yelled after him. "Don't forget to tell him not to let the drunks free."

By the time Zane came back, Rand, Amanda, and Henry had already mounted and were waiting for him.

The pride swelling inside her filled her with a warm glow as she slid a glance at Rand, sitting straight and tall on his horse, and watched Zane approach, both in full "Ranger" mode.

The sight of them never failed to stir her.

Zane came directly to her and gripped her thigh. "If you're going with us, you'd better do everything we tell you."

Amanda batted her lashes. "Everything, Ranger?"

He scowled up at her. "I mean it, Amanda. If you get hurt, I'll paddle your ass good."

Amanda nodded. "Deal, because if you get hurt that's what I'll do to you."

Before he could respond, she cupped his jaw. "Now that I've found you, I don't want to lose either one of you. I've got my own Texas Rangers and I'm keeping them."

Zane slid his hand down her thigh and looked toward her scabbard.

Rand rode close. "I already checked. She's ready."

Zane looked anything but convinced. "We're gonna talk about this when we get back." He shot a glance at Henry and smiled. "It'll be real nice having two sharpshooters watching our backs."

When Henry beamed, Zane patted her thigh. "You stay back with that rifle when the shooting starts. You don't have to be close to be dangerous and I don't want you getting hurt."

Amanda grinned and started out, looking over her shoulder. "Ranger, when we get back, you and I are going to get real close and I'll show you just how dangerous I can be."

THE END

Siren Publishing, Inc.
www.SirenPublishing.com